D1020214

THE QUEST FOR SS433

ALSO BY DAVID H. CLARK

HISTORICAL SUPERNOVAE

SUPERSTARS

APPLICATIONS OF EARLY
ASTRONOMICAL RECORDS

THE QUEST FOR SS433

DAVID H. CLARK

VIKING

VIKING
Viking Penguin Inc., 40 West 23rd Street,
New York, New York 10010, U.S.A.
Penguin Books Ltd, Harmondsworth,
Middlesex, England
Penguin Books Australia Ltd, Ringwood,
Victoria, Australia
Penguin Books Canada Limited, 2801 John Street,
Markham, Ontario, Canada L3R 1B4
Penguin Books (N.Z.) Ltd, 182–190 Wairau Road,
Auckland 10, New Zealand

First published in 1985 by Viking Penguin Inc.
Published simultaneously in Canada

LIBRARY OF CONGRESS CATALOGING IN PUBLICATION DATA
Clark, David H.
The quest for SS433.
1. SS433 (Astronomy). I. Title.
QB841.C587 1985 523.8 83-40660
ISBN 0-670-80388-X

Grateful acknowledgment is made to Macmillan Publishing Company, A. P. Watt Ltd., and Michael B. Yeats for permission to reprint two lines from W. B. Yeats's poem entitled "The Secret Rose" from *The Poems of W. B. Yeats,* edited by Richard J. Finneran.

Printed in the United States of America by
R. R. Donnelley & Sons Company, Harrisonburg, Virginia
Set in Baskerville

DEDICATED TO SUZANNE, MATTHEW,
ANDREW, AND STEPHEN

FOREWORD

Until this century, a small number of rich patrons allegedly financed most astronomers, and these scientists owed an almost servile allegiance to their benefactors. Today, the situation is reversed: most astronomy is financed by a large number of considerably poorer patrons—the taxpayers of developed nations—and all too often the scientific benefactors seem oblivious to their debt. Scientific results are often not properly distilled for the public who purchased them, and the methodology of science today, the excitement when it succeeds and the frustration when it fails, is rarely discussed with them. *The Quest for SS433* is a payment on the astronomers' debt to their public patrons, for it describes the evolution of an important and exciting discovery in modern astrophysics.

Luck, fate, and coincidence can play important roles in modern scientific methodology. Certainly in the discovery of the unusual properties of SS433 this was true, and it was particularly true in the case of my own role, as David

Clark relates in the following pages. Although my first and only meeting with him, on a cloudy Sussex day more than six years ago, lasted for only about thirty minutes, his recollection of it is almost identical to my own in every detail. Had my scheduled observing time on the Isaac Newton telescope ended even one day earlier, we would not have met; Clark would still have been en route from Australia, fresh from his and his colleague Paul Murdin's discovery of the spectacular spectrum of SS433. Indeed, had the stubborn English coastal clouds and fog rolled back for even a few hours the previous night, I would have worked at the telescope until dawn, slept through the daylight hours, and returned to the United States lacking the clue that involved me in the entire adventure described in this book.

Lest it appear, however, that such capricious factors dominate the methodology of modern astrophysics, Clark points out that one of the charms of the tale that follows is that, in hindsight, this discovery was inevitable. A variety of researchers were independently moving toward recognition of the strange nature of SS433 throughout the decade of the 1970s, utilizing techniques of visible light, radio, and X-ray astronomy. As with many scientific discoveries, hindsight shows that the path to the solution was remarkably crooked at times; only the principals involved and the precise dates were chance. Clark and I were favored in this particular lottery.

Clark explains how SS433 achieved what he dubs "Very Important Star" status: a (sometimes brief) recognition by the astronomical community that this is *the* fascinating object of the year for further study. In each of the several years since that occasion, new contenders have appeared for this title: an intense burst of energetic gamma radiation from the nearby Large Magellanic Cloud; a pair of closely spaced quasars caused by a grand optical illusion of General Relativity; a pulsar spinning so rapidly that we receive flashes of radio radiation one thousand times per second. Now that we have had the opportunity to view several successors to the VIS title, we have the chance to attempt some absolute assessment of the importance of SS433 to astronomy. Will its status be only short-term, as is the case for many celebrities, whether scientific theories or movie stars, or will it truly remain a unique, prototypical object of basic import to astrophysics? It is difficult to remove my personal bias when answering this question; no scientist wants to believe that his work will be widely viewed as prosaic, at least during his own lifetime. However, there seem to be certain quantitative clues that SS433 will remain a prominent part of the astrophysical scene for a long time. The first such indication is that no second member of the SS433 class has yet been found. Astronomers (including Clark and myself) differ on exact details of whether a handful of other catalogued galactic X-ray and radio sources, such as Circinus X-1, share certain specific properties in common with SS433, in particular their evolutionary history. But I believe everyone agrees that the primary SS433 observational phenomenon is still unique: nothing else in the universe exhibits features in the spectrum that wander back and forth on a time scale of days. The other VISs have all been duplicated; we now know of many gamma-ray-burst sources, a half-dozen double and even triple quasars, and further ultrarapid pulsars.

A second clue to the import of SS433 is that observational and theoretical work conducted since the first few years of research documented in *The Quest for SS433* has supported and expanded the concept that the object may be a miniature version of a far grander example of astrophysical violence, namely, the powerful quasi-stellar objects. Perhaps this evidence is due to the "bandwagon effect": it becomes increasingly difficult to oppose an attractive theory. If the analogy is valid, SS433 is assured a permanent niche of importance in astronomy, simply because the quasi-stellar objects are so distant from us that certain absolute limits are imposed on the level of detail with which we may study them. In SS433 we have a bright, nearby example available for extremely detailed observation via a large variety of sensitive astrophysical techniques.

Just a few days after my meeting with Clark, from which I emerged with the clue that triggered some of the events described in this book, my summer's visit to England was abruptly terminated, one month early, by the unexpected death of both my parents. During the long plane flight home, unaware of the import of my conversation with Clark, I reflected upon what a complete waste of time that summer had been. How wrong I was! SS433 was to influence both my professional and my personal life more than I imagined possible by an astronomical object. In *The Quest for SS433* we see the same impact on David Clark's life, and glimpse the excitement of modern research in astrophysics.

Bruce Margon

ACKNOWLEDGMENTS

Mediocrity knows nothing higher than itself, but talent instantly recognizes genius.

—SIR ARTHUR CONAN DOYLE, *The Valley of Fear*

En route to the discovery of SS433, I was fortunate to work closely with two exceptionally talented astronomers: James Caswell and Paul Murdin. To each of them I offer my sincere thanks for their patient tuition, and for their sharing with me the excitement of astronomical research.

To name in the text everyone associated with the study of SS433 would have led to confusion. I have, therefore, restricted myself to those individuals who made contributions of particular relevance to my version of the unfolding drama. Often I have named just one person from an observing team, usually the individual with whom I had direct dealings. I hope that all those astronomers who contributed to unraveling the mysterious nature of SS433, but who are not named in the text, will not be offended. Their manifold contributions are here acknowledged.

I wish to thank my agent, Felicia Eth, of Writers House, for helpful advice, and my editor, William Strachan, for his thorough reworking of the manuscript. I also wish to thank Bruce Margon, Paul Murdin, William Zealey, Andrew Fabian, Frederick Seward, John Shakeshaft, and E. R. Seaquist for reading parts of the manuscript, suggesting changes and improvements, and correcting a number of errors or misunderstandings. Responsibility for any remaining or inadvertent misrepresentation of events is, of course, mine alone. Above all, I wish to thank my wife, Suzanne, for all her help and encouragement.

CONTENTS

"Where shall I begin, please your Majesty?" he asked.
"Begin at the beginning," the King said gravely, "and go on till you come to the end: then stop."

—LEWIS CARROLL,
Alice's Adventures in Wonderland

THE QUEST FOR SS433

PROLOGUE

It is a riddle wrapped in a mystery
inside an enigma.
—WINSTON CHURCHILL,
Broadcast Talk, 1 October 1939

Observing on any big telescope is always an exciting experience for a professional astronomer. The dramatic advances in the design of optical telescopes with new sophisticated instrumentation have been such that any astronomer with a carefully prepared program of observations is almost assured of dramatic results if the skies remain cloud-free. But some results can be more dramatic and spectacular than others, and lead to the discovery of often totally unexpected phenomena. This was certainly the case in June 1978 when I was observing on the giant Anglo-Australian Telescope in northwestern New South Wales, Australia, with my long-time scientific collaborator and close friend Paul Murdin.

The observations we had planned for the long winter night of June 28 were a mixture of astronomical sources and phenomena that for a variety of reasons had attracted our interest. Included in our observing program was an object we then knew as "A1909+04." This unexciting label gave the catalogue number of a peculiar celestial source of X-rays that also emitted radio waves and that we believed might mark the site of an ancient stellar explosion of almost unimaginable proportions. Our objective, given the rather inexact position we had from X-ray and radio observations, was to attempt to find the star responsible for the strange emissions. The vague position we had calculated encompassed several very faint stars, plus a somewhat brighter one. A few days before our trip to the telescope, Murdin had drawn attention to the single bright star on existing photographs of that region of sky: "It seems to have a flag on it reading, 'Hey, look at me!' "

Never suspecting that the obvious "flag-waving" star could possibly be our quarry, we wasted precious telescope time looking first at the faintest stars, which proved to be ordinary. I supervised the operation of the telescope; Murdin controlled the detector analyzing and recording the star light. As the telescope was eventually directed toward the single bright star within the area of interest, and as the instrument analyzing its light revealed certain peculiarities, Murdin excitedly proclaimed our success in a manner not totally in keeping with his usual cool professional approach, but nevertheless engraved on my memory: "Bloody hell! We've got the bastard!"

Just what an extraordinary star the "bastard" was did not become apparent until months later, by which time a host of astronomers world-wide were training their telescopes on it to record its unusual signature. Theoretical astronomers rapidly converged on a complex system able to explain the strange emissions; this involved a compact object, possibly a black hole (the astronomers' favorite candidate for unusual phenomena) orbiting a giant star. Gas from the giant star swirled onto the compact object like water flowing down a drain with the tap at the other end of the bath left running. But some of this material was then ejected from the system at unprecedented speeds in two finely collimated "jets" that swept around the sky every 164 days like a giant garden sprinkler (see Figure P1). The popular press produced a steady flow of superlatives to herald the recently discovered unusual properties of the object, now redesignated "SS433." It was described as "the most bizarre object in the Galaxy," "a truly unique discovery," "a star that seems to be coming and going at the same time," "164-day stellar wonder," "enigma of the century." Reflecting its new-found VIS (Very Important Star) status, the story made the science columns of *Newsweek* and *Time*; self-styled experts on the star passed their judgments in the columns of the popular scientific press; international astronomical conferences debated the nature of this strange object. Where would it end? And how had it all begun?

This account of astronomical discovery, the quest for SS433, begins in Sicily, at an astronomical conference on the subject of the giant stellar explosions called "supernovae." Supernovae and related astronomical phenomena lie at the heart of this story. The conference was a starting point in the quest for SS433, an entrance to the maze that would have at its end one of the strangest cosmic phenomena yet identified.

But SS433 was a star whose "moment had come." Several groups of astronomers were converging on its unusual properties by a variety of paths. Had Paul Murdin and I never pointed the Anglo-Australian Telescope at it, its enigmatic nature would still soon have been revealed.

My quest had started very much earlier than that of most other researchers, back in 1972. The six-year journey from first tentative ideas to observational reality forms an astronomical detective story in which history must judge

FIGURE P1. SS433—ENIGMA OF THE CENTURY

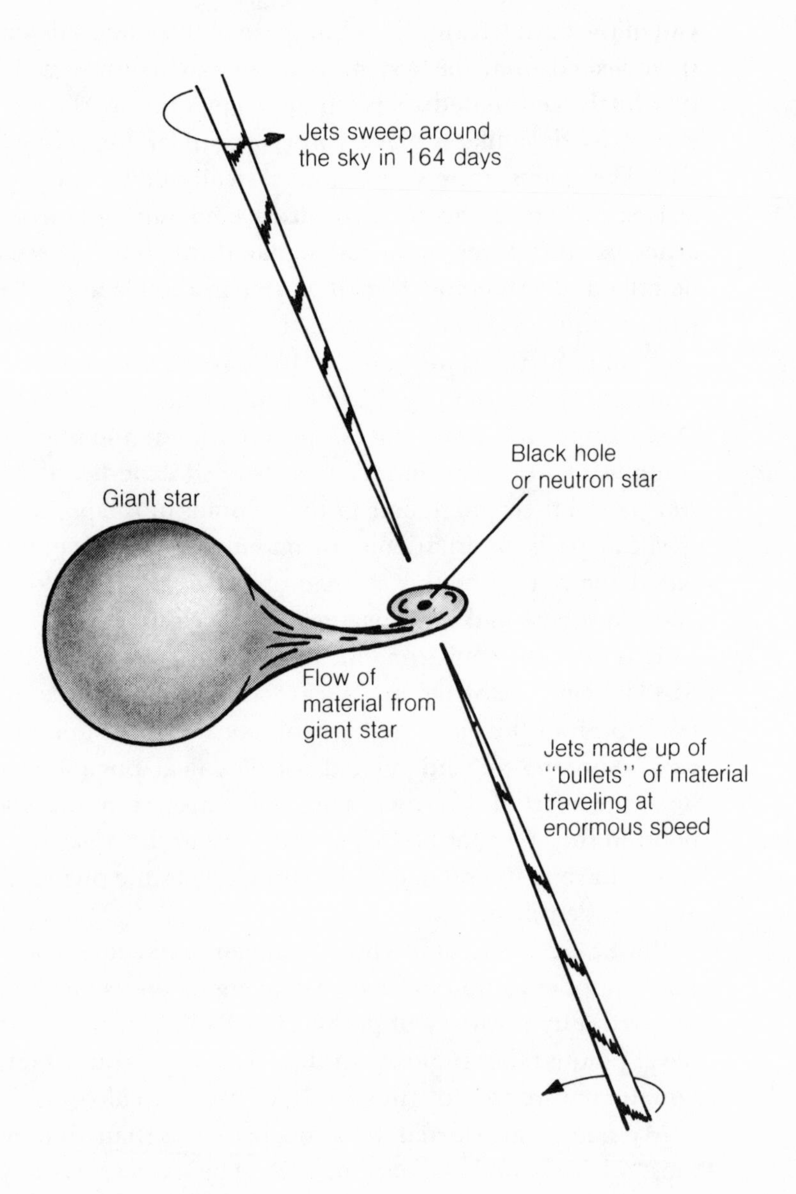

who played the major roles as the drama unfolded—as the quarry was pursued, the evidence collected, and the final judgment made. It is a story full of false trails, personal intrigue, professional competitiveness, claims and counterclaims for precedence and recognition, and, overriding all else, an air of great excitement as astronomers came to realize that they were exploring a totally new celestial phenomenon. The universe could never look quite the same again.

1 SICILIAN SUPERSTARS

When shall the stars be blown about
the sky,
Like the sparks blown out of a smithy
and die?
—W. B. YEATS,
The Secret Rose

Ask most people what they associate the island of Sicily with, and answers might range from the Mafia to almonds, olives, and citrus fruits; ask a professional research scientist, and he is likely to mention the E. Majorana Centre for Scientific Culture. This international scientific conference center is located at Erice, a quaint medieval town perched atop a rocky prominence on the northwestern coast of the island, and it would seem that this ancient monastery town exists today almost solely for the benefit of tourists and as a center for international scientific conferences. Why Erice was chosen as a place where research scientists from all over the world could gather to discuss and argue over advancements in their various subjects I do not know, but there can be no doubting that the center offers everything scientists look for in a location for one of their international meetings. Conferences are very much part of the established and privileged life style of modern research astronomers, who try to justify regular attendance at such meetings on the basis that forefront research requires the periodic sharing of ideas and active debate on new results by members of the international astronomical community. If a conference can be held at a resort offering natural beauty, historic interest, good restaurants, relative isolation from the excesses of the tourist trade, and good conference facilities, so much the better. Erice has all of these features in abundance, and more.

In May 1978, the E. Majorana Centre for Scientific Culture was selected as the site for an international astronomical conference on the subject of supernovae. A supernova represents the spectacular death throes of a certain type of star, which, having reached the end of its normal life span of some tens to thousands of millions of years, blows itself apart in a spectacular explosion. It was known that even as stars die as supernovae they might give birth to strange and enigmatic systems known as pulsars and black holes; it would soon be learned, with the discovery of the mysterious object that was to be designated "SS433," that they could create even more bizarre offspring.

The conference was to occupy a full two weeks, and the day before it was due to begin, the majority of the fifty or so participants, from more than a dozen countries, gathered at the airport in Rome to take the afternoon flight to Palermo, the capital of Sicily. Most of the world's top experts in the field were there, astronomers referred to by us lesser scientific mortals as the "mega-pundits." Palermo's airport has a notorious safety record, and someone commented that if this flight fell victim to the Palermo jinx, most of the world's know-how on supernovae would be wiped out at a stroke. He quipped that it would be an appropriate end for experts on stellar explosions "to go out in a blaze of glory." Those of us who were nervous air passengers found little comfort in his joke. The short flight took us within sight of the volcano Mount Etna, undergoing a period of significant activity at that time. One of our number noted that, by his quick calculations, the energy released in a typical supernova explosion was about a billion billion billion times that of a major volcanic eruption. Nature's terrestrial violence is dwarfed on the celestial scale.

The long ride from the airport to Erice gave us the chance to start talking about the topic that would be at the center of our thinking for the next fortnight. The vast majority of professional astronomers live the cliché that astronomy is not merely a job but very definitely a way of life dominating every waking minute. Their seventeenth- and eighteenth-century post-Renaissance counterparts were usually gentlemen of private means or under patronage, motivated by the desire to find an order in the heavens and explore the marvels of God's creation. By contrast, modern-day astronomers are more often than not ambitious young professionals dedicated to personal advancement and addicted to the excitement of astronomical research with the powerful new instruments modern technology has provided them. The wife of an astronomer colleague tried to persuade me once that all the astronomers she knew (including, presumably, her husband and me) were merely "egomaniacs," wanting no more than to see their names in the papers as the discoverers of new phenomena, to be invited to conferences and meetings to talk about their famous theories and discoveries, to get their names in the history books—to be recognized as very important people. Perhaps she is right, in part, but I hope there is still a little of the Renaissance spirit in what we do. Somehow this busload of modern-day researchers did not strike me as being merely egomaniacs; there seemed a clear commitment to a cause, which was to become even more apparent in the days to come.

The subjects to be discussed at the Erice supernova meeting could be divided into four broad areas: first, the nature of the supernova explosions themselves; second, the theories of why certain stars explode; third, the form of the debris ejected in the outburst, the so-called supernova remnant, and its effect on the interstellar environment; and, fourth, the question of what was left, if anything, at the site of the explosion—the stellar remnants. It was the debate of this final question that was to prove important in the quest for SS433.

Stars accumulate in giant conglomerates called "galaxies." Our sun is one of some 100 billion stars making up our galaxy, the Milky Way (often referred to merely as the "Galaxy," from the Greek *galaxias,* Milky Way). But our galaxy is just one of billions of similar such gigantic structures making up the observable universe, and galaxies themselves tend to gather in clusters.

Galaxies come in a variety of forms: some have a characteristic spiral structure, others are ellipsoidal in structure, and some have an irregular form. The Milky Way is a spiral galaxy, displaying intertwined spiral arms—edge-on it is discus-shaped (see Figure. 1.1)—about 100,000 light-years in diameter. (The light-year is the usual unit used by astronomers to describe the enormous distances in the cosmos. A light-year is the distance traveled by a pulse of light, at the speed of 300,000 kilometers per second, each year. It is equivalent to about ten trillion kilometers.)

Stars in our galaxy are believed to explode as supernovae about once every twenty years or so on average. The reason so few of these are observed on Earth (not a single supernova within the Galaxy has been detected since the advent of the telescope in A.D. 1609) is due to the obscur-

FIGURE 1.1. THE GALAXY

EDGE-ON VIEW

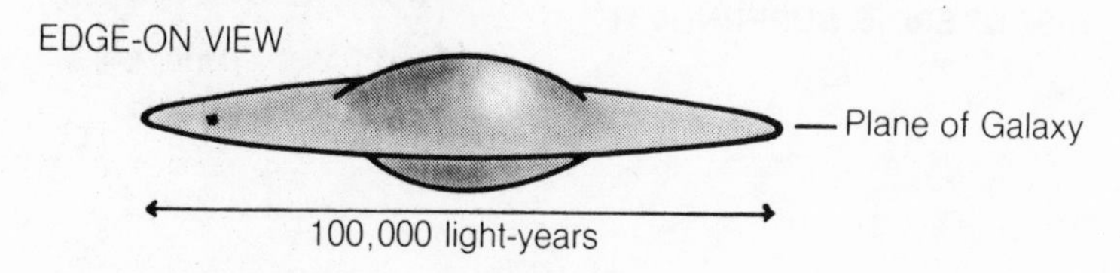

BIRD'S-EYE VIEW

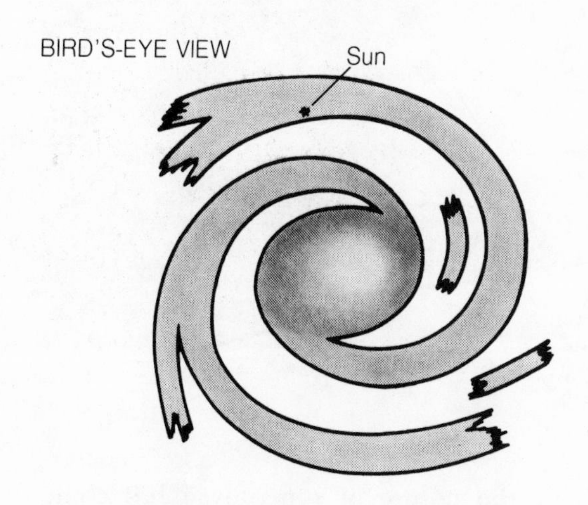

ing blanket of dust that permeates the disk of the Milky Way, screening all but the nearest outbursts from view. An analogy can be made to car headlights in fog. Without the fog, distant vehicles can be sighted; with the fog, only the closest can be seen. However, the galactic dust is very directional, being concentrated along the plane of the Milky Way and toward the center of its discus shape. Thus supernovae in the plane of the Galaxy could be seen with the naked eye only if they lay within about 20,000 light-years of the Earth; they would be invisible if they lay close to the center or on the remote side of the Milky Way. Looking out of the plane of the Galaxy toward galaxies even at vast distances, the "fog" is sufficiently thin for supernovae to have been sighted in large numbers over recent decades (see Figure 1.2). Most of what has been

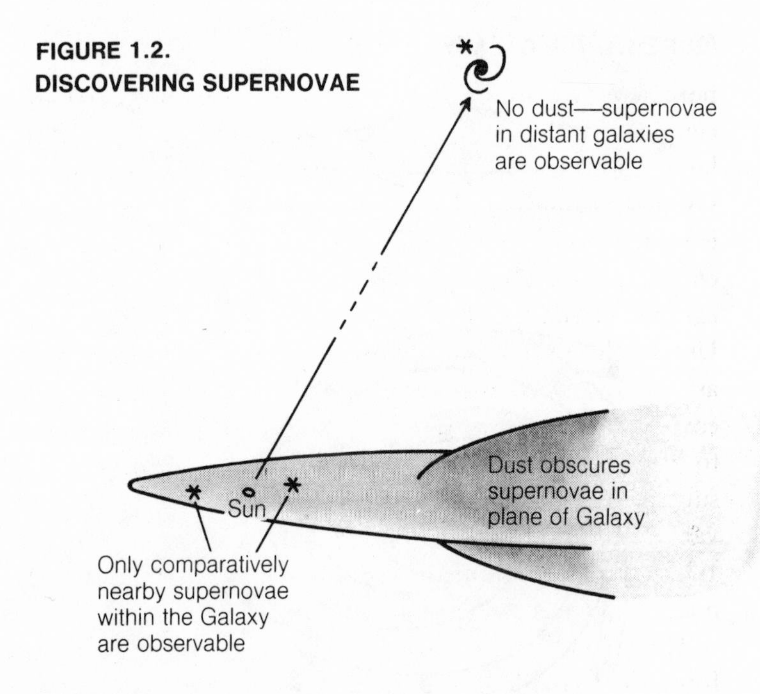

FIGURE 1.2.
DISCOVERING SUPERNOVAE

determined about the nature of supernovae has come from their observation in distant galaxies.

The Erice presentations on the nature of supernovae were based on these modern observations of explosions in external galaxies. By repeatedly photographing selections of galaxies, the appearance of a suddenly brightening star can be noted. At its maximum light, a supernova can outshine the combined light of all the other 10 to 100 billion stars in a typical galaxy. This technique of comparing photographs of galaxies at different times was pioneered in the 1930s by the remarkable Swiss-American astronomer Fritz Zwicky, working at the California Institute of Technology. Zwicky was the father of modern supernova research, and indeed coined the term "supernova." The systematic survey for supernovae that he initiated evolved to the major Mt. Palomar Observatory survey responsible for the discovery of 75 percent of the more than 400 supernovae detected in distant galaxies over the past half-century. (In the future, supernovae should be detected in large numbers with new computer-controlled automated systems currently under development.) Once a supernova is found, preferably early in its outburst, news of its discovery is rushed to observatories world-wide by coded telegrams circulated by the International Astronomical Union, the professional body overseeing the interests of astronomy. Once astronomers are alerted to the new discovery, there are two types of observation it is important to make. The first is to measure how the brightness of the supernova varies, day by day, week by week; a plot of varying brightness is referred to as a "light curve" (Figure 1.3) and the technique of studying the brightness of astronomical objects as "photometry."

The second type of observation is to separate the light from the exploding star into its component colors—to form a spectrum. It is a well-known phenomenon that if a beam of white light is passed through a slit and a prism, it spreads into the continuous rainbow of colors from violet

FIGURE 1.3. A SUPERNOVA LIGHT CURVE

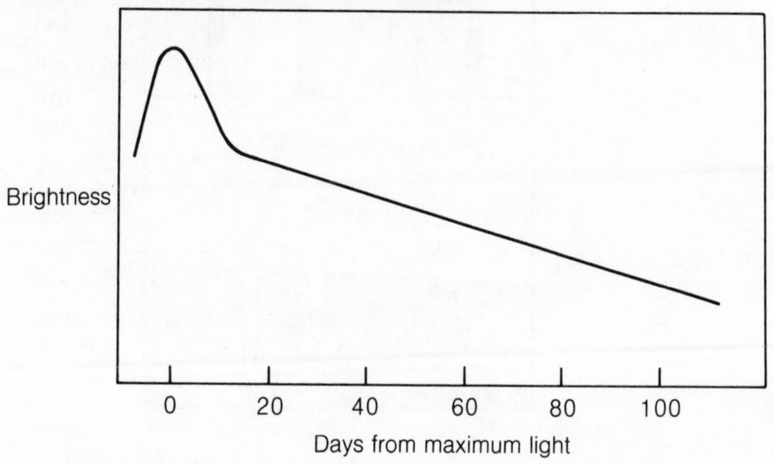

FIGURE 1.4. SPECTRA

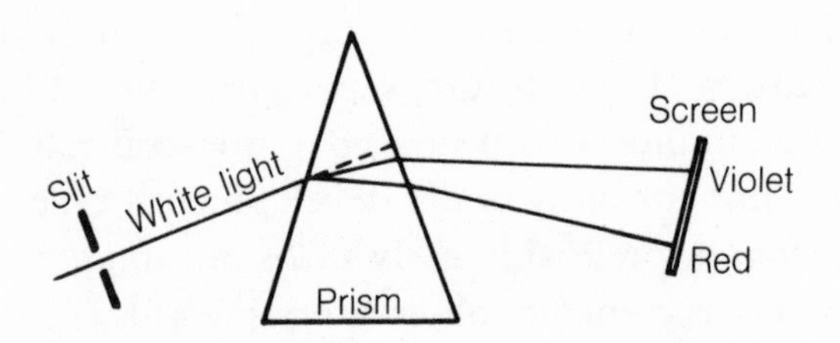

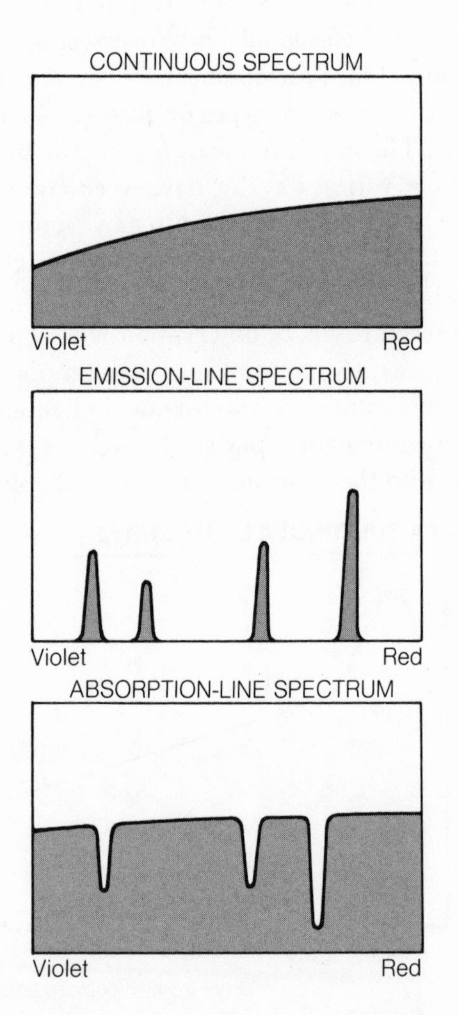

to red, forming a "continuous spectrum" (see Figure 1.4). This analysis, known as spectroscopy, of the light emitted by any source isolates the component colors, which are characteristic of the material emitting the light.

Experiments in the seventeenth and eighteenth centuries revealed light to be a form of wave; it displayed certain properties, notably interference, normally associated with waves. The properties of common examples of waves (water waves or waves on a stretched string) are well known. They are characterized by the distance between adjacent crests (the wavelength), by the height (amplitude) of the wave, and by the number of crests passing a stationary observer each second (the frequency). The wavelength of a particular light wave determines its color. Spectroscopy separates a source of light into its components of different wavelength.

For example, a hydrogen gas lamp shows a characteristic purplish hue; when the light is passed through a slit and a prism, then focused onto a screen, an image of the slit will be seen separately in red (the H-alpha line), blue (the H-beta line), and violet (the H-gamma and delta lines). These various components, seen against a black background, are an emission-line spectrum (see Figure 1.4). Each chemical element when converted to a gas has a characteristic emission-line spectrum—a unique signature that will identify it unambiguously. When a white light source shines through a gas, and a spectrum is formed, the continuous spectrum is found to display dark bands at just the positions where the gas's emission lines would be if it were radiating. This is an absorption-line spectrum. The spectroscopic analysis of light from stars and galaxies, achieved by placing a spectrometer at the focus of a telescope, has proved to be a tool of great power for astronomers.

The spectroscopic analysis of light from a supernova can give details of the temperature of the emitting material, its composition, the speed with which it is expanding away from the site of the explosion, and the distance to the supernova.

Studies of the spectra and light curves of large numbers of supernovae show that they come in two principal varieties: Type I and the Type II. Type II supernovae are intrinsically less luminous than Type I, and characteristically fade more rapidly; they occur only in spiral galaxies like the Milky Way. Type I supernovae occur in all forms of galaxy.

Type I supernovae are characterized by the *absence* of emission from hydrogen, the most abundant element in the universe, in their outburst spectra. In the Milky Way, Type I and Type II supernovae are believed to occur with about equal likelihood. Supernovae, although comparatively rare in any particular galaxy, must be exploding at the rate of about ten every second in the observable universe.

The conference progressed to its second area of discussion, the consideration of why certain stars explode. Several brilliant American theorists dominated this field, among them Roger Chevalier, who was to feature in the SS433 saga. Chevalier, from the Kitt Peak Observatory, had, in addition to making outstanding theoretical contributions to supernova research, shown himself to be a talented observer. With another talented young observer, Robert Kirshner, he made observations that were to prove an interesting sidetrack along the path to SS433.

Despite a few remaining uncertainties, the picture presented by the theoreticians at Erice provided plausible explanations for why stars explode. The Type II supernovae are produced by very massive stars, ten to twenty times more massive than our sun. A star produces its energy in a central core at temperatures so extreme (hundreds of millions of degrees) that certain nuclear burning processes can occur. These are the "fusion reactions"—the type of nuclear burning harnessed by man in thermonuclear (hydrogen) bombs. But a star's fuel reserves, although enormous, are nevertheless finite, so that a star about twenty times the mass of the sun will expend them all in about ten million years. When this happens, there is no longer any energy to sustain the star's structure, and the central core collapses under the action of gravity, the universal attractive force acting between all matter. The core crunches together in a fraction of a second to a state of extreme density, forming a "neutron" star, which might be observed as a "pulsar." In collapse, the core initially overshoots neutron-star density, then bounces back, producing an outward-moving "shock wave." (A familiar example of a shock wave is that set up by an aircraft flying beyond the speed of sound, which produces the sonic boom.)

What about the outer envelope of the star? Having lost the supporting core, it collapses behind it—just as surely as a building would collapse if its foundations were knocked from under it. But before collapsing onto the newly formed neutron star, it encounters the outward-moving shock wave, which blasts it into space at speeds of thousands of kilometers per second. In this way the bulk of the mass of the dying star is ejected outward like shrapnel from a bomb, an act of stellar suicide witnessed as a Type II supernova (see Figure 1.5). Other models have been proposed for Type II supernovae, but the conference was persuaded that core bounce was the current best bet.

The likely explanation for Type I supernovae is less certain. Stars about the mass of the sun or slightly larger do

FIGURE 1.5. EVOLUTION OF A MASSIVE STAR

Star burns nuclear
fuel in its central core

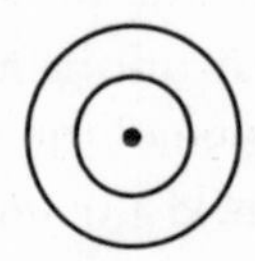

When all nuclear fuel
is expended, central
core collapses

"Core bounce" drives
a "shock" outward,
initiating explosive ejection
of outer envelope . . .

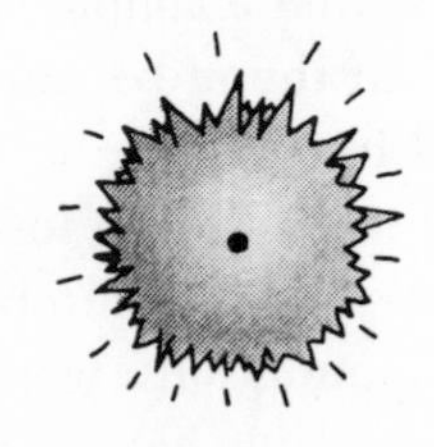

. . . as a Type II supernova

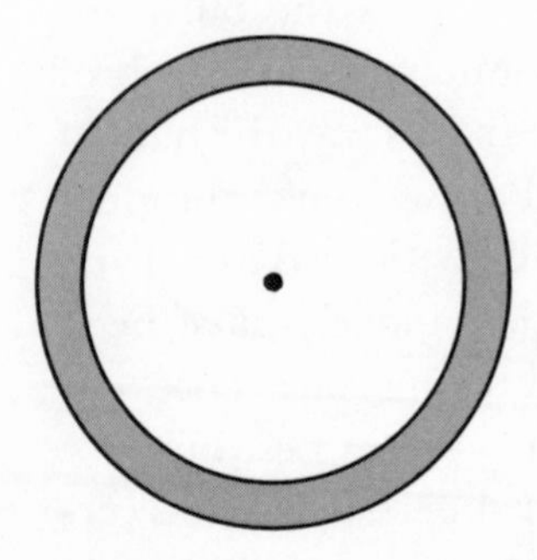

Thousands of years later,
expanding shell may
be seen as an extended
"supernova remnant";
collapsed central core
may be seen as a "pulsar"

not die as catastrophically as the really massive stars, but evolve more sedately over billions of years to become "white dwarfs," burned-out receptacles of nuclear garbage. Nine hundred and ninety-nine stars out of every thousand are believed to evolve eventually to white dwarfs. Stars are often formed in pairs, each star orbiting the other and forming a "binary system." In some such systems the two stars are close enough for matter to be transferred from one to the other under the action of gravity. Any such close binary system in which one of the stars has already evolved to become a white dwarf is a potential Type I supernova candidate. Transfer of material from the normal companion star back onto the white dwarf is believed in certain situations to trigger an explosive nuclear reaction, which blasts the white dwarf to smithereens (see Figure 1.6).

Thus if the U.S. theoreticians were correct, Type II supernovae are created by massive stars, leaving a compact stellar remnant—a neutron star/pulsar—at the site of the outburst. Type I supernovae are formed from some close binary systems containing a white dwarf, where the white dwarf is completely destroyed in the holocaust. The en-

FIGURE 1.6. PROGENITOR OF TYPE I SUPERNOVA?

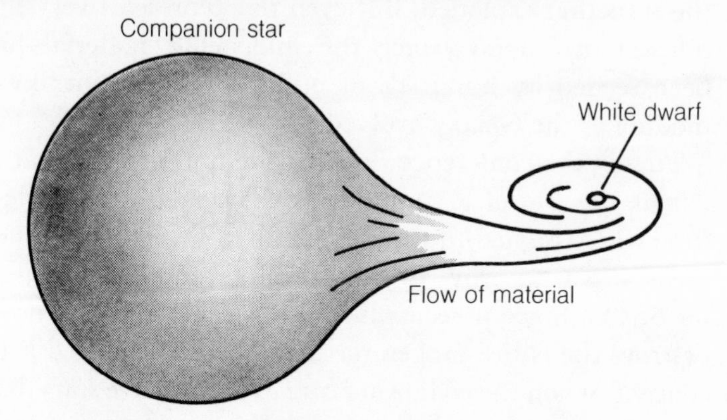

ergy released in each supernova explosion is almost beyond comprehension. The total destructive capacity of the combined nuclear arsenals of the world's superpowers would be dwarfed an unbelievable number of times by the energy of a typical supernova.

As the conference moved to its second week, the emphasis shifted from the stellar explosions themselves to their aftereffects. What is left after the explosion and what is its impact on the interstellar environment? The debris showering outward from a supernova, referred to as the "supernova remnant," emits a variety of radiations—radio waves, visible light, infrared, ultraviolet, and X radiation. These radiations are all known as "electromagnetic waves"; all traveling with the velocity of light and differing only in their wavelength. Each radiation signature from a supernova remnant tells us something different about the physics of the expanding debris. As the expansion continues, the material from the exploding star is diluted by interstellar matter swept up in the expansion, so the radiations from older supernova remnants (older than a thousand years) may be telling us more about the tenuous material that lies between the stars than about the stars that exploded. But even this represents very significant astronomy, since the interstellar material has been seeded by hundreds of millions of supernovae exploding as the Galaxy evolved.

Finally the conference debated the question of what is left at the site of a supernova explosion. Although less time was assigned to this subject than to the three other areas, it was to prove of critical importance in the quest for SS433. Since it seems likely that a Type I supernova destroys the entire progenitor white dwarf, the need is to concentrate on the collapsing core of the massive stars that precipitate Type II supernovae. The presupernova star would be rotating sedately in space, making one revolution every few score of days. But as the core collapses, it spins up like a pirouetting ice skater. The compact neutron star is left spinning with remarkable rapidity, making tens or even hundreds of revolutions each second. By a mechanism still understood only in part, the neutron star emits a finely collimated beam of radio waves, which sweeps around the sky like a lighthouse beacon. If the Earth lies in the path of the rotating beam, the neutron star will be observed as a pulsar. Pulsars caused great excitement in astronomy when they were first discovered, in 1967, and it did not take too long to associate pulsars and supernovae. A pulsar was found near the center of the famous Crab Nebula, the entangled web of debris from a stellar explosion witnessed in A.D. 1054, and also at the center of a very much older supernova remnant in the constellation Vela. Both these radio pulsars were later found to pulse in the optical range as well. Until comparatively recently, these were the only two pulsars unambiguously identified with supernova remnants; a third association was discovered in 1982.

There are more than 130 known supernova remnants in the Galaxy, and over 400 pulsars. The fact that there are many more pulsars known than supernova remnants is not a problem; pulsars live for millions of years, whereas the extended supernova remnants fade after a mere 100,000 years or so. But why out of 130 known supernova remnants are only three associated with pulsars? Well, only the Type II supernovae are expected to produce pulsars; pulsars are more difficult to observe when at large distances; and, finally, the pulsar "beam" may not sweep through the direction of the Earth. Hence the smallness of the number of associations is not entirely unexpected.

American theoretician Stirling Colgate posed the question as to whether neutron stars, although not always observable as pulsars, may be seen in some other way. "Back-of-envelope" calculations he had carried out suggested that young neutron stars might be hot enough to emit X-rays, which should be detectable by a big new NASA X-ray observatory that was soon to be launched. His calculations were to prove remarkably prophetic. He then raised another tantalizing possibility—that the stellar remnants of supernovae may manifest themselves in ways none of us had yet contemplated.

The idea of nonpulsar stellar remnants of supernovae was not a new one, although it took Colgate to stimulate renewed debate on the possibility. The idea had long been advocated, although the evidence was admittedly slim indeed. It did seem that "pointlike" radio sources (not observed as pulsars) were often seen near extended supernova remnants, certainly more often than one might expect if they were merely random background sources (for example, distant galaxies). The peculiar properties of one of these, known as Circinus X-1, was described to the conference by my observing colleague Paul Murdin. Murdin was co-discoverer of the optical pulsar in Vela (only the second optical pulsar identified, after that in the Crab), which he had also detailed to the conference, so his interest in the stellar remnants of supernovae was well established. I described several other interesting objects I knew of. One of these was a supernova remnant called "W50," which had a point radio source (*not* a pulsar) near its center; another was a remnant called "G127.1+0.5," which also displayed a central point source.

The long and often heated debate that followed went nowhere. What possible reason was there for associating the point radio sources and supernova remnants, argued some; surely all one was seeing was the chance positional coincidence on the sky of an extended supernova remnant and a distant background source. More data were urgently needed. No one would believe mere positional coincidences without clear evidence linking the point radio sources and the supernova remnants. Identification of optical stars with the point radio sources might provide the "missing link," since so much can be learned from optical spectroscopy.

If the outcome of the Erice debate on the subject was inconclusive, it nevertheless served a useful purpose. The challenge had been set to find the missing link. Our hooks had been baited and our lines were about to be cast. Chevalier and Kirshner decided to search for the missing link in G127.1+0.5. They were about to pull in what they decided was just an "old boot." Paul Murdin and I decided to search for the missing link in W50, and we were about to hook the big one—SS433! But there were others, not at Erice, who also had their lines in the water—and their lines would shortly become entangled with our own.

2
THE SMOKING GUN

"A long shot, Watson; a very long shot!"
—SIR ARTHUR CONAN DOYLE, *Silver Blaze*

Within days of returning to England, I was packing my bags again to fly to Australia, where Paul Murdin and I had been assigned a period of observing time on the Anglo-Australian Telescope, the AAT. The temptation to use this observing time to follow up many of the problems raised at Erice (and in particular the missing-link mystery) was to prove irresistible, although in truth the time had been assigned to us to investigate a rather different set of problems.

The long flight to Australia gave me plenty of time to reflect on the supernova stellar-remnant problem, and to think back over the previous years of research that had led to the conclusion that stellar remnants may be seen in forms other than conventional pulsars. My introduction to supernovae had come some six years earlier, when the study of their radio remnants had been suggested to me, then a novice radio astronomer, by Professor Bernard Mills of the University of Sydney, Australia. Mills was one of the pioneers of radio astronomy in the 1950s, the designer of giant radio telescopes of a unique kind. I had been fortunate, in 1972, to gain a research fellowship to work with him for two years, and he was astute enough to realize that if I was to achieve anything significant during the limited period of the fellowship, I would need to work closely with someone established in the subject; it was arranged that this should be James Caswell, a British radio astronomer who had been working at a nearby government research establishment for several years. From my point of view it was an excellent choice. Jim was a patient tutor and an admirable observing colleague.

Together we set out, through 1972 to 1974, to survey in a systematic fashion all the radio supernova remnants in the southern portion of the Milky Way. The tools of our work were the giant sixty-four-meter-diameter "dish" radio telescope at Parkes in western New South Wales, and the Mills Cross radio telescope at Molonglo, near Australia's capital city, Canberra. The Mills Cross is a remarkable instrument. Each crossarm is about a mile long, and it takes over an hour to walk around the telescope's periphery. The Parkes radio telescope is of more conventional design, but an engineering marvel nevertheless.

Radio astronomy—viewing the heavens by means of radio waves rather than visible light—had evolved dramatically after World War II by using the new instrumental techniques in radio receivers and aerials developed at that time. It was technology that extended the range of man's senses and gave him a new look at the universe. The science of radio astronomy had, in fact, had its beginnings somewhat earlier, in the experiments of a Bell Telephone Laboratories' radio engineer, Karl Jansky, during 1931–32. Jansky was investigating the nature of radio noise, particularly that originating in thunderstorms, which interfered with communication by radio. In addition to noise of terrestrial origin, he recognized "a hiss in the phones that can hardly be distinguished from set noise." His observation led him to conclude that "the direction of arrival of these waves is fixed in space, i.e. that the waves come from some source outside the solar system."

Later, in 1935, Jansky was able to report that "radiations are received any time the antenna is directed towards some part of the Milky Way system, the greatest response being obtained when the antenna points towards the centre of the system. This fact leads to the conclusion that the source of these radiations is located in the stars themselves or in the interstellar matter distributed throughout the Milky Way."

Jansky's accidental discoveries passed unnoticed at the time by most of the astronomical fraternity. The postwar re-emergence of radio astronomy was led by the new breed of wartime-trained radio engineers, skilled in the radio direction-finding and radar techniques so easily adapted to radio astronomical investigation. The first discrete celestial radio-wave source was identified in 1946, in the constellation Cygnus, and was designated "Cygnus A." By the late 1950s, extensive surveys of the radio sky had resulted in the publication of a series of catalogues of radio sources, and several associations of radio sources with optical objects had been proposed. Within the Milky Way, the first source of radio emission identified was a supernova remnant—the Crab Nebula. The radio emission in supernova remnants arises from the interaction of energetic particles with magnetic fields, a process known as "synchrotron emission"; the emission is also referred to as "nonthermal," to distinguish it from the more familiar thermal emission from a hot gas.

I would like to think that the survey of galactic radio supernova remnants Caswell and I completed was successful. We discovered thirty new remnants, were able to reject twelve objects previously identified as supernova remnants as not being so, and produced improved data on many other objects, including the remnant W50. By about mid-1973 we had accumulated sufficient data to disclose an intriguing fact: pointlike radio sources were often found lying either within or close to the periphery of remnants. With the by-then-accepted association of supernovae and neutron stars, it seemed a tantalizing possibility that some of these might be pulsars.

I approached the two pulsar hunters in Mills's team, Michael Large and John Sutton, with the list of these mysterious pointlike radio sources near remnants in the hope that they could check them out with their sensitive detection equipment. They returned from a hastily arranged expedition to Molonglo with a catalogue of null results, and I was left feeling rather foolish. In fact, two of the sources on that list were later revealed as SS433 and Circinus X-1—objects that would create enormous interest in astronomy—but since they were not pulsars, they did not trigger the Large and Sutton detectors.

Things were not looking good, and I have no doubt that I would have pursued the idea no further had it not been for Caswell's encouragement. His "gut reaction" that there must be something in the number of associations of pointlike (nonpulsar) sources with extended supernova remnants was at least based on many years of research in radio astronomy.

The arguments for and against association went as follows. Certain distant galaxies, the "radio galaxies" (like Cygnus A) are powerful radio emitters and because of their extreme distance look pointlike, despite their enormous size, to most radio telescopes. (In reality, when observed with very high spatial resolution, a radio galaxy is often found to have a bright central "nucleus" plus two oppositely directed "jets" emerging from it.) The distribution of radio galaxies is uniform over the entire sky, and the universe does appear to be very homogeneous. Thus, when one looks through the plane of the Milky Way and sees lots of pointlike sources, one can estimate how many of these are likely to be distant radio galaxies on the basis of their expected uniform distribution. But what we had found was that in the vicinity of supernova remnants many more pointlike objects were being found than would have been expected had they all been merely distant radio galaxies. To this point I do not believe there was any dispute. I am sure it was accepted by all those aware of the situation that a significant fraction (perhaps as much as one-third) of the pointlike sources detected must therefore lie within the Galaxy. But were they *physically associated* with the supernova remnants? Certain pointlike radio sources lying within the Milky Way were expected, some of which might be pulsars. But there was another class of small-diameter radio object, called "compact HII regions," which could confuse the issue. Supernova remnants are in general large extended systems covering a significant area of sky, so there is a distinct likelihood that any foreground or background pulsar, compact HII region, or distant radio galaxy might appear to lie in proximity to the remnant when viewed in two dimensions but not actually be associated in three dimensions (see Figure 2.1). Here was the enigma—and the basis for controversy. Additional information physically linking any particular pointlike source with its "nearby" remnant was needed.

FIGURE 2.1.

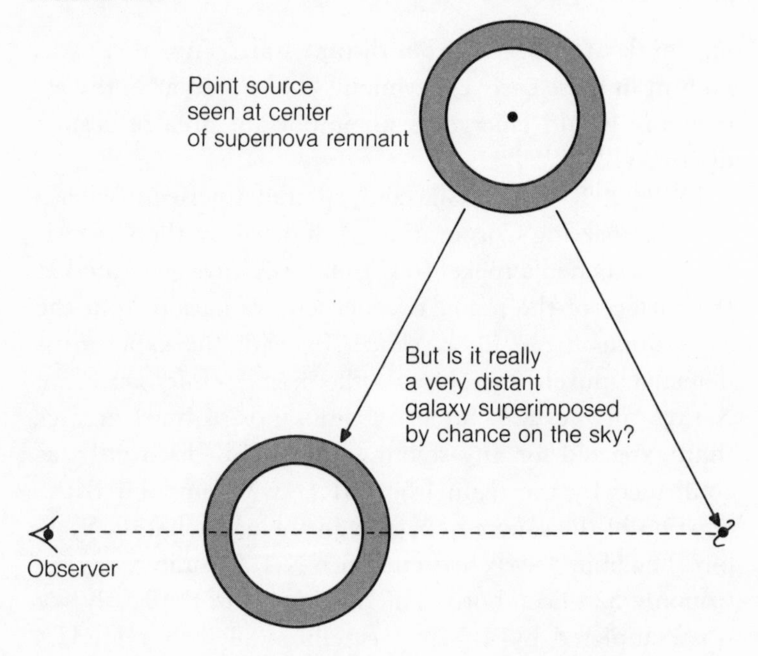

After the earlier setbacks, I doubt whether my interest in the mysterious excess of pointlike radio sources could possibly have been maintained had it not been for an announcement in early 1974 about a source of cosmic X-rays. In the early 1970s, astronomy was being revolutionized by the new discipline of X-ray astronomy. In fact, the research had begun shortly after World War II, when a group of researchers from the U.S. Naval Research Laboratories (NRL), using captured German V-2 rockets, detected X-rays from the sun. X-rays do not penetrate the Earth's upper atmosphere, so they could have been detected only by placing detectors on rockets. The sun turned out to be a comparatively weak source of X-rays, and the detection held out little prospect of detecting similar levels of radiation from distant stars. Thus there was no hint in these early experiments that nonsolar X-ray astronomy would emerge as an important area of cosmic discovery.

In 1962, Riccardo Giacconi, of the American Science and Engineering Corporation, supported by the U.S. Air Force, launched a rocket to search for X-rays generated at the surface of the moon by energetic radiation from the sun—lunar X-ray fluorescence. Instead, the experiment detected, purely by chance, the first cosmic source of X-rays, at a level of intensity thousands of times greater than expected for any stellar source. This discovery was confirmed by the team from NRL, who pinpointed the position of the source of X-rays in the constellation Scorpio. The object was christened Sco X-1. Cosmic X-ray astronomy had been born. The first survey of the X-ray sky was completed by a NASA satellite called "UHURU," launched in 1970. X-rays have now been detected from a host of celestial objects, both within the Galaxy (neutron stars, the debris from stellar explosions, bright X-ray stars like Sco X-1) and beyond (haloes around normal galaxies, clusters of galaxies, galactic jets, quasars). X-ray astronomy has revealed a range of cosmic phenomena never thought possible prior to its inception.

The surprise announcement of 1974 was related to a source of celestial X-rays called "Circinus X-1." A greatly improved position in the sky had been obtained by UHURU for this X-ray-emitting star, which, Caswell realized, showed it to be exactly coincident with one of the "mystery" pointlike radio sources we had found lying on the periphery of one of our newly discovered supernova remnants, G321.9-0.3 (see Figure 2.2). Circinus X-1, which Murdin later described to the Erice meeting as an

FIGURE 2.2.

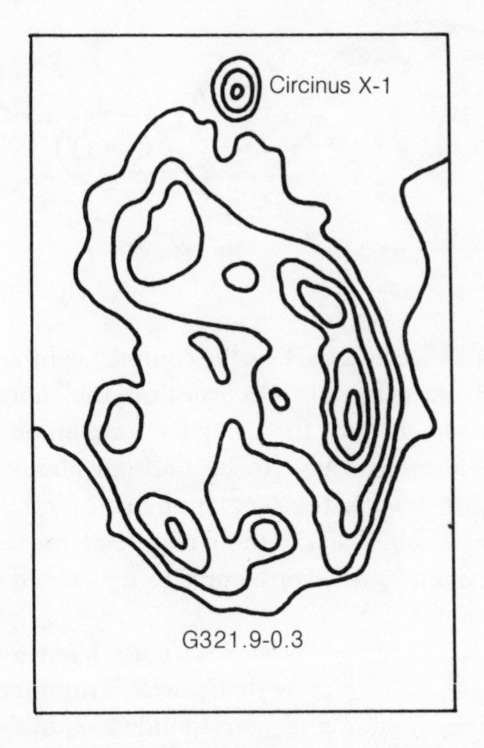

extremely interesting X-ray object, was highly variable in intensity, often flaring brilliantly. The X-ray data alone required that it lie within the Milky Way and at not too extreme a distance. The exact positional coincidence with the newly discovered radio object argued that at least this mystery pointlike source was not just a background galaxy. Here was something to work on—but was it enough on which to construct a new theory of stellar remnants?

The stellar objects within the Galaxy that were strong emitters of X-rays, like Sco X-1, had been known for some time to be close binary systems—not unlike the probable precursors of Type I supernovae, but with a neutron star,

FIGURE 2.3. X-RAY STAR

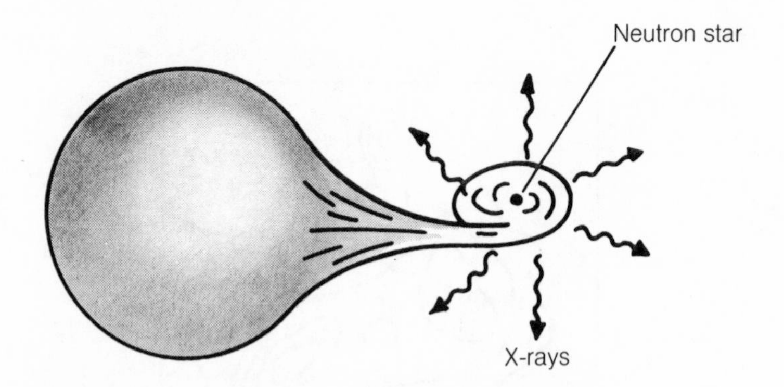

rather than a white dwarf, as the compact companion (see Figure 2.3). As material spills over from the "normal" star and swirls down onto the compact companion, it emits X-rays. What was found to be unusual about Circinus X-1 compared with the large number of other known X-ray binary objects was the strength of the associated radio emission, and its proximity to an extended supernova remnant.

But my two years at Sydney were up. I was sorry to be breaking the close ties with Caswell. Although we remained firm friends and corresponded on many astronomical problems of mutual interest, close transglobal scientific collaborations are very difficult to maintain. I moved to England, to the Mullard Space Science Laboratory (MSSL), about fifty miles south of London. I had spent eighteen months at the laboratory prior to joining Mills, so I knew what I was returning to. I arrived in late August 1974, missing by a few days a California astronomer, Bruce Margon, who had just left after a twelve-month visit. He had gained the reputation of being a talented, energetic, and ambitious young man determined to make the "big time" in astronomy. I eventually met Margon in July 1978, in an accidental encounter that paved the way for his discovery later that year of the unique properties of SS433, which would set it apart from all other stars and place Margon in the position of prominence in astronomy to which he had aspired. Andrew Fabian, a talented young X-ray astronomer known to me from my previous visit, had also just left MSSL. He had joined the brilliant theoretician Martin Rees, who had recently succeeded the incomparable Fred Hoyle at the prestigious Institute of Theoretical Astronomy at Cambridge, England. In early 1979 Fabian and Rees cracked the code of SS433, and revealed it in all its universal glory. In 1974, however, Margon, Caswell, Fabian, Rees, Circinus X-1, W50, and the pointlike radio sources were but unconnected threads yet to be woven into the web that would eventually enmesh SS433.

Artists record their creativity on canvas, poets in verse; research scientists record theirs in papers published in learned journals. Publishing a paper is the accepted way of announcing new discoveries, recording details of new observations, postulating new theories. The best scientific journals do not accept papers for publication directly, but first have them assessed by one or more independent "referees," who check them for errors, originality, soundness of argument, and so forth.

My most pressing concern on getting to MSSL was to see that the last of the Molonglo-Parkes supernova-remnant research was prepared for publication. Caswell and I had managed to get some reports of our observations into print before I left Australia, but there was still the detailed interpretation to complete. One requirement was to compare the radio observations with the appearance of the sky as viewed through optical telescopes. Advice from an optical astronomer was needed. An MSSL colleague suggested that a visit to the home of optical astronomy in

England, the Royal Greenwich Observatory (RGO), was the obvious starting point; indeed, he knew one of the RGO astronomers from student days. This was my introduction to Paul Murdin, and the start of an enjoyable and productive collaboration in optical observations of supernova remnants. Shortly after our first meeting, he moved to the recently completed Anglo-Australian Telescope for three years. As one of the AAT "pioneers," he was thus able to acquire an important early insight into its remarkable performance and capabilities that would greatly assist our later research.

Among the material I was keen to publish at this time was the discovery of the pointlike radio source associated with the highly variable X-ray object Circinus X-1. As already noted, this lay just outside the boundary of one of the recently discovered Molonglo-Parkes radio remnants, so if the extended remnant and pointlike source (Circinus X-1) were indeed associated, this fact had to be explained. Actually, theory had already predicted the possibility of a supernova "stellar" remnant lying outside a supernova "extended" remnant. If one started with a binary system, and one of the stars exploded as a Type II supernova, creating a neutron star, the system left (a normal star plus the neutron star) would be seriously disturbed. Indeed, in certain cases the binary would be completely disrupted, the neutron star being hurled off in one direction and the normal star in the opposite direction. But in other cases the two stars would remain gravitationally bound after the supernova, but would together be flung from the site of the outburst at enormous speed. Rather than the stable presupernova circular orbit of one star about the other, the postsupernova "runaway" system would contain the residual neutron star in a highly eccentric elliptical orbit about the normal companion (see Figure 2.4). A description of the possible evolution of such a system into something resembling Circinus X-1 was developed in collaboration with my office companion at MSSL, John Parkinson. We decided that Circinus X-1 might just be the runaway stellar remnant of the extended supernova remnant G321.9-0.3. Circinus X-1 might be traveling at a relatively sedate 500 kilometers per second—much less than the initial speed of the shock from the supernova of thousands of kilometers per second. But over tens of thou-

FIGURE 2.4. RUNAWAY STARS

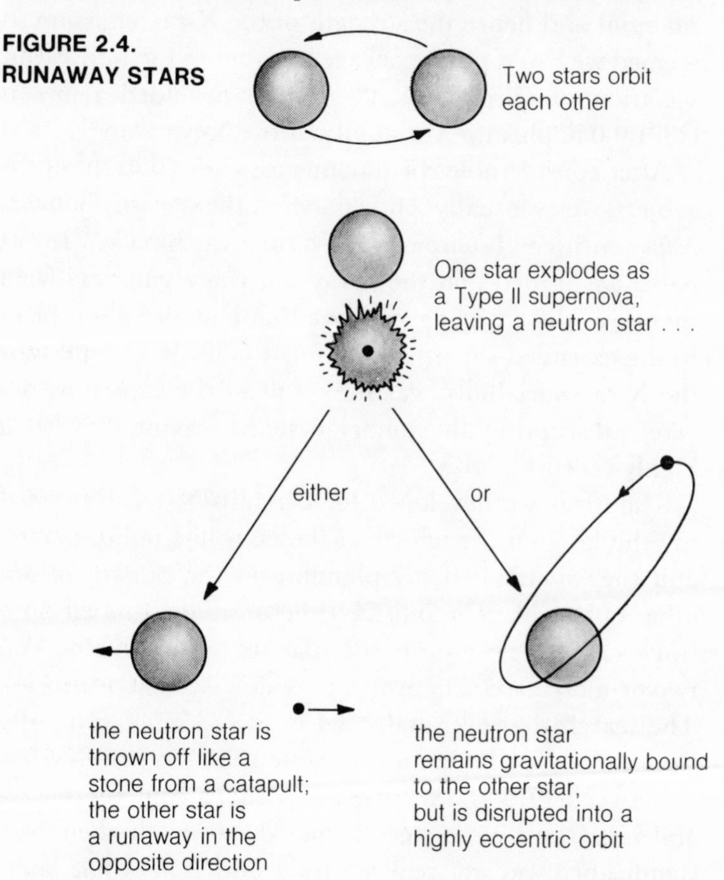

sands of years the shock would slow to a speed of just a few tens of kilometers per second, and could eventually be overtaken by the runaway star system in an astronomical version of the "hare and the tortoise." Thus, for the runaway star from an ancient supernova event that occurred probably more than about 50,000 years ago, the fact that it lay outside the extended remnant did not in itself present a problem. Besides, we argued, since the distance between the normal star and its compact companion would vary around the elliptical orbit, so must the exchange of material and hence the strength of the X-ray emission. It seemed we could put a package together to include the association of Circinus X-1 and the extended remnant G321.9-0.3, plus the variability of the X-ray source.

After considerable correspondence with Caswell on the subject, we eventually sent a paper to the scientific journal *Nature* entitled "Is Circinus X-1 a runaway binary?" In the paper we argued that the X-ray star was a runaway from the site of the ancient supernova that had also given birth to the extended supernova remnant G321.9-0.3, and that the X-ray variability was the result of the supernova severely disrupting the binary system, leaving it with a highly eccentric orbit.

The ideas we developed for Circinus X-1 conditioned my thinking on the nature of the pointlike radio sources, and they dominated my planning in the pursuit of another object like Circinus X-1, because ideas based on a single case are necessarily speculative, but when based on two or more cases can evolve to widely accepted theories. The search that eventually led to SS433 arose primarily from this desire to find a companion for Circinus X-1.

Between 1975 and the Erice supernova conference, several important clues were gathered, although their true significance was not realized fully until somewhat later.

Nevertheless, they can usefully be recalled here. One was related to the nature of the supernova remnant W50. The map of this remnant that Caswell and I published in 1974 from observations with the Molonglo radio telescope depicted a bright "banana-shaped" ridge of emission, rather than a familiar near-symmetrical remnant. Near the bright ridge was a pointlike source. Later, we were accused of having misled other astronomers by publishing a map showing just the bright ridge. In truth, the only ones who could have been misled were those who looked at the map of the remnant only, without reading the accompanying text, where we stated quite clearly that "this ridge may be part of an old large supernova remnant which remains visible only in this extremity." This interpretation was soon confirmed by a young Indian radio astronomer, Thangasamy Velusamy, who as part of his doctoral dissertation mapped W50 at a somewhat higher radio frequency, using the giant 300-foot-diameter radio telescope at the National Radio Astronomy Observatory (NRAO) in Green Bank, West Virginia. Velusamy's map revealed for the first time the true extent of W50. The bright ridge lay along the northern rim of a melon-shaped remnant, with the point source plumb in the center. This pioneering work tended to be ignored by others later in the SS433 saga—a cruel injustice.

Why had Velusamy been able to determine the true extent of W50, whereas our Molonglo map had failed to reveal it? The reason is quite simple. In addition to the discrete sources of radio emission within the Galaxy (supernova remnants, pulsars, etc.), there is a diffuse galactic background emission that "shines" weakly over the whole sky but is strongest along the plane of the Galaxy. The background radiation is most intense at low radio frequencies. Thus, at Molonglo the weak emission of W50 could be distinguished above the diffuse background emission only along the bright northern rim. Velusamy's map was made at more than double the radio frequency, where the galactic radio background emission had faded proportionately more than the supernova remnant's emission. Hence the whole remnant revealed itself in Velusamy's observations, although his map showed less detail of the bright northern rim (see Figure 2.5).

But what of the pointlike radio source at the center of W50? Although this was eventually to lead us to SS433, in 1974 there was controversy surrounding this object. Caswell and I had believed we were the first to identify and position this pointlike radio source. Yet on Velusamy's map of W50 he had annotated it as "4C 04.66." The "4C" in this label referred to the fourth catalogue of cosmic radio sources prepared by the world-famous radio-astronomy observatory at Cambridge. Earlier Cambridge catalogues of radio sources had been criticized because of some inaccuracies and the inclusion of a few spurious sources; but the third and fourth catalogues had the reputation of being very reliable. We were therefore mystified by the 4C label Velusamy had given to the point source at the center of W50. We found that despite the reliability of the catalogue, the 4C 04.66 position was spurious (caused by confusion of the point source at the center of W50 and a bright feature in the northern rim of the remnant). Thus Cambridge had *not* beaten us to the discovery of the point radio source at the center of W50, and Caswell and I were the first to identify its true nature and position it with reasonable accuracy. This "error" on the part of the Cambridge group is rather amusing in view of their later prominent role in determining with great accuracy the position of the radio source at the center of W50 (later to be iden-

FIGURE 2.5. MAPS OF W50

CLARK AND CASWELL MAP

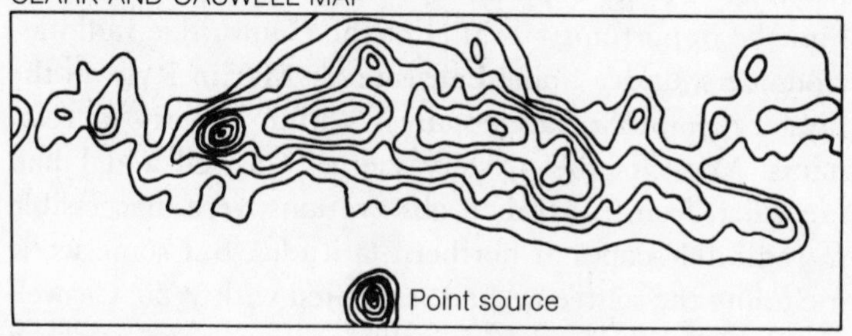

VELUSAMY MAP

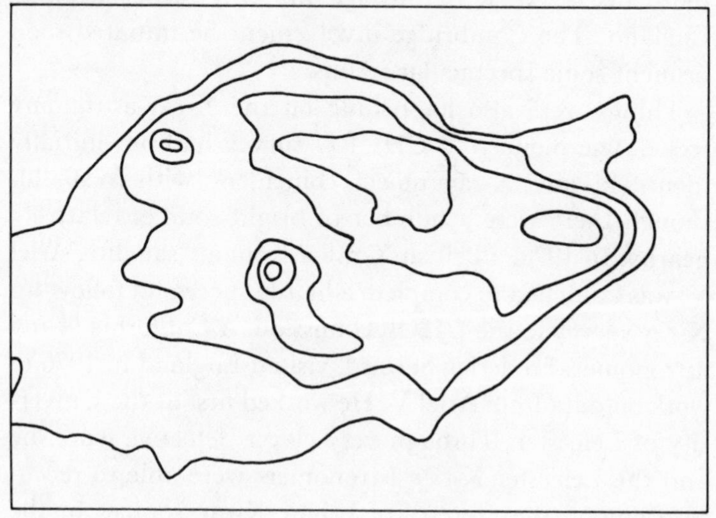

tified with SS433) and their being the first to measure its spectacular radio variability.

In 1975, Jim Caswell came, on a short sabbatical, to the radio-astronomy observatory at Cambridge, where he had carried out his doctoral research. His visit gave us the chance to get together to complete much of our

Molonglo-Parkes supernova-remnant work. It also gave him the opportunity to interest the Cambridge radio astronomers, under Nobel Laureate Sir Martin Ryle, in the mystery pointlike radio sources within supernova remnants. Many of the mystery sources Caswell and I had identified from Australian observations were inaccessible to radio telescopes at northern latitudes, but some were, including the source we had associated with W50. Caswell also had a list of other pointlike sources near northern remnants he knew of through his own earlier work in England. The Cambridge involvement he initiated soon brought some spectacular results.

Things were also happening on the X-ray-astronomy scene. The pioneering UHURU survey had not initially identified any X-ray object coincident with W50, although there were a number of bright sources relatively nearby. In 1975, a British X-ray-astronomy satellite, Ariel V, was launched to complete a highly successful follow-up X-ray survey to the UHURU mission. A California X-ray astronomer, Frederick Seward, visited England in 1976 to work on data from Ariel V. He worked first at the University of Leicester. Through very clever detective work, he and the Leicester X-ray astronomers were able to recognize among the "forest" of bright X-ray sources in the constellation Aquila a faint X-ray "sapling" at the site of W50 that had been missed by UHURU. The intensity of the X-ray emission, although weak, was variable. Despite some uncertainty about the exact location of the X-ray source, it seemed extremely likely that it coincided with the pointlike radio source at the center of W50. The X-ray object was labeled "A1909+04"—the "A" referring to its discovery by the Ariel V satellite, and the numbers giving its celestial co-ordinates and defining its position in the sky. (In a most remarkable prophecy, Seward and the Leicester astronomers suggested that A1909+04 might be an exotic stellar remnant of W50.) After six months at Leicester, Seward joined us at MSSL for a short period. I recall spending with him a very pleasant warm evening during the magnificent English summer of 1976 beside a swimming pool near the laboratory. While our wives and children cooled off in the pool, Seward explained in some detail how A1909+04 had been discovered, and I passed on all I knew about the supernova remnant W50 and the pointlike radio source at its center. Had he followed up his X-ray discovery by looking for the optical star behind A1909+04, the prize of SS433 would have been his. However, he was to take the lead in X-ray observations after its eventual unmasking, and his role in this was a crucial one.

During 1976, a special meeting of the Royal Astronomical Society, the bastion of British astronomy, was held to discuss some of the important discoveries that had been made up to that time with Ariel V. One of the contributions to the meeting was made by John Shakeshaft, from the radio-astronomy observatory at Cambridge. Following Caswell's initiative in instigating a study of the pointlike radio sources within supernova remnants, Shakeshaft and his colleagues had found that the source within W50 flared erratically. Such behavior is rather unusual for radio sources, the vast majority of which shine with constant radio brightness. Here was a supernova remnant, apparently associated with a pointlike radio source, with highly variable intensity that emitted X-rays. Caswell and some colleagues in Australia had by then found that the radio emission from the Circinus X-1 source also flared. The similarities between Circinus X-1 and A1909+04 were starting to appear suggestive indeed, despite the fact that Circinus X-1 was a very bright X-ray source at maximum intensity, whereas A1909+04 was comparatively weak. Both showed variable X-ray emission (not by itself too unusual for galactic X-ray sources); both were associated with pointlike radio sources that varied spectacularly in intensity (this *was* unusual); and it was possible that both were associated with extended supernova remnants (if proven, this would be a most exciting result).

Although Seward, Caswell, and I had failed to follow up the W50 point source by looking with an optical telescope for the star system responsible for the strange emissions, Cambridge astronomer John Whelan had not been so neglectful of Circinus X-1. Using the best estimates of positions for the radio point source and the X-ray source, he and several colleagues searched with the giant Anglo-Australian Telescope for the associated "star." When they viewed the area of sky near Circinus X-1, they noticed that one star on the telescope's television monitor was, although very faint, somewhat brighter than on the photograph of that region of sky they had brought with them. When they took a spectrum of the star's light, the reason quickly became apparent. Not only was the star "red" (that is, the continuum emission was stronger at the red end of the spectrum), but it had the very intense red emission line characteristic of hydrogen—the H-alpha emission line (see Figure 2.6). The TV camera emphasized the red emission more than the photograph, and so the star had looked comparatively brighter on the monitor. Other weaker-emission features in the spectrum were due to helium. The star was exactly coincident with the point radio source. There could be absolutely no doubting that the point radio source, the peculiar star, and the X-ray source Circinus X-1 were one and the same object—almost certainly a complex binary system containing a normal star and a compact star in orbit around each other. The emission lines in the optical spectrum were then believed to be

FIGURE 2.6. WHELAN'S SPECTRUM OF CIRCINUS X-1

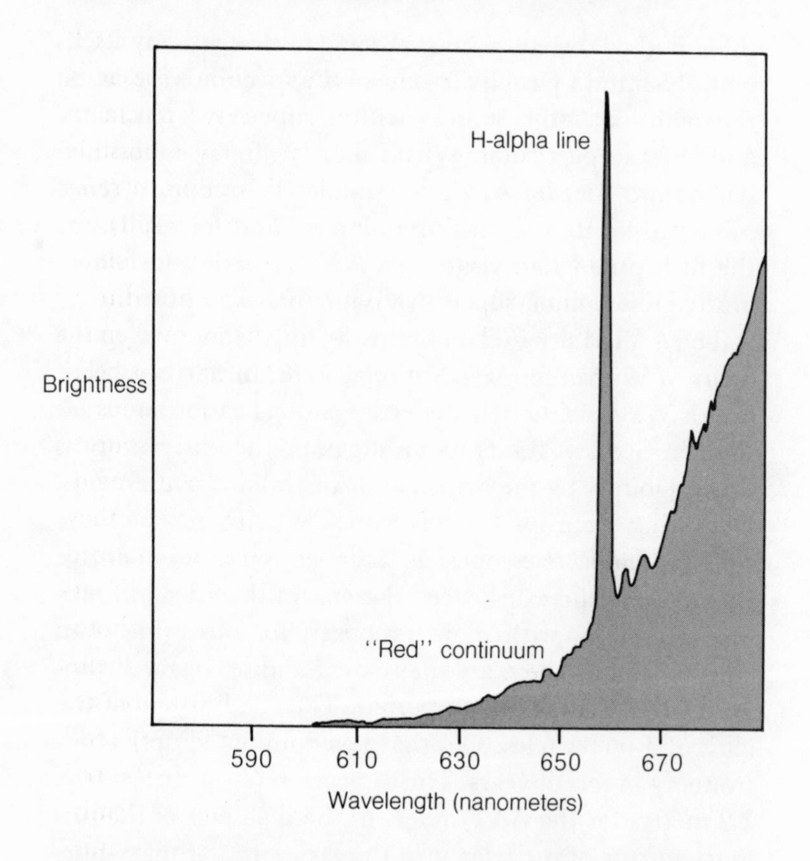

produced in the gas being stripped from the normal star of the binary, some of which would fall onto the compact star and emit X-rays. The fact that the continuum was red did not imply that this was the intrinsic color of the star; rather, the scattering of a star's blue light by dust in the tenuous medium between the stars tends to redden it. (Stellar reddening is exactly analogous to the reddening of the sun at sunset.)

This was the state of affairs at the time of the Erice supernova conference in May 1978, where Paul Murdin presented to the conference a detailed description of Circinus X-1 and I passed on some of the speculative ideas on the pointlike radio sources within supernova remnants, and W50 in particular. When, shortly after, I found myself bound for the Anglo-Australian Telescope, I determined to locate the missing link once and for all. It was the fifth time I had visited the AAT to carry out collaborative research on supernova remnants with Murdin.

The AAT is situated on Siding Spring Mountain, in the heart of Warrumbungle National Park, in northern New South Wales, although the observatory headquarters are sited in Sydney. As its name suggests, the observatory is funded jointly by the British and Australian governments. Observing time on the telescope, as with most of the world's major telescopes, is assigned on a competitive basis; "scientific excellence" dominates the selection process, although, with more proposals for observing than time available, there are many outstanding research programs that cannot be supported. The AAT is one of the class of 4-meter telescopes that has dominated optical astronomy in recent years. The dimension (more accurately, 3.9 meters for the AAT) refers to the diameter of the primary mirror of the telescope; the larger the primary mirror, the greater its light-gathering capacity and hence the fainter (and usually the more distant) the objects that can be observed. (The light-gathering capacity of a 4-meter telescope is about a millionfold that of the fully dilated pupil of the human eye.) However, it is not merely the size of the AAT that sets it apart. The telescope, under computer control, is able to point with remarkable precision for a telescope of its size to a given position in the sky and accurately track under computer control that position for the extended periods required for observations of very faint objects. During observation, the telescope is under the control of a "night assistant"; the astronomer operates the sophisticated instruments and computers acquiring data.

Each minute of observing time on a big telescope is precious (and extremely expensive), and time cannot be wasted searching the sky for the objects to be observed. It is therefore important to have accurately determined positions and "finding charts" (photographs) for pertinent areas of sky, so that the telescope can be pointed accurately and quickly at the objects to be studied. I arranged to visit Murdin at the observatory headquarters in Sydney several days before our observations were scheduled, so we could complete planning them in minute detail. At this point, fate had a final card to play. We had requested originally to make our observations with an instrument called the "Image Photon Counting System" (IPCS). Sophisticated electronic devices have replaced the photographic plate in many (but certainly not all) aspects of astronomy, and the IPCS is particularly suited for use in spectroscopy of extended astronomical objects such as supernova remnants. Murdin and I had used it with considerable success for all our previous observing sessions on the telescope. A few days before our observing run was scheduled, the IPCS failed catastrophically after an astronomer failed to power it down according to accepted practice at the end of a night's observing, and it soon became apparent that the instrument would take many weeks to repair. At this point, Murdin's considerable knowledge of the telescope and the various instruments available proved invaluable, and before I had even arrived in Australia he had arranged for another instrument, called the "Image Dissector Scanner" (IDS), to be fitted to the telescope for our observing run. The IDS is better suited to the observation of stars than extended objects, in contrast to the IPCS; thus, quite apart from the challenge of seeking the missing link, we found ourselves forced to depart from the program of observing extended remnants for which we had been awarded the time, and to substitute an observing program concentrating on stellar objects.

We prepared our finding charts with maximum care, using existing photographs of the southern sky produced by a British telescope of the Schmidt type, also located on Siding Spring Mountain; for the northern portion of the sky we used photographs from a similar Schmidt telescope on Mt. Palomar. Although planned initially as a "scout" telescope for the AAT and to prepare a photographic atlas of the whole of the southern sky (the Palomar Schmidt had produced the standard photographic atlas for the northern sky), this Schmidt telescope had also done much forefront research in its own right. When preparing the finding chart for the W50 point radio/X-ray source, the radio position we used was not that from the radio maps of W50, but a very much more accurate position I had determined in collaboration with Sydney astronomer David Crawford, in compiling a catalogue of point radio sources close to the galactic plane. To our amazement, when Murdin measured the Schmidt finding chart, there was a comparatively bright star almost exactly coincident with the point radio/X-ray source. I can recall vividly that he put a circle around it with a grease pencil on the photographic enlargement we had made, noting: "It seems to have a flag on it reading, 'Hey, look at me!' " But could things be that simple? The star Whelan had found corresponding to Circinus X-1 had been extremely faint and difficult to find. Surely the star corresponding to the W50 point radio/X-ray source could be expected to be equally elusive? I doubt whether either of us took the "flag-waving" bright star too seriously. Instead, we noted the large number of extremely faint stars in the region, any one of which we supposed might be our quarry. Whelan was in Sydney at this time, having just returned from the telescope where he had been reobserving Circinus X-1. When I described to him the evidence for an object of the Circinus X-1 type at the center of W50 from existing radio and X-ray data, he boldly predicted that we were on to a winner.

The 300-mile journey from Sydney to the AAT is usually by air to the nearby town of Coonabarabran, followed by a twenty-mile car ride through the spectacular scenery of the national park. The stately dome of the AAT dominates the mountaintop, with the Schmidt telescope plus numerous smaller telescopes nearby. Visiting astronomers stay at a comfortable lodge; the sign outside, "Quiet please: astronomers asleep," is one's introduction to the routine of working nights and grabbing what sleep one can during the morning hours before the afternoon preparations for the next night's observing.

The June 1978 observing run started as had all others, with high expectations and a sense of excitement at being back in control of such a wonderful telescope. The W50 point radio/X-ray source featured about the middle of our list of a large number of objects (mostly related to supernova remnants) for study. Although we had never used the IDS previously, it proved to be straightforward to operate. The night of June 28 was beautifully clear, and we hoped for another fruitful night's observing. A minor technical fault had developed in the telescope, however. The IDS is designed to take a spectrum of a star through a given aperture, with a second aperture looking at a nearby portion of the sky; then the apertures are switched. This technique is used so that any background "sky" light can be subtracted from the true spectrum of the star. A switch on the control console used to offset the telescope from one aperture to the other had failed, and would operate only if held firmly in place during the whole of an observation. It seemed ironic that the performance of a highly sophisticated computer-controlled telescope could be compromised by the failure of a single switch. But help was at hand—literally! A young Scot named Frederick Watson had an observing session following ours, and because he had not used the telescope previously, he had arrived early to see how things were done. His introduction to the AAT, one of the world's most advanced automated telescopes, was to be a night spent with his finger firmly on the aperture offset button.

As the night progressed, we worked steadily through our observing schedule, eventually moving to W50 as Aquila reached the optimum position in the sky for observing. With the telescope slewed to the new position, the field on our finding chart was immediately recognizable on the telescope's TV monitor. There at the center of the field was the bright flag-waving star. Convinced that any candidate for the W50 point radio/X-ray source would be, like Circinus X-1, extremely faint, we initially skirted around the bright star to take spectra of fainter stars in the field. They were all boringly ordinary. Obviously the brighter star was worth a careful look, although we did not wish to risk the sensitive IDS by shining too much light onto it. Paul was monitoring the IDS output as I supervised the operation of the telescope and Fred kept his finger firmly on the aperture offset button. As the telescope was nudged gently to the image of the flag-waving star, and before the IDS had started recording data, a spectrum similar in many ways to that of Circinus X-1 revealed itself on the computer displays. "Bloody hell!" screamed Paul. "We've got the bastard!"

3 THE MORNING AFTER . . .

"You see but you do not observe. . . .
It is a capital mistake to theorize
before one has data."
—SIR ARTHUR CONAN DOYLE,
Scandal in Bohemia

The Royal Greenwich Observatory is housed in a medieval moated castle nestled in the Sussex downs of southern England. It is hard to imagine a more idyllic site for a research establishment—nor a less suitable one for a modern observatory. In its favor, the remoteness of the castle and its picturesque setting are highly conducive to original research, offering the same isolation from the "real world" as the cloistered university or a medieval monastery. The spectacular scenery, the beautiful Elizabethan gardens, the country walks, and the quaint village pubs within easy reach are a bonus that no astronomer could fail to appreciate. On the negative side, the climate of Britain, with its almost perpetual cloud cover, is not well suited to optical astronomy; in addition, the marshland adjacent to the observatory is often mistbound in winter, and lights from the nearby towns of Eastbourne and Hastings contaminate the night sky. The original observatory, founded in 1675 and sited in the Thames-side royal park at Greenwich, is now a museum; its working telescopes were moved from smogbound London to the supposed clear air of Sussex after World War II. In addition to the refurbished older telescopes, a large new telescope, named after Isaac Newton, was built. But the new site did not offer all that had been hoped for; sadly, there is little to distinguish between London smog and Sussex mist, or London lights and Eastbourne illuminations. A more enlightened attitude now exists (aided by the new global freedom that has resulted from comparatively cheap and convenient international air travel), and Britain's new major telescopes are sited on remote mountaintops in Hawaii, Australia, and the Canary Islands (to where the Isaac Newton telescope had now been transferred).

I moved from the Mullard Space Science Laboratory to the Royal Greenwich Observatory in September 1977. Returning there in early July 1978, after two weeks at the Anglo-Australian Telescope, I found a message from an ex-MSSL colleague, Greg Parkes. He was visiting RGO and wanted to see me. At the appointed time, I heard him climbing the spiral staircase to my office high in the castle's central turret, overlooking the main entrance, where a drawbridge once spanned the moat. He was accompanied by a smartly dressed young American wearing sunglasses, who was introduced to me as Bruce Margon, from the University of California, Los Angeles, known to me previously only by the reputation he had earlier gained at MSSL. The two men had just completed a week's observing run on the Isaac Newton telescope—or, more exactly, a week's *non*observing. The Sussex skies had lived up to their reputation and remained cloudbound for the entire week allocated to their observations. Margon had by this time no doubt resigned himself to returning home to California empty-handed; he could hardly have imagined that he would in fact return with the biggest astronomical catch of his life. His introduction to SS433 was purely chance—a case of being in the right place at the right time, and fortuitously talking to the right people. But fate could hardly have placed evidence of this stellar wonder in more receptive hands, for he was to play the role of supersleuth in the SS433 saga.

Parkes and Margon were interested to learn how my trip to the AAT had gone, and of any new results Paul Murdin and I might have obtained. Good scientific research should (and usually does) involve the sharing of ideas, so I had no hesitation in telling them about our exciting discovery of the strange emission-line star we believed to be associated with the supernova remnant W50.

The evidence I was able to show them consisted of just two spectra. The first was in yellow-to-red light, and the second in violet-to-green light. The "red" spectrum was the one we had observed first, on the night of June 28–29, 1978, and that had so excited us because of certain similarities to Circinus X-1. The "blue" spectrum had been obtained on the following night. The red spectrum was dominated, as in Circinus X-1, by strong line emission associated with hydrogen—the H-alpha line, with a wavelength of 656.3 nanometers (one nanometer is a billionth of a meter). Other, weaker, lines were readily identified with helium. The vast majority of stars do not show emission lines; rather, their spectra show just continuous emission with various absorption features. So the appearance of strong emission lines set the star apart as other than ordinary, and likely to be the optical counterpart of the peculiar radio/X-ray star. The fact that the emission lines were associated with hydrogen and helium was not in itself of great surprise, these being the two most abundant elements, accounting for 98 percent of the material in the universe. But there were unusual features in the red spectrum that belied easy identification. These appeared to be broad, highly structured "bands" of emission, rather than discrete lines (see Figure 3.1).

Even as observations were being made at the telescope, Murdin had pored over books in the observatory's library, trying to decipher the strange spectral signature. But none of the standard codes would fit. His first guess had been that the star might be one of a peculiar type of object known as a "Wolf-Rayet star." The Wolf-Rayet stars (named for their French co-discoverers of 1867 C. J. E. Wolf and G. A. P. Rayet), are very rare, very hot objects. They are thought to be extremely massive stars that have become bloated and unstable, approaching senility, puffing off their outer layers in the form of a "stellar wind" or perhaps shedding them to a companion star. But the Wolf-Rayet picture did not fit, because, although such stars do exhibit broad emission features somewhat analogous to those in our red spectrum, they are usually charac-

FIGURE 3.1. THE FIRST SPECTRUM OF SS433

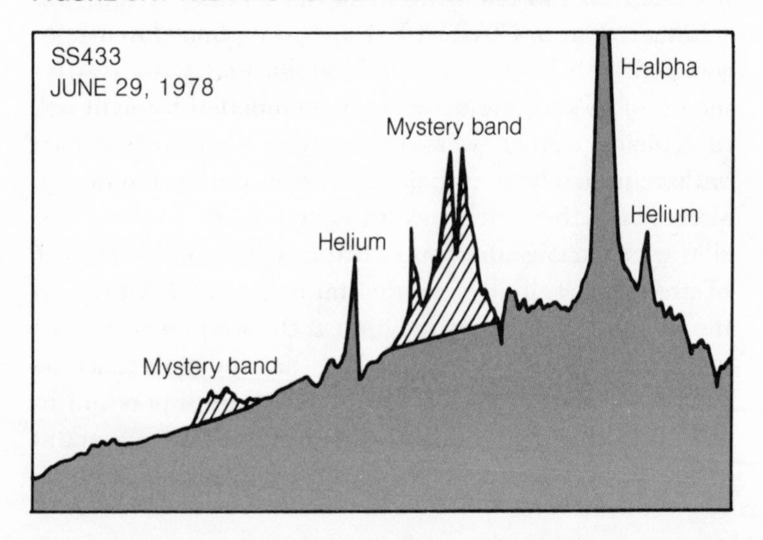

terized by the absence of hydrogen emission; yet this strange star was dominated by intense hydrogen emission. Also the mysterious bands were in the wrong place in the spectrum for a Wolf-Rayet star. Murdin's rapid perusal of the literature failed to reveal any clues to the peculiar broad emission features, but, these apart, we were tempted back to the similarities with Circinus X-1, particularly the intense emission lines from hydrogen and helium. The star appeared so bright that it hardly seemed possible that it could have escaped discovery in the searches of the heavens for peculiar emission-line stars. Perhaps the best known of such surveys at that time was the one compiled in 1970 by L. Wackerling. When Murdin hurried back to the library to check this catalogue, he found that the strange star was not included. We were, at that stage, sadly unaware of another list of peculiar emission-line stars, published the previous year—the little-known and then totally unacclaimed catalogue by Bruce Stephenson and Nicholas Sanduleak. One year later, there was not a professional astronomer in the world who had not heard of the "SS catalogue."

Since the red spectrum of the new star seemed so mysterious, we decided to look the following night (our last on the telescope) at a blue spectrum, hoping that it might unravel the star's secrets. We might have learned these earlier had we continued to concentrate our attention on the red emission.

Margon and Parkes were intrigued by the evidence I had on display. Margon's main interest in astronomy was the study of stars with associated X-ray emission, and since he was soon to return to California to make observations on telescopes there, he asked me for a position for the new star. I gave it to him and told him also of the radio observations at Cambridge. It was Bruce Margon's lucky day; I had just handed him a winning ticket in the universal lottery. He would use his prize well.

It is possible to announce a spectacular new discovery to the astronomical world via the telegrams and airmail circulars issued through the International Astronomical Union. Murdin and I had agreed that the "birth" of the "bastard" star would be announced by this means; but first we had to check a few details of its pedigree. For example, we had to be absolutely certain that the peculiar emission-line star, the variable pointlike radio source, and the Ariel V X-ray source A1909+04 were definitely one and the same object. Certainly the peculiar properties of the strange trio suggested they must be the same system, but to be absolutely certain it would have to be shown that they were *exactly* coincident in the sky. There was no hope at that stage of getting a precise position for the X-ray star; the Ariel V position was necessarily somewhat uncertain because of the nature of the instrument that made the discovery. However, we could now measure the position of the proposed optical counterpart with high precision. What was needed was an extremely accurate radio position (the Molonglo result of 1974 was not accurate enough for the purpose, despite its having been adequate for us to locate the star), and I knew exactly where to go for it. Within minutes of Parkes and Margon leaving me, I was on the phone to John Shakeshaft at the radio-astronomy observatory at Cambridge. It was, to repeat, Shakeshaft who had reported the discovery of the variability of the pointlike radio source at the center of the supernova remnant W50, two years previously, following the monitoring of the source that Caswell had initiated at Cambridge.

The radio telescopes at Cambridge are of a special design, known as "aperture synthesis" instruments, pioneered by the Cambridge radio astronomers. Such radio telescopes are able to determine positions of celestial radio sources with remarkable precision, especially Cambridge's vanguard 5-kilometer instrument. Shakeshaft was extremely interested to learn of the discovery of the optical counterpart, and knowing the importance of verifying the association by confirming the exact positional coincidence of the star and the pointlike radio source, he was happy to agree to reveal the accurate radio position determined with the 5-kilometer telescope.

Positions of astronomical objects are given in terms of the celestial equivalent of longitude and latitude for terrestrial locations. The equivalent of longitude is known as "right ascension" (RA), and the equivalent of latitude is called "declination" (dec). Right ascensions are measured relative to a reference position in the constellation Pisces; declinations are measured relative to the so-called celestial equator (defined by the Earth's equatorial plane intersecting the celestial sphere). Since the Earth's attitude in space varies with time, it is necessary to refer celestial positions to a particular epoch if a meaningful comparison is to be made of positions determined at different times. This reference epoch is the year 1950. For reasons that are not of concern here, right ascension is measured in hours, minutes, and seconds of time, whereas declination is measured in degrees, minutes of arc (60 minutes to a degree), and seconds of arc (60 seconds to a minute of arc).

The accurate celestial position Shakeshaft gave me for the point radio source at the center of W50 was, in 1950 co-ordinates: right ascension, 19 hours 9 minutes 21.273 seconds; declination, 4 degrees 53 minutes of arc 53.1 seconds of arc. (The position, just north of the celestial equator, fortuitously placed the star within reach of most

Northern *and* Southern Hemisphere telescopes.) The right ascension of the mystery star agreed exactly with Shakeshaft's position, but the declination differed by almost one second of arc. The accuracy of the Cambridge 5-kilometer telescope radio position was claimed to be better than a tenth of a second of arc, and that of the optical star about a quarter of a second of arc. I was sorely troubled by the discrepancy. Murdin was still in Australia, and I cabled him immediately to get him to check the optical position as determined with high precision by the AAT. At the same time, I had experts at RGO use sophisticated measuring machines to determine the position of the star on Schmidt photographs and also on photographic plates specifically taken for the purpose with one of the small RGO telescopes. All of these sources gave the same result: a right ascension identical with the radio position, but a declination of 4 degrees 53 minutes 54.0 seconds.

Although it seemed to be inconceivable that a peculiar emission-line star and a highly variable point radio source should lie so close together and not be one and the same object, the slight positional discrepancy raised doubts in my mind. I cabled Murdin again. There could be no doubt about the optical star's position, and it seemed impossible that the Cambridge radio position could be in error bearing in mind the exceptional precision of the instrument and the Cambridge radio observatory's reputation for producing data of high accuracy and reliability. Murdin shared my concern, and we decided not to submit the result for release by IAU circular as planned. The last thing any astronomer wants to do is lay claim to a significant new discovery, only to be forced later to withdraw the claim as new information becomes available. The astronomical world had to wait a few more weeks for news of a genuine birth. But when the birth notice came, it was to be announced by someone else.

Colleagues at RGO and a number of distinguished visitors to whom I showed the data took a great interest in the strange spectral signature of the new star. Of particular interest were the peculiar band features that seemed impossible to identify uniquely with the characteristic emission from any of the known elements. It would eventually be these strange bands that set this star apart from all others.

The optical counterparts of the majority of strong X-ray stellar systems tend to be highly variable in their output, and it was obviously extremely important to be able to look at the star again to see how it might have changed. But here we had a problem. Time on British telescopes is assigned competitively in advance, and there is always a delay of many months between submitting a proposal to observe on a telescope and finally getting on the telescope to carry out the observations. Since the strange star would be hidden in daylight from early December to February, had we followed the normal course we would not have been able to monitor it again until March 1979 at the earliest. We knew that we had made an important discovery, and were not prepared to wait. Consequently, Murdin asked a colleague in Australia, David Allen, who was about to observe on the AAT, whether he would take other observations of the star for us as a personal favor. This he generously agreed to, and new observations were made between July 13 and 16, 1978. The new spectra again showed the bright emission lines of hydrogen and helium, but the peculiar emission bands were gone, although a strange variable "wing" seemed to have emerged on the H-alpha line. So the star did, as we suspected it would, vary in its line output. By itself such variability was not surprising, being a well-known phenomenon for the optical counterparts of galactic X-ray stars. We were led to suppose that the bands apparent in our first spectra must be made up of a confused conglomerate of emission lines from well-known elements (for example, helium and iron) at high temperatures, with conditions in the star system varying so that sometimes they were suitable for producing these "high-excitation" lines and sometimes they were not.

Although Murdin and I had stepped back while on the verge of announcing the discovery through the IAU circular system because of the apparent radio/optical positional discrepancy, we pressed ahead with getting our data prepared for publication, so that it would receive the appropriate recognition. We hoped that in the time it would take for the paper to be published (typically, several months) the positional-discrepancy problem would be resolved. A first draft of the paper had in fact been prepared in record time. At the end of the exciting night on the telescope during which we had first stumbled on the bastard star, we wandered at sunrise back to the lodge to try to gain a few hours' sleep before our final night's observing, and Murdin joked, "I expect you to have a paper reporting this discovery written up by breakfast." It was a challenge that could not be ignored. When he arrived at the breakfast table five hours later, the draft of a short paper I had entitled "A1909+04—a companion for Circinus X-1?" awaited his perusal. The title I had chosen reflected my conviction that the star was a similar system to Circinus X-1, the pursuit of such an object having been our clearly defined goal from the outset.

When I left Australia a few days later to return to the RGO, Murdin continued work on the draft. The first thing he changed was the title; he called it "An unusual emission-line/X-ray source/radio star possibly associated with a supernova remnant." The change in title was not significant (although it summarized better the nature of the strange star), since the emphasis of the paper remained the same: the fact that we had found a peculiar emission-line star we believed was associated with a highly variable radio source and X-ray source, situated at the center of the supernova remnant W50. We argued that the peculiar star was the stellar remnant left from the gigantic stellar explosion, which had also produced the extended supernova remnant W50. The similarities to Circinus X-1 were stressed throughout the paper. We decided that rather than publish our discovery spectrum showing the peculiar emission bands that we could not explain satisfactorily, we would show only a spectrum from July 15–16, where they appeared to be absent. A picture of the new star's red spectrum alongside a red spectrum we had obtained several years earlier of Circinus X-1 emphasized the spectral similarity, with the strange bands absent (see Figure 3.2). Since we intended to apply for more telescope time in early 1979 (the earliest we could hope to get back on the AAT given the vagaries of the time-allocation procedure) to investigate the strange emission bands, we thought it premature to attempt to explain them at this stage. In the draft paper we dismissed them thus: "The higher excitation spectrum is variable; details will be given elsewhere."

It was a tragic oversight! By the time we got to look at the star again, the mystery bands had alerted the astro-

FIGURE 3.2.

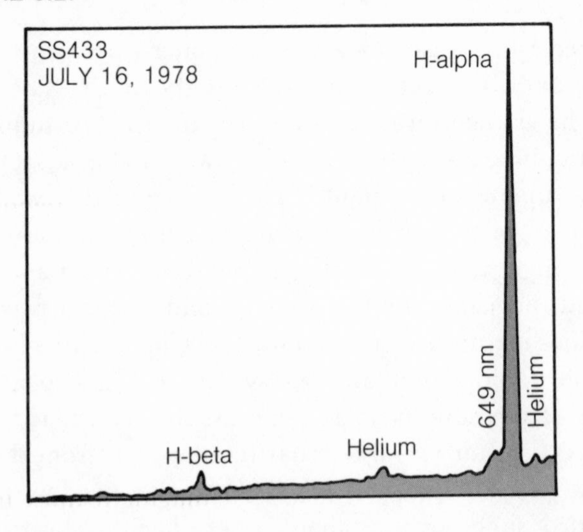

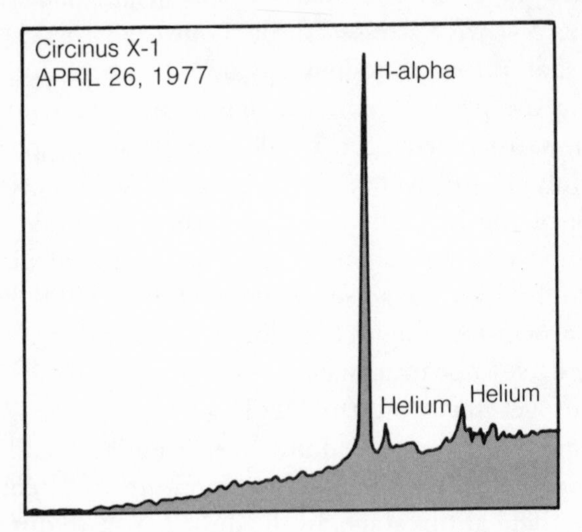

nomical world to the existence of a completely new type of stellar phenomenon.

Within three weeks of our observations, Murdin sent me his final version of our paper. (He had toyed with the idea of ending the paper by thanking Fred Watson, who had spent the night with his finger on the button, for "digital assistance.") I had merely to check it, make a few minor alterations and additions, and send it in early August to the editor of *Nature,* where three years previously Caswell and I had published our ideas on Circinus X-1 that suggested it was a new form of stellar remnant of a supernova. I learned later that *Nature* sent the new paper to John Shakeshaft for review. This choice had a significant impact on the SS433 story. Since Shakeshaft had a keen personal interest in the object, he was better placed to assess our paper than probably anyone else in Great Britain at that time. In addition, I imagine it must have encouraged the Cambridge radio astronomers (Ryle, Shakeshaft, Hine) and Caswell to finish a paper they had long been preparing, which described several pointlike radio sources they suggested might possibly be associated with supernova remnants, including the pointlike radio source at the center of W50.

Murdin and I ended our paper:

> The Molonglo-Parkes survey of supernova remnants [by Clark and Caswell] revealed a statistical excess of point radio sources within or close to the periphery of supernova remnants. Apart from the Crab and Vela pulsars, none has been identified as a pulsar within the detection limits of existing surveys, but two have now been identified optically with unusual emission-line objects and with X-ray variables [Circinus X-1 and A1909+04]. This suggests that such objects represent an identifiable sub-class of supernova stellar remnants.

This, of course, was the view Caswell and I had shared for five years, so it was hardly surprising that the Ryle,

Caswell, and Shakeshaft paper submitted to *Nature* a few weeks after ours concluded in similar vein:

> It seems likely that most of the sources we investigated represent an important new class of radio star. The relationship of these sources to the other galactic X-ray sources and to pulsars is not yet clear although, if either [A1909+04] or [Circinus X-1] is indeed a member of the new class, then the other galactic X-ray binary systems (with or without detectable radio emission) may, in some cases at least, also be the stellar remnants of supernovae, perhaps having outlived their supernova remnant shells.

The near-simultaneous publication of the paper by Paul Murdin and myself (in the November 2, 1978 issue of *Nature*) and that by Caswell and the Cambridge radio astronomers (in the December 7, 1978 issue) was no coincidence (although later newspaper and magazine accounts of the discovery of SS433 were to claim that it had been). Both pieces of research had had their ultimate origins in the work Caswell and I had undertaken four years previously. Although Caswell's route through the "maze" to our ultimate quarry was a very different one from mine, we had commenced the journey of discovery together. Of course, Caswell and company could (and indeed should) have published their data on the radio variability of the W50 pointlike source at least a year earlier. Although their preliminary results had been announced by Shakeshaft at the Royal Astronomical Society meeting, they had never been submitted for publication. It was an oversight the Cambridge radio astronomers must later have sorely regretted. Had they followed up their discovery of radio variability immediately, SS433 would have been unmasked almost two years earlier.

In early September 1978, I was invited to talk at a conference at the High Altitude Observatory in Boulder, Colorado, on the topic of long-term variations in the sun's output (an astronomical topic I then had a strong interest in). Before going, I sent a letter to Kirshner at the University of Michigan, telling him of the strange star within W50 and suggesting he observe it. I provided him with the position of the star and details of our discovery spectrum. At the Erice meeting, just three months earlier, he had been rather suspicious about suggestions that there were stellar remnants of supernovae that manifested themselves in guises like Circinus X-1. My letter to him was not too diplomatic, I recall. I was feeling smug, and wanted to make a big deal of our success in finding another object of this type. At any rate, he ignored the suggestion to make new observations of the W50 source. A few years later he admitted to me the unfortunate error in judgment he had made: "I let SS433 slip through my fingers." I have no doubt that had he accepted the challenge of the new star and studied it with his characteristic vigor, he would have been the first to reveal its intriguing secrets.

En route to Boulder I stopped off in Boston to visit my old friend Fred Seward. The prime purpose of the visit was to discuss observations of the X-ray emission from supernova remnants that might be made with the major new X-ray astronomy satellite shortly to be launched by NASA. (Once in orbit, it was named the Einstein Observatory, to commemorate the centenary of the birth of one of the world's greatest scientists.) Seward held an important position in the project. Since he had been co-discoverer of the X-ray source A1909+04, I was naturally eager to tell him the exciting news of the strange emission-line star that appeared to be associated with it, and give him a copy of the paper we had submitted to *Nature.* His interest in A1909+04 and W50 had persisted over the years, and he had already made plans to observe them with the Einstein instruments. In view of his pioneering role in discovering A1909+04, and thus helping to pave the way to SS433, it was only justice that he lead the Einstein observations of it.

There was another astronomer in Boston I hoped to see: William Liller, of the Harvard Observatory. He had earned a reputation for being a skilled interpreter of archive photographs of the sky taken at regular intervals over many decades by the Harvard Observatory. Archive data can be of great importance in studying the way the brightness of certain stars may vary over years or even decades, for such variations are often periodic, that is, a star's brightness varies in a repetitive manner. The new mystery star varied in its emission-line spectrum; that we knew. It was highly likely that the total light it radiated would vary also, and I hoped Liller might be able to check this for me. Although I missed him in Boston, he arrived in Boulder to speak to the solar variability meeting. I gave him positional details of the new star and a copy of our paper. Although it was our first meeting, he willingly agreed to check the archive data. In fact, it was to turn out that he had already scrutinized the archive for this very object; in Boulder he failed to recognize, merely from the celestial co-ordinates I had given him, that it was a star he was already familiar with. Others, for very different reasons, had been homing in on its remarkable nature and had already solicited his assistance in studying its long-term variability.

When I returned to RGO in mid-September 1978, three important letters awaited me. One was from the editor of *Nature* confirming that our paper had been accepted for publication, and would appear in print in a few weeks' time. The second was from Bruce Margon, dated September 6, 1978; he asked for further details of the mystery star—a finding chart and a copy of our paper. He ended: "I have some observing time at the end of this month (September 29–30), and if you feel it's important I can take another spectrum then." Margon's spectral observations of September 29–30, 1978, and later were to reveal the most remarkable properties of this most remarkable star. "Supersleuth" was about to strike.

The third letter was from Kirshner, enclosing a paper he and Roger Chevalier had just completed writing, based on observations they had made in late August, entitled "The Central Source in the Supernova Remnant G127.1+0.5." Just as Murdin and I had left the Erice supernova conference committed to follow up many of the issues raised there, so had Kirshner and Chevalier. In probing the missing-link mystery, they had decided to investigate the central pointlike radio source in the supernova remnant G127.1+0.5, that had been discovered by Caswell—one of the peculiar supernova remnants discussed at Erice. The Kirshner and Chevalier paper reported the spectrum of the optical object to be coincident with the central pointlike radio source. They interpreted this as being a distant galaxy, the positional coincidence with the supernova remnant being mere chance. Kirshner's letter had crossed with mine to him, so at the time of sending me his new paper he was unaware of the mystery star in the center of W50. Had he known of it, I'm sure he and Chevalier would never have concluded their paper (in *Nature* a fortnight after ours) as they did:

> Because G127.1+0.5 was the most compelling case for a compact radio source associated with a supernova remnant, the demonstration that this object is a

> chance event makes it seem likely that other suggested radio objects near supernova remnants may well be just the superposition of background sources on galactic remnants.

There is always an element of competition between observing teams pursuing similar goals, even if it is to be hoped that such competition is "friendly." Thus, although I held both Kirshner and Chevalier in high esteem, I could not resist the temptation to draw attention to their blunder. I quickly prepared a short contribution to the popular scientific magazine *New Scientist,* describing our results on the strange new star in W50 and its similarities to Circinus X-1, discussing the variable pointlike sources Ryle, Caswell, and Shakeshaft had suggested might be associated with supernova remnants, and presenting the Kirshner and Chevalier counterargument based on their observations of just one of these. All these results were viewed in the light of their impact on the question of whether supernovae might produce stellar remnants other than pulsars, and whether at least some pulsars might be formed by means besides conventional supernovae. My article ended:

> While astronomers shape up for a continuing confrontation on the matter, with the UK team leading the US 2–1 after the first round, the long-accepted one-to-one correspondence between supernovae and pulsars seems ready to receive the knock-out punch.

My self-satisfaction at having "scooped" the U.S. team knew no bounds, but I was soon humbled. The U.S. astronomers actually had the last laugh. Of eight objects in the Ryle, Caswell, and Shakeshaft list, only two, SS433 and Circinus X-1, could be positively identified as galactic. The remainder are all now thought to be background sources.

My next opportunity to boast about the new star was during the final week of September. A meeting was held at the University of Cambridge, where British observers were given the opportunity to report on their recent observations with the Anglo-Australian Telescope; this "AAT Symposium" was a yearly gathering. In my talk to the meeting, the new star was just one of many observational topics I presented. However, I did draw attention to the peculiar variable emission bands in the star as being worthy of further investigation, and pushed my idea that we had a new type of stellar remnant for supernovae. But events taking place on the other side of the Atlantic were rapidly to overtake my attempts to generate interest in the star on this basis alone.

Things were looking good. We had a major new discovery, giving credence to our stellar-remnant ideas. The paper reporting it would soon be published. We had alerted several interested astronomers on both sides of the Atlantic to its significance. We had beaten a competing U.S. team to finding one of the proposed new class of stellar remnant. And now I had openly reported the result to a gathering of British astronomers. Surely I had good reason to feel pleased.

Back at RGO, a colleague hailed me in the library. "Hey, Dave, have you seen this IAU circular?" I read the small postcard he handed me. I sat down and read it again. I could not believe it. The sky had just fallen in on my self-endowed glory.

4

SUPERSLEUTH AND CO.

"It has long been an axiom of mine that the little things are infinitely the most important."
—SIR ARTHUR CONAN DOYLE,
A Case of Identity

Circular number 3256 from the Central Bureau for Astronomical Telegrams, International Astronomical Union, read:

> E. R. Seaquist, David Dunlap Observatory; P. C. Gregory, University of British Columbia; and P. C. Crane, National Radio Astronomy Obervatory, report the detection and subsequent observations of highly variable radio emission from object No. 433 in the list of H-alpha emission objects by Stephenson and Sanduleak [published in 1977 in a supplement to the *Astrophysical Journal*]. Observations at several frequencies were made between 1977 August 15 and 1978 June 30. . . . Observations on 1978 June 30 show possible variability (approximately 20 percent) during a single day. . . . The radio source position (1950.0) is —

right ascension = 19 hours 9 minutes 21.3 seconds (± 3 seconds)
declination = 4 degrees 53 minutes 53.5 seconds (± 1 second)

X-ray, optical and infrared observations are strongly urged.

The position left no doubt. It was the same star. *Our* star! The seemingly abandoned waif we had found was not illegitimate after all. It had previously been found and listed in a catalogue totally unknown to us. From this time forth, the 433rd entry in a barely known catalogue became known as "SS433." The bastard star would be nameless no longer. This single object would put the SS catalogue in the history books of astronomy.

It might well be asked why the object came to be known as SS433, rather than, for example, 4C 04.66 (even if the 4C position was significantly in error); or CC493 (after radio source number 493 in the Clark and Crawford catalogue of 1974, with a position accurate enough for the optical counterpart to have been found); or A1909+04 (Fred Seward's X-ray discovery from Ariel V in 1975); or W50-X (from its location at the center of W50); or some other name. Well—it just happened that way. (Stephenson and Sanduleak did not use the "SS" nomenclature in their catalogue; nor did Seaquist in his IAU circular. Yet the next IAU circular referring to the object was titled "SS433," and one suspects that the circular editor may have arbitrarily introduced this abbreviation for convenience, thus inadvertently creating a piece of astronomical history.) In the end, the name is unimportant, and any one of the above suggestions might have served equally well, especially since the special nature of the star was highlighted via its association with the variable point radio source/ X-ray star and W50. It would in truth have been the source of intense study even if there had not been an SS catalogue, since it was already being observed by Paul Murdin and me, Bruce Margon, and others, in ignorance of its inclusion in the SS catalogue prior to IAU circular 3256. However, SS433 does slide off the tongue rather more easily than A1909+04 or even CC493.

Devastated by the IAU circular, I scoured the library to find out what I could about the background of the Stephenson and Sanduleak result. Bruce Stephenson and Nicholas Sanduleak are from the Warner and Swasey Observatory of Case Western Reserve University, in Cleveland. In the 1960s, astronomers there had initiated a systematic survey of the central plane of the Galaxy to identify those few in a hundred stars that display emission lines, and, in particular, H-alpha emission. Their technique used a device called an "objective prism," an optical element mounted on a telescope that smears slightly the colors of any star image on a photographic plate. In a conventional photographic plate the star images appear as spots of varying brightness; on a plate where an objective prism has been used each star image appears as a tiny trail of varying color (red to violet) and provides some spectroscopic information. While crude in comparison with spectra obtained by conventional means, showing a thousandfold or more greater spectral detail, objective-prism surveys do enable a vast number of stars to be studied simultaneously. They have proved invaluable in identifying certain classes of cosmic object with emission lines (for example, extragalactic objects such as quasars, and galactic objects such as peculiar emission-line stars).

In 1975, one of the Case astronomers, Lawrence Krumenaker, published finding charts of selected emission-line stars from the Cleveland survey. One of these would resurface as SS433, but, unfortunately, Krumenaker made an error in determining the position of the star, so that even if astronomers had wished to follow up his work they would never have been able to find it. Then in 1977, Stephenson and Sanduleak published a catalogue of 455 stars from the Cleveland survey that showed H-alpha emission. Number 433 in their catalogue was this time accurately positioned, and was one of only twenty-two objects in the list for which the H-alpha line was indicated as being strong (the criterion used later by Seaquist as the basis for his search for associated radio emission). The possibility that a helium line might have been detected was also noted. But why had these bright stars with strong line emission not all been included in the Wackerling catalogue, the source of our fruitless search at the AAT? Stephenson and Sanduleak themselves provided the likely reason:

> A sizable proportion of the stars whose H-alpha emission we call strong ought to have been found in previous surveys if their emission intensity has been constant, and hence they are probably variable.

There was nothing else in the Stephenson and Sanduleak paper that hinted at the imminent rise to fame of the star they had numbered 433.

It was clearly important that Murdin and I take account of this new development. I wrote immediately to the editor of *Nature* and asked him to add the following footnote to our paper before publication:

> Seaquist et al. note that our optical candidate for A1909+04 is no. 433 in the catalogue of Stephenson and Sanduleak.

At least we would be spared the embarrassment of having overlooked this fact. However, I was desperately disappointed that the IAU circular from Seaquist alerted the world to the fascinating new object ahead of our *Nature* paper, particularly when we had decided against releasing an IAU circular ourselves two months earlier because of the apparent radio/optical positional discrepancy. (It was infuriating to learn some months later that the Cambridge radio position had not been as accurate in its declination estimate as had been claimed. An improved determination eventually placed the radio source exactly coincident with the optical star.)

My initial reaction of disappointment at finding that the star had been previously catalogued (albeit its association with the pointlike radio source and X-ray star at the center of the supernova remnant W50 had not been realized, nor a high-resolution spectrum obtained) soon changed to one of sheer frustration—that Seaquist and his colleagues could be claiming a new discovery for something many of us had known about for years. The pointlike radio source had been identified (and accurately positioned to better than 10 seconds of arc) from Molonglo observations five years previously, and its extreme variability had been known for over two years from the Cambridge observations. Seaquist made no mention of W50 or of A1909+04 in his circular. I sat down and wrote him a rather discourteous letter pointing out that his detection was not new and criticizing his oversight of various facts. It was a letter I now feel ashamed of. There was, after all, no reason Seaquist should have known of the Molonglo results; they were published in the *Australian Journal of Physics,* hardly compulsory reading for professional astronomers. In addition, the X-ray source was just one of many listed in an Ariel V survey of the constellation Aquila, and, had I not worked with Seward at MSSL in 1976, I would not have known of it. Moreover, the Cambridge evidence of extreme radio variability was known only to those who had heard of Shakeshaft's presentation to the Royal Astronomical Society. Just as Murdin and I had been completely unaware that the star had been catalogued a year earlier, Seaquist and his colleagues had understandably been unaware of the previous detection of the pointlike radio source, its well-studied variability, its long-known location at the center of a supernova remnant, and its likely association with the variable X-ray source A1909+04.

The star SS433 is many millions of years old. Its light takes on the order of 10,000 years to reach us. In the domain of such a time scale, it scarcely seems plausible that teams of astronomers, working totally independently and in ignorance of the work of each other, could converge on the same object from different directions at essentially the same time. Another unlikely thread in the story is that at the time I was working in Sydney with Jim Caswell on the Molonglo-Parkes survey of supernova remnants, Ernie Seaquist was visiting Australia from Canada and working with Caswell in a totally different area of radio-astronomy research. Four years later, the paths of the three of us crossed again, unexpectedly, at SS433.

A letter from Liller arrived in early October in response to my request to him in Boulder. It contained a preliminary analysis of the Harvard archive data, and revealed the intriguing fact that he had been approached three months earlier by Seaquist about SS433. (Liller had not realized at Boulder that my request regarding A1909+04 and Seaquist's earlier request regarding SS433 in fact referred to one and the same object.) A copy of a letter he had received from Seaquist was enclosed, which gave some background to the Canadian's interest in the star. It seems that he and his colleagues had initiated a program of looking for radio emission from H-alpha-emitting objects, and stumbled on the extreme radio variability of SS433 purely by chance.

When Seaquist's reply to my rather irritable letter eventually arrived, it was a polite expression of gratitude for acquainting him with work already done on the star and its likely association with W50 and A1909+04. His disappointment at finding that what he had thought was entirely original work was already being undertaken independently elsewhere, or had already been completed, must have been as extreme as mine on reading circular 3256. His courteous letter ended with the suggestion that we should keep in contact over developments in our future independent observations. But in the months to come, as the pace quickened in the quest to unravel the mysteries of SS433, contact between many competing observational teams was to prove minimal as each strove for ascendancy. Egomania was, on occasion, to take precedence over Renaissance inquisitiveness. Seaquist and his colleagues, having in part initiated the excitement with their release of circular 3256, were to remain aloof from the competition, blatant opportunism, and claims and counterclaims to priority. When they eventually published their paper on observations of the radio variability of SS433, it contained the most balanced and accurate account of the true path to SS433 of any of the pioneering papers on the object.

The introduction to the paper by Seaquist and his colleagues (with my italics added) began:

Recently Seaquist et al. [IAU circular 3256] reported the detection of variable radio emission from the peculiar H-alpha emission object no. 433 in the list of Stephenson and Sanduleak (1977). These observations were part of a radio survey of about twenty objects from this list described as *strong* in H-alpha. SS433 was the only detection. *At virtually the same time* Clark and Murdin reported *their earlier* discovery of an unusual emission line star associated with a variable unresolved radio source possibly associated with the variable X-ray source A1909+04 and the radio supernova remnant W50. *By coincidence* our *independent investigations* concerned the same star SS433.

Shortly after the paper by Clark and Murdin appeared, Ryle et al. reported the results of an extended series of observations of a number of compact radio sources possibly associated with supernova remnants. One of these (1909+04) is also the source associated with SS433.

It is noteworthy that the source 4C 04.66 is very near SS433 and that it is probably the same radio source [in spite of a positional discrepancy]. . . . Radio maps of this region [Velusamy 1975, Clark and Caswell 1975] show only the SS433 source, and so it is reasonably certain that 4C 04.66 is the same source.

Clark and Murdin found that SS433 has a red continuum dominated by broad strong emission lines, some of which are variable. The nature of some of these lines suggests that SS433 is associated with the X-ray source A1909+04, and several aspects of the behaviour of this object are similar to the radio and X-ray binary Circinus X-1. Margon et al. have made extensive spectroscopic observations of SS433 which confirm the conclusions made by Clark and Murdin, and also

> *investigate other more bizarre aspects of the emission line behaviour.*

In fewer than three hundred words Seaquist and his colleagues had given a totally accurate picture of the parallel paths to SS433, and the true order of the main events up to the point where the observations of Margon were shortly to reveal its most remarkable properties. But now supersleuth was about to take center stage.

Bruce Margon took his first spectrum of SS433 on the night of September 29–30, 1978 (three months after our chance encounter at RGO) on the 3-meter Shane telescope at the Lick Observatory, in California, and had given notice of this observing session in his letter to me of September 6. He recorded later that his primary intention in this first spectroscopic observation was simply to confirm our AAT results. Although he may not have taken note of the strange emission bands in the AAT spectrum I had shown him at RGO, it was the appearance of these strange features in his own data that immediately attracted his attention. He wrote later, referring to his first spectrum:

> To my surprise, also present in the spectrum were very prominent emission lines not familiar to me. This was a disquieting state of affairs. Which spectral lines appear in a stellar spectrum depends on the abundance, the temperature and the density of the individual elements in the star. In astrophysical situations there is some variety in these parameters, but it is not infinite; accordingly the stellar spectroscopist gets accustomed to the appearance of certain familiar spectral lines. To encounter spectral emission lines at completely miscellaneous wavelengths is an

experience somewhat akin to a driver suddenly finding that his familiar homeward-bound freeway has all new exit ramps.

Murdin and I had encountered these unfamiliar exit ramps, but had chosen to ignore them, deciding that even if we appeared to be on an unfamiliar freeway, we could still find our way home to announce an interesting new discovery. To Margon's great credit, he realized immediately that he was definitely on the correct freeway, and those new exit ramps just had *no* right to be there. Whereas Murdin and I had (in hindsight) foolishly chosen to ignore, at least temporarily, that which we could not explain, Margon was determined to get to the bottom of the new-exit-ramp problem. We were to play the role of Micawber, waiting for something to turn up; Bruce had decided to take on the role of Sherlock Holmes.

The astronomers at the various campuses of the University of California are privileged to have their own observatory, the Lick Observatory, where time is made freely available to tenured staff. This comparative ease of access to telescopes (in stark contrast to the system British astronomers have been forced to live with) was crucial to Margon's desire to get to the bottom of the SS433 mystery. Also crucial was the co-operation of colleagues already assigned time on the Lick and other telescopes. Margon, with characteristic vigor, quickly convinced colleagues of the exciting nature of SS433 and the urgent need to subject it to close scrutiny. SS433 was obligingly sufficiently bright that it could be studied even with comparatively small telescopes, and the next significant step occurred when Margon's associate Remington Stone used the small 0.6-meter Lick telescope between the nights of October 23 and 26, 1978. There again, in addition to the easily identified intense emission lines from hydrogen and helium, were the strange emission band features—the new "exit ramps." One prominent feature showed up at a wavelength about 50 nanometers shorter than that of the intense H-alpha line at 656 nanometers, and another at about 100 nanometers longer. That these features were not at the same wavelengths as in the September 30 spectrum was surprising enough; more startling was that over the space of the four nights they displayed a distinct "drift" in wavelength (see Figure 4.1). Both features had drifted, in opposite directions, *away* from the intense H-alpha feature. It must be stressed how totally unprecedented such spectral variation was; nothing like it had ever been seen before. This was a new cosmic phenomenon, previously unknown to the human experience. Such totally new phenomena are discovered comparatively rarely in astronomy—perhaps at most just once or twice a decade.

The observations were difficult to assimilate. It was all very well having a freeway where new exit ramps suddenly appeared, but for these exit ramps to drift along the freeway night by night was a seemingly impossible situation. The whole thing was very perplexing to any astronomer who, while quite used to variations in the intensity of a star's emission, was conditioned to believe that random wavelength variations such as these could not happen. Margon made one very important deduction. Since the mysterious drifting features were only slightly less prominent than the familiar hydrogen lines in the spectrum, he argued that on a simplistic view they might therefore be attributed to a chemical element with cosmic abundance comparable to hydrogen. But there is no such element. Because hydrogen is far and away the most abundant element in the universe, could the unidentified

FIGURE 4.1. SPECTRUM OF SS433 RECORDED ON THREE DIFFERENT NIGHTS

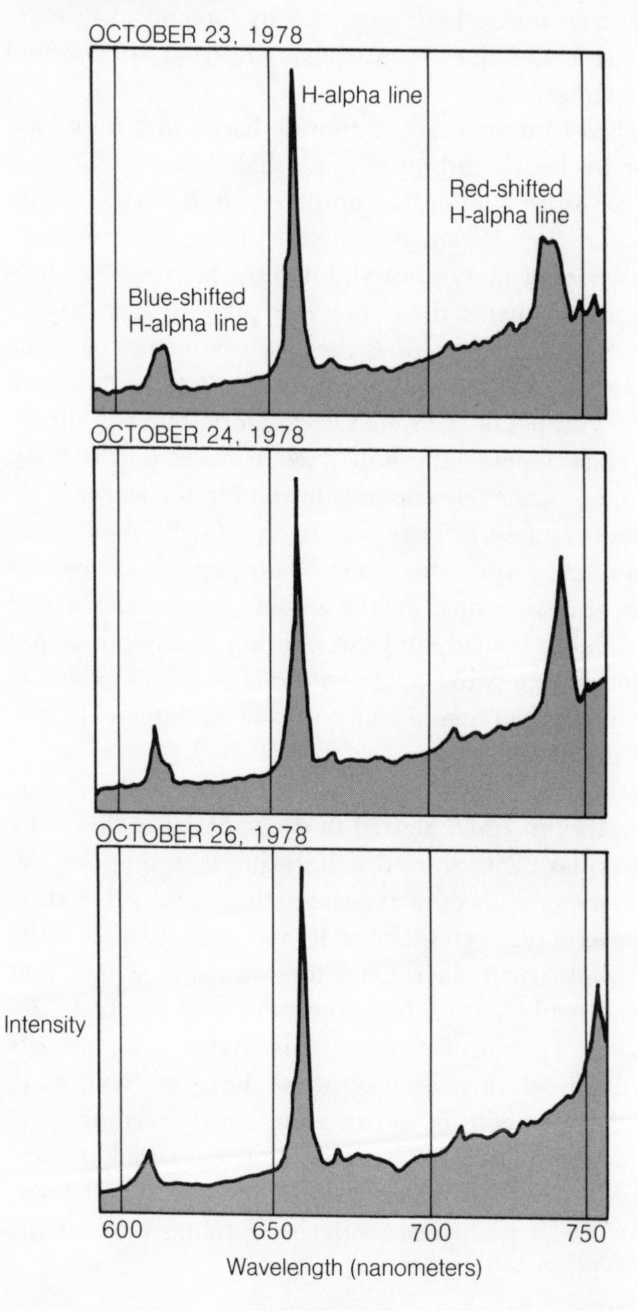

lines also be due to hydrogen, and by some means the familiar emission lines were displaced from the normal wavelengths?

By then Margon realized that he had a first-class mystery on his hands and rapidly marshaled additional assistance at other California campuses, at Berkeley, Santa Cruz, and San Diego. A score of distinguished astronomers whose primary research interests spanned the whole of astronomy altered their observing plans to gaze in wonder at SS433. In late 1978 these astronomers "beat the tar" out of SS433, using not only the 3-meter and 0.6-meter telescopes of the Lick Observatory, but also the famous Hale 5-meter, the Kitt Peak 4-meter, and the Mt. Wilson 2.5-meter telescopes. (On the big telescopes, only very short exposures were required.) Murdin and I continued to play Micawber. Our *Nature* paper had now appeared, and we waited for the accolades to flow, unaware that while we waited, and did nothing, truly spectacular discoveries were being made on the U.S. West Coast. Yet the unmasking of SS433 was not to be entirely a California affair.

Augusto Mammano and his colleagues at the Asiago Observatory in Italy, alerted to the vagaries of SS433 by IAU circular 3256, started monitoring it. Using the 1.2- and 1.8-meter telescopes at Asiago, they obtained twenty-three spectra between October 10 and December 10, 1978. They would then have been unaware of the fact that spectra already existed from the AAT and the Lick Observatory. By mid-November, the Italian astronomers were sufficiently mystified by what they were witnessing in the SS433 spectrum to call attention to startling spectral changes in two IAU circulars. These circulars indicated that they had fallen initially into the same trap as Murdin and I had, incorrectly interpreting most of the peculiar bands that belied easy interpretation as transient high-excitation features from various known elements. For example, they proposed various high-excitation lines of iron and manganese. So much for the appearance of "freeway exit ramps" overnight. (They later made amends for these early errors in interpretation with some first-class observational data, which would be important in understanding the nature of SS433.) Even if the Italians initially gave no clue to understanding the phenomenon, they did allude to the drifting exit ramps; their second IAU circular ended:

> A diffuse band appeared around 590 nanometres on November 5 and it was displaced towards 589 to 587 nanometres on November 6 and 7. On November 10 and 11 the band separated into two lines at 587 and 591 nanometres, the latter being much the stronger.

This was the first published reference to drifting features in SS433. The story was starting to sound like something from Lewis Carroll, with SS433 resembling the Cheshire Cat. In California, the White Rabbit was still in a hurry. He was racing to an "important date"—in Munich.

From December 13 to 19, 1978, a major astronomical conference—the Ninth Texas Symposium on Relativistic Astrophysics—was held in Munich, West Germany. This series of conferences was conceived in 1963 by a group of Texas academics (hence the name), but this was the first time in the history of the illustrious sequence of meetings that a venue outside the United States had been chosen. A wide range of topics was to be covered. One set of presentations was on X-ray astronomy, and Margon was scheduled to give a talk entitled "Optical Counterparts of Compact Galactic X-ray Sources." The bulk of his talk covered the various types of comparatively well-studied X-ray/optical systems. No surprises so far. But with the flair of a seasoned showman, he kept his prime trick until last:

> I will conclude by briefly mentioning some very recent data of my own, in collaboration with my colleagues at the University of California, on a newly identified optical counterpart that perhaps may presage some of the future surprises in this field. The optical counterpart of A1909+04, a weak and rather undistinguished X-ray source, has recently been identified with a peculiar emission line star that is also a variable nonthermal radio source. The object has been previously catalogued as SS433. . . . In agreement with the discovery observations [Clark and Murdin], we found the spectrum to be dominated by hydrogen and helium emission, variable on a time scale of days.

Margon then went on to describe the mysterious unidentified bands:

> The most perplexing property of these features is seen when spectra obtained on three or four consecutive nights are displayed sequentially. The features change their wavelengths daily by very substantial amount! . . . It is, to phrase it mildly, very difficult to interpret these spectral changes in the context of any previously known stellar spectrum.

The impact on the astronomers present in Munich was, from all accounts, dramatic. Nothing like the drifting features had ever been seen before. Here was a new and exciting challenge to theoretical astronomy, and it would not take long for the theorists to respond. Several mind-boggling explanations came forth within a matter of weeks.

Margon must have left Munich well satisfied—he and SS433 had stolen the show. The universal acclaim was well earned, and at future conferences this new double act would top the bill.

I was not at Munich, but did not have to wait long to learn of Margon's spectacular new data. In early January 1979, he sent me a draft version of a paper entitled "The Bizarre Spectrum of SS433" that he and his colleagues were submitting to the *Astrophysical Journal.* A short note accompanied the paper:

> Dear Dave,
>
> Many thanks for putting me on to this interesting object. If you have any comments on the manuscript, we'd be happy to incorporate them.
>
> Sincerely,
> Bruce Margon

As I read the paper, I grew furious. First, in referring to the moving features (the peculiar bands Murdin and I could not identify), the authors had written: "These features were absent in spectra obtained ten weeks earlier by Clark and Murdin." Not so! Second: "Our data argue against an association of the system with the nearby supernova remnant W50, or a similarity to Circinus X-1, contrary to several previous suggestions." How could this be, when the similarity to Circinus X-1 (in terms of X-ray/radio variability and so on) and the situation in a supernova remnant had been what attracted us to the object in the first place? There were other irritants. Margon had invited comments; and he got them. His reply was courteous, noting:

> The confusion about whether or not the strange spectral features were present in your data is partly one of nomenclature. Your *Nature* article did clearly state that the "higher excitation" spectrum was variable, and by this we assumed that you meant the identified helium lines, etc., vary in intensity (which we also see). It wasn't clear to us that you had observed any unidentifiable features. . . . Also, we think that the moving lines are probably H-alpha, and therefore weren't mentally oriented to identifying them with your "higher excitation" features. . . . Anyway, the one simple change that I was able to make to the manuscript in this regard is to remove the statement concerning whether the mysterious features were present in your spectrum.

He was right, of course. Murdin and I had not confessed in our *Nature* paper to any unidentifiable features, preferring instead to cover our ignorance with the vague allusion to "variable high-excitation lines." But Margon was true to his word, and the reference to the mysterious features not having been seen in the AAT spectra was removed. Also removed in the published paper was the suggestion that SS433 and W50 were not related. Even the supposed lack of similarity to Circinus X-1 was mildly phrased.

It had been a clever piece of detective work on Margon's part to suggest that the peculiar moving (drifting exit ramp) features might be the normal hydrogen lines somehow displaced in wavelength and then made to drift with time. But how can wavelengths change—how can an emitting source change color? There is one well-understood way, which occurs when a source of waves is moving. The most familiar manifestation of this phenomenon is the change of pitch noticed by a stationary observer when a source of sound approaches and passes. Thus, for example, when a police car approaches with its siren on, the sound waves are "bunched up" ahead of it (in the sense that the distance between adjacent sound-wave crests is shortened)—that is, the wavelength is decreased and the sound is of higher pitch than when the siren is stationary. When the source of sound is receding, the waves are "stretched out" (in the sense that the distance between adjacent wave crests is lengthened), thereby increasing the wavelength and making the pitch lower (see Figure 4.2).

FIGURE 4.2. THE DOPPLER EFFECT FOR SOUND

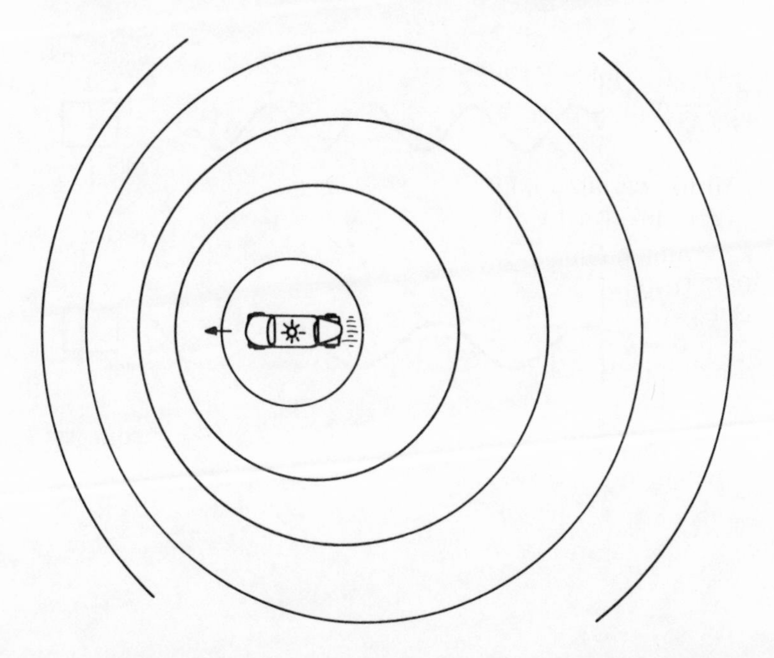

As it is with sound waves, so it is with light waves. If a source of light (for example, a star or a galaxy) is approaching an observer, the wavelength (defining the "color") of any characteristic emission is decreased; the light is said to be "blue-shifted" (emission features shift toward the blue end of the spectrum). When the source is receding, the light is "red-shifted." The greater the speed of approach or recession, the greater the degree of blue shift or red shift (see Figure 4.3). Thus the measurement of wavelength shift conveniently provides the velocity of the light source. However, it is normally only when the speed of the light source is an appreciable fraction of the speed of light that the effect is discernible or significant. The phenomenon was first formulated mathematically by Christian Doppler in 1842, and now bears his name—the "Doppler effect."

FIGURE 4.3. THE DOPPLER EFFECT FOR LIGHT

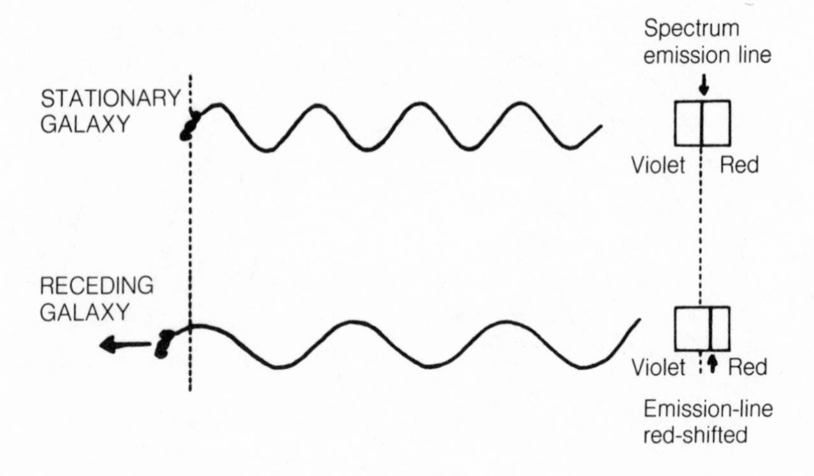

Margon and his colleagues considered the possibility of a Doppler origin for the peculiar drifting features in SS433, but initially dismissed this; the consequences of the moving features resulting from the Doppler effect seemed too absurd even to contemplate. They looked instead at an alternative way to describe wavelength shift, known as the "Zeeman effect," which was proposed in the draft Margon sent me.

In the Zeeman effect (named for Dutch physicist Pieter Zeeman), the emission lines from any light source situated in a strong magnetic field are split into multiple components shifted with respect to the normal emission wavelength. It was argued that the normal hydrogen and helium lines of SS433 were produced in a location different from that of the moving features, these originating in a strong magnetic field produced by the compact star in a close binary system. If the location of the emitting region responsible for the moving features changed with respect to the magnetic star, a change in wavelength could result—the features would drift. Although strong magnetic fields in compact objects (neutron stars or white dwarfs) are well known, the magnetic-field strengths required in SS433 would have been enormous. There were other difficulties. By the time Margon's paper appeared, the Zeeman splitting explanation for the moving features had been dropped.

So what could cause the moving features? Theories worthy of the most imaginative science-fiction writer were about to place SS433 in the superstar class. Enter the Jet Set!

5
THE JET SET

"How often have I said to you that when you have eliminated the impossible, whatever remains, however improbable, *must be the truth."*

—SIR ARTHUR CONAN DOYLE, *The Sign of Four*

The idiosyncrasies of the wavelength shifts that Bruce Margon and the Asiago astronomers had been observing in SS433 during the final months of 1978 must be looked at. First, some of the moving features seemed to be moving to shorter wavelengths, whereas others moved to longer wavelengths. Were these shifts due to the Doppler effect? If so, how could a star possibly be "coming" and "going" at the same time? Additionally, the strange features, if they were indeed hydrogen, were seen on Margon's spectra of October and November 1978 to be very significantly displaced from the normal hydrogen lines. Such large red shifts or blue shifts would imply enormous speeds; at least on the order of 40,000 kilometers per second, according to Margon's calculations. If a star were to attain just 1 percent of such a speed, it would rapidly escape from the Galaxy. Not only would the star need to be simultaneously coming and going, but it would also need to be traveling, in both directions at once, about one hundred times faster than any star had been observed to move before! If this was not enough, there was the final problem that the unfamiliar features drifted by substantial amounts from night to night. If the Doppler effect was invoked, it required that the already enormous velocities would need to be changing by about 1,000 kilometers per second each day. As Margon recalled later, "In short, Doppler-shifted hydrogen emission seemed [at this time] a poor explanation of the observations."

Such concerns did not inhibit the theorists, however, and one can only marvel at the depth of imagination that enabled models to be produced based on the Doppler effect despite the apparently insurmountable problems originally envisaged. Precedence for some of the novel explanations of SS433 that appeared in the early weeks of 1979, following Margon's presentation to the Munich meeting, is hard to establish. Of course, it is entirely possible that similar theoretical explanations evolved entirely contemporaneously (as with the parallel and independent observational discoveries). Certainly it would appear that theoreticians in Cambridge, England, and in Israel arrived at similar conclusions on a similar time scale.

In late January, a copy of a paper that had been submitted for publication was sent to me by Andy Fabian. His co-author was Martin Rees. The paper was provocatively titled "SS433: A Double Jet in Action?" What Fabian and Rees had done was to take the model usually invoked to describe the structure of radio galaxies, and propose that it might apply to a stellar system. In the pioneering surveys of radio astronomy, extragalactic radio sources had been found to be divided broadly into two groups. First there were the "normal galaxies," with radio output that could be almost completely ascribed to emission from a conglomerate of sources such as those detected in our own galaxy, plus a weak radio halo. Then there were the "radio galaxies," such as Cygnus A, with enormous intrinsic radio output, on the order of 100,000 times greater than that of our galaxy—although only one in a million galaxies is a radio galaxy. The early radio telescopes were unable to resolve the detailed structure of the radio galaxies. But by the 1950s, radio telescopes were being linked electrically, enabling them to record features in radio sources too small to be distinguished by individual telescopes alone. The emission from radio galaxies was found to originate in a central nucleus with diffuse blobs on either side—radio galaxies that looked like cosmic dumbbells. As detail on a finer scale was observed, the central nuclei (clearly sites of violent activity, of uncertain origin) were seen to display fine "jets" protruding in opposite directions and terminating in the diffuse blobs (see Figure 5.1). What Fabian and Rees were now proposing was that mystery star SS433 might also exhibit a double-jet system. Their paper began:

> We discuss the possibility that the remarkable moving emission lines of SS433, found by Margon et al., originate in cool blobs accelerated in a double jet. . . .

FIGURE 5.1. RADIO JETS

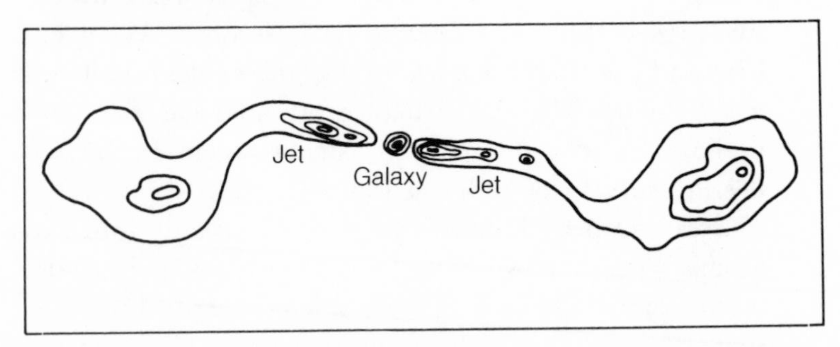

A double jet! Why not? A central object ejecting matter in two opposing beams—what a neat way of getting around the coming-and-going problem. It seemed so simple a solution; the normal hydrogen and helium lines could come from the presumed binary system at the heart of SS433, from which (by means yet to be explained) two opposing beams of matter were ejected. Matter in the beam approaching would give blue-shifted line emission, whereas the beam receding would give red-shifted features. It was so beautifully simple (see Figure 5.2).

The origin of the jets? Well, that still had to be thought about. And how could matter be accelerated to speeds of many tens of thousands of kilometers per second? That still had to be answered also. What about the fact that the red- and blue-shifted features drifted in wavelength? Allow the speed of ejection of the emitting blobs in the jets to vary, so that the Doppler-shifted lines could drift backward and forward. But surely any mechanism that could accelerate the blobs to the enormous velocities implied would heat the gas in the blobs to such high temperatures that they would not emit the conventional hydrogen and helium lines. True, and the blobs would have to be allowed to cool somehow. What about the surrounding supernova remnant W50? No problem. The binary star supposed to be at the heart of the jet-emitting system could contain the stellar remnant of the supernova explosion that produced the extended supernova remnant. Fabian and Rees had absolutely no doubts about the model.

> We attribute the features either side of the H-alpha line to cool gas trapped within the approaching and receding jets.

FIGURE 5.2. INITIAL FABIAN AND REES MODEL

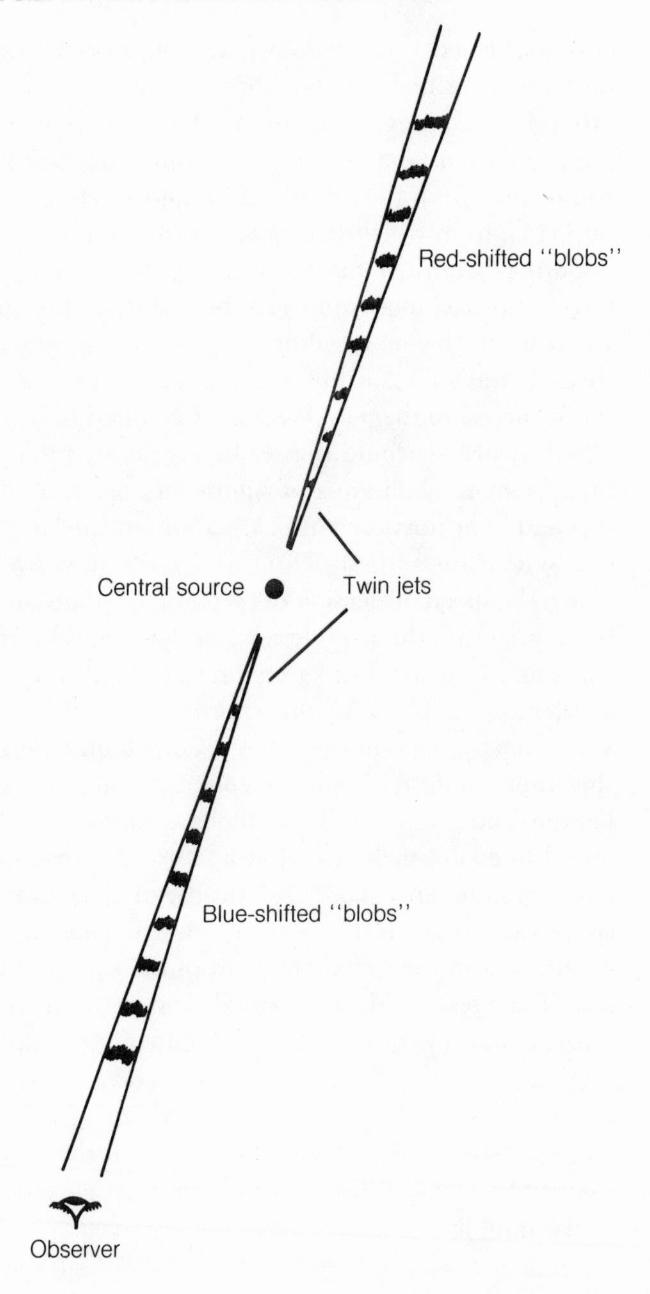

They concluded with a number of predictions:

> If the moving features in the optical spectrum of SS433 do indeed indicate a rapidly-changing Doppler effect, then better spectra ought to reveal other lines with the same shift. . . . SS433 may have an extended radio structure. The detection of such a feature, or any directionality in the variable radio component, would clarify the non-thermal processes occurring in the jet.
>
> Our interpretation of SS433 suggests that the X-ray and radio variability of some other galactic compact sources (e.g. Sco X-1, Circinus X-1) may also involve unsteady jets. Such objects would acquire added astrophysical significance if they indeed involve, on smaller lengthscales and timescales, the same basic physical processes as the collimated outbursts in radio galaxies.

These suggestions were soon to prove quite remarkably prophetic—it was an astonishing piece of crystal-ball gazing.

In the same week that I received the Fabian and Rees paper, another reached me from Mordehai Milgrom, of Israel's Weizman Institute of Science. It was called "On the Interpretation of the Large Variations in the Line Positions in SS433." Milgrom had interpreted all the data then available on the moving lines, from Margon's work and also that of the Asiago astronomers, and had made a startling deduction. He found that the drifting lines moved symmetrically about a fixed mean position (at slightly longer wavelength than the H-alpha line)—that is, the motion of the blueward-moving feature was a mirror image of the redward-moving feature (although the "mirror" point was not exactly at the H-alpha wavelength) (see Figure 5.3). Milgrom, like Fabian and Rees, favored the Doppler effect as the means by which the lines were displaced, but argued that the movements in wavelength were due to variations in the *direction* of the emitting material rather than variations in its speed, as had been suggested by Fabian and Rees. For example, if the jets of the Fabian and Rees model were directed exactly toward and away from the observer, the maximum possible red shift and blue shift would be measured, but if the jets then swung away from this direction, both red shift and blue shift would decrease. Indeed, if the jets were "rotating," the red-shifted and blue-shifted components would then cross when the jets were directed at right angles to the observer's line of sight; then red-shifted and

FIGURE 5.3. MILGROM'S DEDUCTION

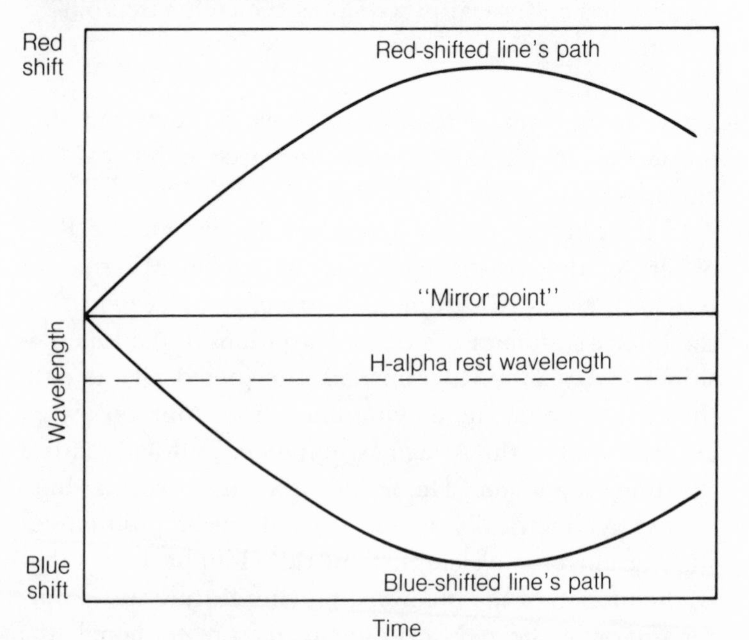

blue-shifted components would be interchanged—that is, what was the blue-shifted (approaching) jet would have become the red-shifted (receding) jet, and vice versa (see Figure 5.4).

FIGURE 5.4. ROTATING JET MODEL

a. Jet A shows maximum red shift; Jet B shows maximum blue shift.

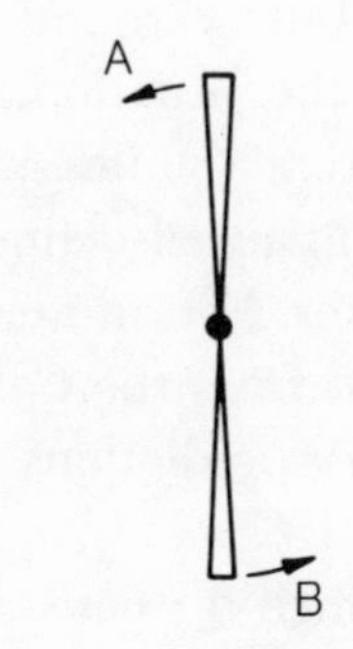

b. Both jets traveling at right angles to line of sight; have common red shift due to transverse Doppler effect.

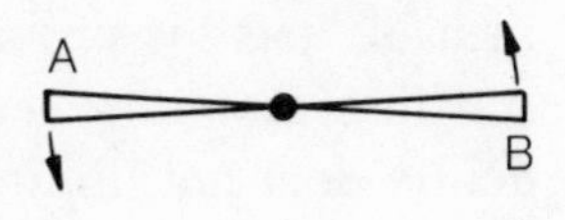

c. Jets reversed compared with a. Jet A now shows maximum blue shift; Jet B shows maximum red shift.

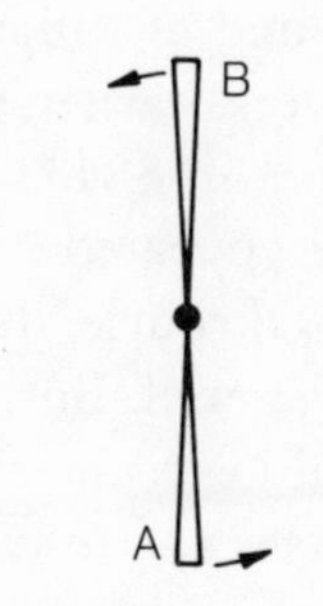

Milgrom did not consider just the idea of the moving components being produced by outward-directed jets from a central source; he also considered the possibility that they might be produced by matter falling inward onto a central object, or, alternatively, that matter might be orbiting around a central object (see Figure 5.5). Whatever the situation, a consequence of Milgrom's analysis was that the line motions would be periodic (that is, repeat in a well-defined way) with a repetition time of a few months. For an analysis based on only a handful of data points from the California and Asiago observations, Milgrom's predictions were later proved to be spectacularly accurate.

Which of these two new theoretical papers was off the typewriter first? I do not know. Indeed, precedence for the idea of "jets" is probably unimportant. The fact that a startling new idea may have been thought of independently does not diminish its originality or quality. What was certain was that the impact of the work of Fabian and Rees and of Milgrom was immediate. What had, only a few weeks earlier, seemed inconceivable—that the moving features in SS433 resulted from the Doppler effect—suddenly appeared not only feasible but also almost believable. Of course, there were still many specific questions to be answered. But, no matter—here were some firm theoretical ideas and definite predictions for observational astronomers to test. After having revealed only tantalizing glimpses of itself for so many years, the mysterious code of SS433 was about to be broken. Fabian, Rees, and Milgrom had made the big breakthrough.

Milgrom had included in his analysis a process called the "transverse Doppler effect," which proved to be critical to the detailed interpretation of SS433. As already noted, if the jets were by chance perfectly aligned with the

FIGURE 5.5. MILGROM'S MODELS

a. IN-FALLING MATERIAL

b. JETS

c. ROTATING RING

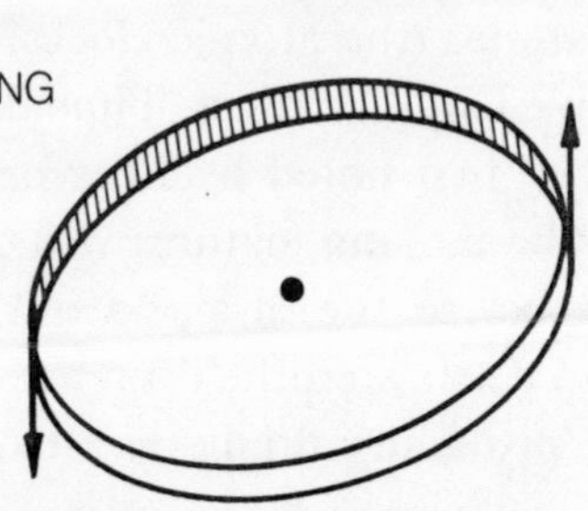

observer's line of sight, then the H-alpha line emitted from the approaching jet would show maximum blue shift, and that from the receding jet would show maximum red shift. Then if the jets rotated so that they were both pointing at right angles to the observer's line of sight (so that neither jet was approaching or receding from the observer), they would merge at the normal H-alpha wavelength (the "rest" wavelength). But this simple interpretation overlooks the enormous velocities in the jets; at such extreme velocities the effects of the special theory of relativity need to be taken into account.

This theory was one of the scientific masterpieces of Albert Einstein. In the domain of special, or restricted, relativity, an effect known as "time dilation" must be taken into account. An imaginary observer watching someone with a clock moving at extreme speed (and the effect is only significant at speeds of greater than about one-twentieth that of light) would perceive the clock to be running slow; the greater the speed, the slower the clock. Even on the atomic scale, atomic clocks would run slow. Thus, fast-moving hydrogen atoms in the jets of SS433 would appear to run slow in their emission processes with respect to our time reference, and so emit, for example, H-alpha light that would appear to us to be of lower frequency (that is, longer wavelength). The time dilation thus appears as a red shift depending only on the velocity of the material (the atomic clocks) in the jets—this is the transverse Doppler effect. Time dilation could thus explain the effect first noted by Milgrom, that the mean wavelength of the moving features was constant, but red-shifted with respect to the H-alpha rest wavelength. The year 1979 had celebrated the centenary year of the birth of Einstein by providing dramatic astronomical confirmation of one of the most startling elements of his theory of special relativity.

The "jet set" had made the first move, but they were not to have it all their own way. A strong contender was emerging, again sponsored by Cambridge and Israeli theoreticians.

Milgrom had offered an alternative to jets in his pioneering paper; he had suggested that, instead, matter responsible for the moving features might be orbiting in a "ring" or "disk" about a central compact object. On the side of the disk where matter is orbiting away from an observer, emission would be red-shifted; on the side of the disk where matter was orbiting toward the observer, emission would be blue-shifted. But what kind of compact object would produce a ring of matter orbiting at the implied enormous velocities? Israeli Amitai Milchgrub and his colleagues provided the answer, and so did Roberto Terlevich and James Pringle from Cambridge.

The only forms of compact stellar objects discussed so far have been white dwarfs and neutron stars (possibly observable as pulsars). However, the maximum mass of a neutron star is just three to four times that of the sun. If the core of a star undergoing gravitational collapse is more massive than this, then gravity triumphs over other natural forces. The core collapses beyond nuclear densities to the ultimate state of compaction, a "black hole"—a body so dense, and with a gravitational field so intense, that even light cannot escape from it.

The concept of a black hole can be envisaged by the following thought experiment. If an object is thrown into the air, it falls back to Earth under the action of gravity. If it could be thrown fast enough, it could escape Earth's attraction and shoot out into space. The minimum velocity the object would require to achieve this is known as the "escape velocity." If the same exercise were carried out on the moon, the object would need to be projected with a much smaller velocity to escape into space, since the moon's gravitational field is not as strong as Earth's. Every astronomical object has an escape velocity, which characterizes the strength of its gravitational field. The gravitational field of a black hole is *so* intense that its escape velocity exceeds the velocity of light. Although one could never expect to observe black holes directly, their presence can be inferred from their effect on the surrounding environment.

Until the advent of X-ray astronomy, black holes seemed to be merely the playthings of mathematics and science-fiction writers—an interesting abstract idea. Then certain X-ray systems were identified that indicated material flowing down onto a compact object that had to be more massive than a neutron star. These observations seemed to demand a black-hole interpretation. The X-rays were coming from the flow of material, not, of course, from the black hole itself. Some argued that if black holes did in fact exist, there would be no limit to their mass, since black holes could only consume material, not regurgitate it, thus becoming more and more massive.

The model the Israeli and Cambridge astronomers were arguing for SS433 involved material orbiting around a black hole. The orbit of the emitting material would need to be so close to the central object that its intense gravitational field would have an effect on the emission. This is a consequence of another of Einstein's theories, the general theory of relativity. In the general theory, a clock runs slow in an intense gravitational field. Thus, in a way analogous to the transverse Doppler effect, emission lines from a radiating gas would be red-shifted. The gravitational red shift produced by the massive black hole being proposed for SS433 would then have the effect of shifting the mean wavelength of the moving features redward of the rest wavelength, as Milgrom had revealed. But *what* a massive black hole! What was being proposed by the Israeli theorists was an object of mass about a million times that of the sun; and by the Cambridge theorists, 300,000 times that of the sun. The massive black hole would be plowing through the plane of the Galaxy at several hundred kilometers per second, "swallowing" (the astronomical term used is "accreting") all matter in its path via an "accretion disk"—a process analogous to water flowing down a drain. This gargantuan monster with insatiable appetite could have come straight from *Star Wars.* Having become adjusted to the idea of jets, I wasn't inclined to join the black-hole brigade without a lot of persuading. Besides, what about the supernova remnant W50? Were we being asked to suppose that a massive black-hole interloper was, just by chance, aligned with a galactic supernova remnant?

The enormous interest in the astronomical community generated by the bizarre spectral properties of SS433, and the "double-jet" and "massive black hole" models proposed to explain them, ensured that when SS433 next became visible in the night sky, in late February 1979, many of the world's telescopes would be trained toward it. Could evidence be produced proving *conclusively* that the Doppler effect was behind the drifting-exit-ramps mystery? Did the moving features drift in a well-defined and predictable manner? Could data be obtained to discriminate between the two Doppler-related models—jets or massive black holes? Could the geometry of the system at the heart of SS433 be defined? The questions were many; the answers would soon be found, given the unprecedented observational attention SS433 was to receive. But for each question answered, SS433 was to reveal new mysteries and raise a host of additional questions. No wonder the astronomical magazine *Sky and Telescope* was to title an article "Does anyone understand SS433?"

Conclusive evidence that the principal moving emission lines were indeed Doppler-shifted hydrogen lines was not long in coming. Bruce Margon's first few spectra of the new observing session showed clearly that *all* the emission lines (and not just H-alpha) had three components: the rest wavelength (undisplaced), a red-shifted (moving), and a blue-shifted (moving) (see Figure 5.6). *All* the proposed red-shifted components (that is, of both hydrogen and helium lines) implied identical speeds of recession, while *all* the proposed blue-shifted components implied identical speeds of approach. Margon, who three months earlier was arguing for the Zeeman-splitting theory on the basis that the Doppler effect was just too complicated to contemplate, was converted immediately by the new observations, writing later:

> This multiple set of coincidences [that is, all lines showing three components and all implying identical speeds of approach or recession on a Doppler interpretation] could be explained *only* by the Doppler shift.

This final piece of code-breaking was achieved independently by another team of astronomers, led by James Liebert, of the Steward Observatory in Tucson, Arizona.

Margon's new data, when compared with previous observations, produced a spectacular new result dramatically confirming a prediction by Milgrom: the velocity

FIGURE 5.6. TRIPLED EMISSION LINES IN SS433 SPECTRUM

Each line has a rest component, a red-shifted component, and a blue-shifted component. The hydrogen-alpha and -beta lines are shown as examples.

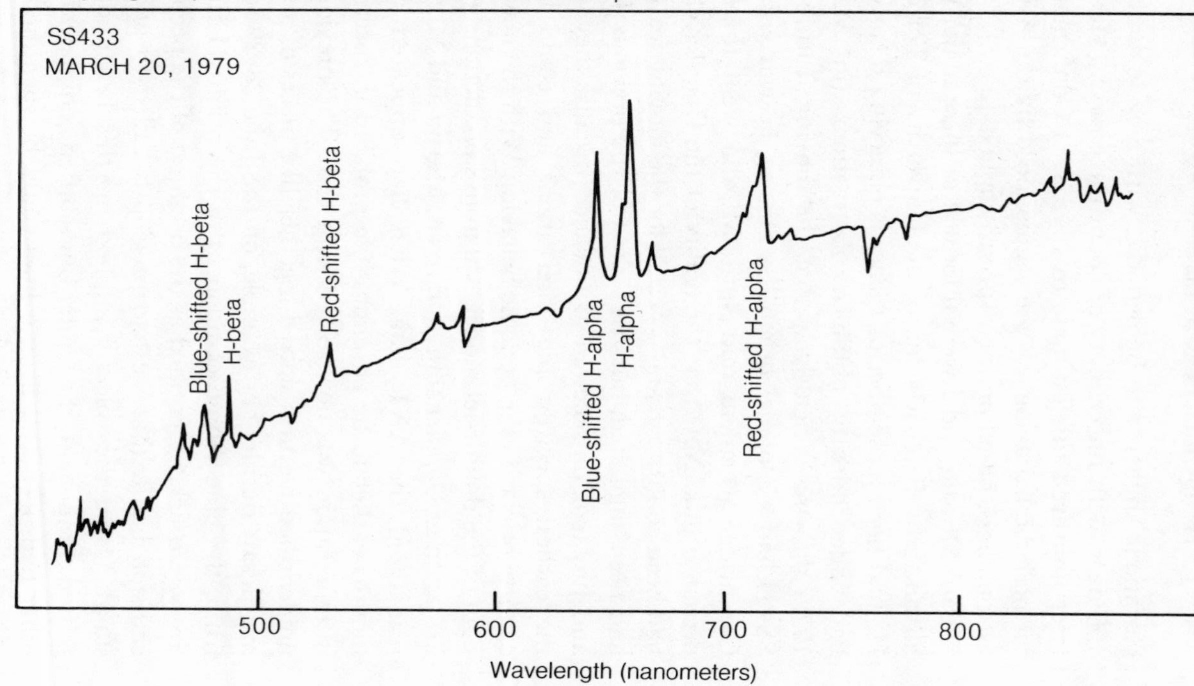

variations appeared to be periodic, with a cycle of about 160 days, with uncertainty of about three days. (Margon later improved this estimate to 164 days.) Confirmation for periodic behavior was soon announced by the Asiago astronomers, based on their spectroscopic data.

Paul Murdin and I were informed of these major new advances by Peter Martin, of the University of Toronto. He had been a member of Liebert's observing team who had independently obtained observations (in March 1979) showing conclusively that the moving features in SS433 had a Doppler origin. By chance, he was visiting Cambridge when, in mid-April, Murdin went there to present a talk. Now that the reality of the Doppler effect had been confirmed, and a period for the moving features had been suggested, our AAT data of the previous June and July took on renewed significance, because they were the earliest spectroscopic observations and could help confirm or clarify the periodic behavior. With the new insight of the double-jet model, Milgrom's predictions, confirmation of Doppler shift, and so on, Martin and Murdin reanalyzed the AAT data. What had appeared nine months earlier to be an impossible problem in spectrum interpretation was now solved with ease. The previously unidentified features slotted together like pieces of a cosmic jigsaw puzzle. For example, on the June 28–29 spectrum, the blue-shifted component of the bright H-alpha line was quickly identified as the brightest of the peculiar emission bands that we had previously failed to understand. Using the velocity implied for this bright blue-shifted component, the fainter blue-shifted components of other hydrogen and helium lines could be identified. It was the same with the red-shifted components. It now all seemed so simple. But what about the July 15–16, 1978, spectrum, which Murdin and I had shown in our *Nature* paper, and for which we thought the peculiar emission features had vanished? The new analysis showed that when we had first looked at our bastard star on the AAT, what were now known to be moving features were drifting back toward the mean (transverse Doppler-shifted) value. When the subsequent AAT spectra were taken two to three weeks later, the blue-shifted H-alpha moving component was just starting to merge with the rest-wavelength H-alpha. The red-shifted H-alpha moving component would still have been beyond the limit of our spectrum, and had thus not confused our ignorance. So, the mysterious unidentified features had *not* disappeared between our first AAT spectra and those taken later. SS433 had cunningly disguised them, so that it could keep its secret a little longer.

Murdin and I were criticized in some quarters of the British astronomical community for not having discovered that the mystery features of our first AAT spectra were "moving," that this remarkable discovery of an entirely new astronomical phenomenon had to be left to the well-publicized follow-up observations in California and the less-well-publicized observations in Asiago. I think in reality such criticisms were unjustified. Given the limited data we had available in July 1978, plus the fact that the moving lines were a totally unknown phenomenon, I doubt whether anyone could have reached conclusions different from ours. It was not really a matter of oversight or slackness on our part; we had merely been outwitted by that damned star. Ernie Seaquist and his colleague Robert Garrison had also been fooled. They had obtained two spectra in July and August 1978 showing the mystery bands but, like us, had failed to recognize their significance.

Armed with the reanalysis of the AAT data, and the

data released by the Asiago astronomers and Liebert, Martin and Murdin decided to see how they could fit them to the double-jet model of Milgrom, Fabian, and Rees. The mathematical basis for this interpretation had been provided by Milgrom. The first assumption they made was that the red shift of the mean of the moving features was due entirely to the transverse Doppler effect. (Remember that this is the result of time dilation of the atomic clocks in the jet material, and depends only on the speed of the material and not on the geometry of the system.) The material in the jets was estimated to be traveling at a quite staggering 80,000 kilometers per second—one-quarter the speed of light. Next, the periodic shift of the moving features was fed into Milgrom's model. Margon's initially announced period of 160 days was used. It was, of course, appreciated that it would be a very unlikely coincidence indeed if the jets were ever exactly aligned with the Earth as they swept around the sky, and the observed Doppler shift would infer a velocity that was merely a component of the true velocity in the jets determined from the transverse Doppler effect. Relating these allowed the direction of the jets relative to the line of sight from Earth to SS433 to be inferred. Finally, the way in which the blue- and red-shifted components drifted backward and forward allowed the nature of the jet "rotation" to be modeled. Combining the AAT and Asiago data showed that the features drifted in an intriguing way. The component believed to be produced by one jet remained red-shifted for most of the 160-day period, crossing over to a blue-shifted mode for only a very short interval; conversely for the component believed to be produced by the other jet (see Figure 5.7). This behavior was fed into the Milgrom model, and it revealed that each jet

FIGURE 5.7. WAVELENGTH DRIFT OF THE MOVING EMISSION LINES

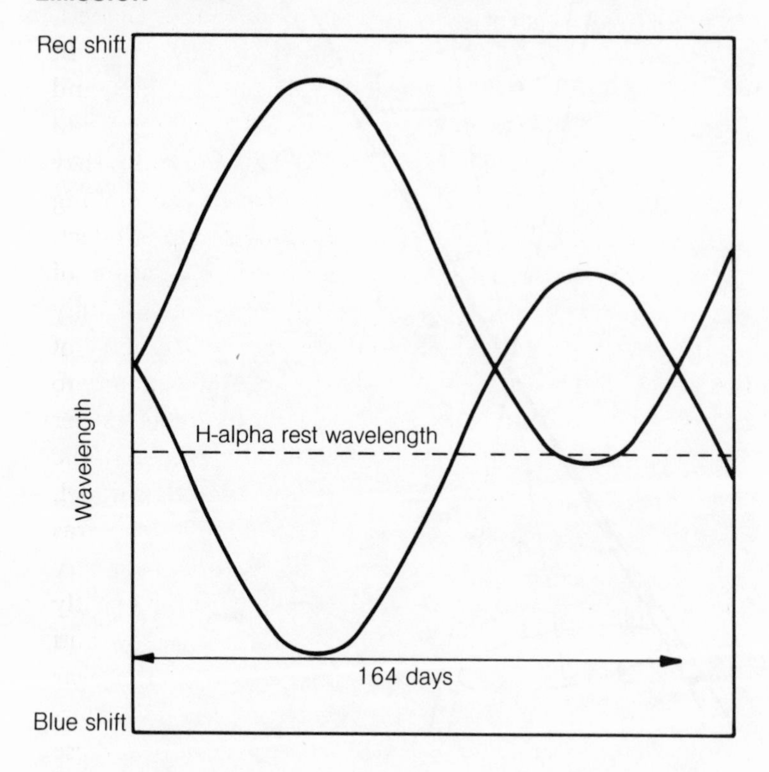

must sweep out a "cone" in the sky. The axis of this cone was inferred to be inclined at an angle of about 80 degrees with respect to the line of sight, and each jet was inclined at about 20 degrees with respect to this axis. Thus one jet would display a blue shift for most of the time as it precessed around the cone, and the other would remain predominantly red-shifted. They would cross over to the reverse velocity for a short interval of the precession, as indeed was observed in the behavior of the drifting features (see Figure 5.8). This geometry allowed predictions

FIGURE 5.8. GEOMETRY OF PRECESSING JETS

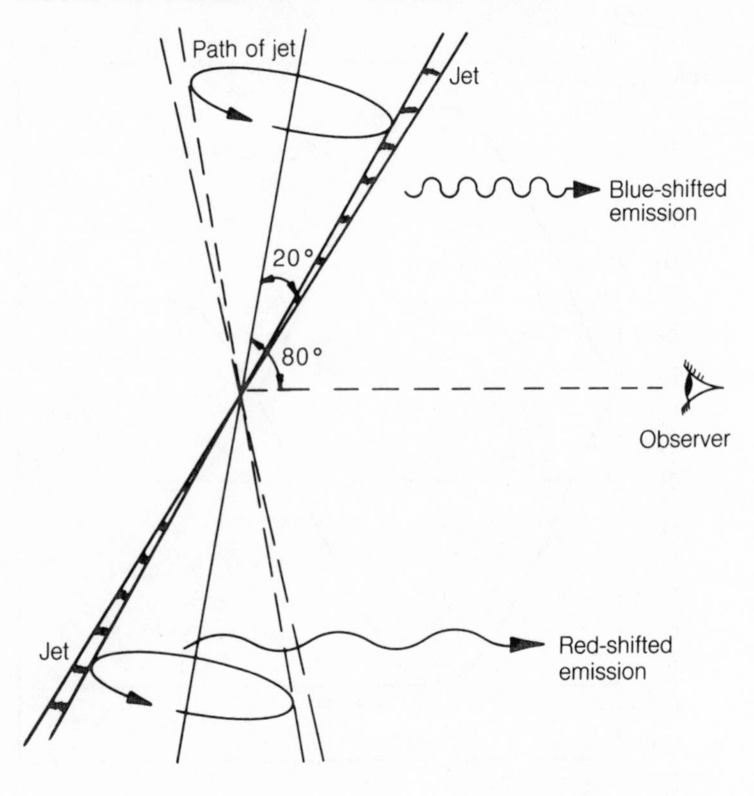

to be made about the future behavior of SS433; an "ephemeris" (an astronomical prediction table) could be produced.

Martin, Murdin, and I met at the Royal Astronomical Society in early May to discuss the validity of the model. It all seemed to fit together so beautifully with the ideas put forward by Milgrom and Fabian and Rees. We had a detailed picture of a star system the likes of which had never been seen before. Not to be left out this time through hesitation, we agreed to release details of the model and its associated ephemeris. An IAU circular was released on May 11, 1979, and read in part:

> P. G. Martin, Institute of Astronomy, University of Cambridge, and P. G. Murdin and D. H. Clark, Royal Greenwich Observatory, report —Following the identification of the moving features in SS433 as velocity-shifted hydrogen and helium lines [by Liebert and colleagues] and announcement of a 160-day periodicity [by Margon and colleagues], we have reanalysed spectrograms obtained with the Anglo-Australian Telescope on 1978 June 29, 30 and July 13, 14, 15, and 17. We find emission systems consistent with this general picture. . . . These data, together with extensive previous results [from Mammano and the Asiago astronomers], suggest a reliable ephemeris that should be useful for identifying the features in the coming months. Underlying this ephemeris might be a model with the following characteristics. The emission arises in two opposing jets [as proposed by Fabian and Rees] flowing away from a central neutron star at a quasi-steady velocity of quarter the speed of light. The latter property accounts for the constant offset in mean wavelength [as noted by Milgrom]. Variable Doppler shifts result from steady precession of the jet axis, which in a period of 160 days sweeps out a cone of opening angle 21.5 degrees centered on inclination 79.1 degrees relative to the line of sight. . . .

Our ephemeris was later proved to be slightly in error—not due to any fault in our interpretation of the data, or in the basic geometrical model, but because we had based our model on Margon's initially announced period of 160 days.

It was inconceivable in the light of all the other parallel activities in the SS433 saga that we would be the only ones to derive the geometric characteristics of the precessing jet model and produce an ephemeris. Inevitably, the ubiquitous Margon had also been working along similar lines, with George Abell, at Los Angeles. Indeed, unknown to us, the paper describing their model had been received by *Nature* on May 9, 1979—two days before the release of our IAU circular. They had fed the wealth of California data, plus the Asiago data, plus our AAT data into the Milgrom model, and had revised the precession period upward to 164 days, thus producing a more accurate ephemeris than we had achieved. However, the essential nature of the geometric model differed little from ours. They had calculated that the angle between the axis of the cones swept out by the jets and the line of sight was 78 degrees (compared with our estimate of 79 degrees), and they had calculated the opening angle of the cone as 17 degrees (compared with our 21.5 degrees). They had, in addition, determined the speed of the material in the jets to be 0.27, rather than our 0.25, times that of light. I learned of these results two weeks after release of our IAU circular, when a preprint of their *Nature* paper arrived from Margon. The Abell and Margon and the Martin and Murdin analyses were classic examples of simultaneous and independent work reaching almost identical conclusions.

Margon reported his detailed findings and their consequences to a meeting of the American Physical Society in April 1979. What for the previous nine months had so excited a few astronomers initially concerned with observing SS433 and interpreting its nature now filtered out to the wider community, catching the imagination of astronomers everywhere. The popular press was not long in joining the excited throng exulting in the wonders of SS433. Reports were flashed through the networks and newspapers of the world. SS433 had achieved superstar status.

INTERLUDE

There were things he stretched, but
mainly he told the truth.
—MARK TWAIN,
The Adventures of Huckleberry Finn

The story so far has, necessarily, been a personal view of the quest for SS433. It could not have been otherwise, since there is no definitive, impartial, well-informed history of the period up to mid-1979 on which to draw. By mid-1979, however, SS433 was "public property," and progress beyond this point can be followed clearly in the wealth of papers published in scientific journals.

An intriguing study was undertaken several years ago by sociologist Stephen Woolgar of the disparate accounts of the discovery of pulsars. The existence of pulsars—radio sources that emit pulses of radio energy at regular intervals from milliseconds to seconds—was totally unforeseen. Although variations in the intensity of a variety of cosmic objects were known, none behaved with such regularity and on these time scales. Radio sources of very small angular diameter often display an effect called "scintillation"—rapid and irregular fluctuations in intensity (analogous to the twinkling of stars). Scintillation results when radio waves emitted by distant cosmic sources pass through structures in the "solar wind," the flux of energetic particles emitted by the sun. It is thus an effect observed predominantly during the day, and its presence can be used to infer that a cosmic radio source has small size. The radio astronomers at Cambridge, England, decided to make use of this fact to search for distant highly energetic galaxies called "quasars," and designed a large sensitive radio telescope specifically for the task. Since scintillating sources were being sought, it was clear that the equipment used to record the cosmic radio signals must be able to respond to rapid variations in intensity. Thus, entirely fortuitously, an instrument became available almost tailor-made for the discovery of pulsars. Observations with the new instrument began at Cambridge in July 1967. Soon it became apparent that a host of scintillating sources could be found—a veritable gold mine in the search for quasars (and a diamond mine for the discovery of pulsars!). Among the hundreds of feet of paper-chart output produced daily, graduate student Jocelyn Bell noticed "a bit of scruff" indicating a possible scintillating source observed at night, the time when scintillation caused by solar wind would not be expected. It would have been only too easy to discount the bit of scruff as man-made interference (the curse of radio astronomers), such as a poorly suppressed automobile ignition or the like. To Bell's great credit, she did not discount the effect; indeed, she noted its systematic reappearance on a number of occasions as the same part of the sky passed overhead. In November 1967, a high-speed chart recorder was connected to the equipment to study the exact nature of the scruff in fine detail. To the amazement of those involved, what appeared were rapid pulses of remarkable regularity evenly spaced by one and a third seconds. The regularity of the pulses again suggested man-made interference, although more and more observations made this an increasingly difficult explanation to accept. So unexpected was the phenomenon that the idea that the regular pulses were "signals" from an "extraterrestrial civilization" was seriously considered, but it was quickly rejected with the discovery of three other pulsed sources. Whereas a single extraterrestrial civilization beaming pulsed signals toward Earth might be a possibility, the idea of a coordinated cosmic conspiracy to do this could hardly be entertained. Systematic observation indicated that the pulses were originating in planet-sized bodies at the distances of the nearer stars in the galaxy. In February 1968, the Cambridge radio astronomers announced their discovery of what are now called "pulsars."

In his study of the discovery of pulsars, Woolgar found that those who had been at the center of the discovery presented stories that, although agreeing in broad outline, differed significantly in important detail. Differences, in both the sequence of events and the inclusion of features believed relevant to the discovery, were quite extensive. Woolgar concluded that the discrepancies did not result merely from differences in emphasis, but that participants in the discovery of pulsars had experienced difficulty in reconstructing and communicating what had taken place. In part, this might be because any written account must tend to relate the path to discovery as being made up of a series of events and revelations, rather than the parallel evolution of ideas. Since events must be recounted sequentially, it might appear that they had occurred sequentially. However, many important steps could occur concurrently, and ideas often evolve slowly over an extended period. Archimedes may have achieved instantaneous insight while taking a bath, but for most researchers the process to scientific discovery is a more protracted, difficult, and less relaxing task.

In writing my story of the quest for SS433, I have been conscious that accounts of the discovery from different participants might be expected to differ, because of the omission by some accounts of events elsewhere considered important, because of differences in emphasis, because of difficulties experienced in reconstructing exactly what had happened, or because relevant material might be excluded for the sake of simplicity. Therefore, my personal story of the early hectic and exciting years of the quest for SS433 might differ in emphasis from such an account presented by, for example, Bruce Margon, Jim Caswell, Fred Seward, Paul Murdin, Ernie Seaquist, or the Asiago astronomers, but no alternative view could dispute the important steps in the parallel paths that led to the discovery of this remarkable phenomenon. These were:

INDIRECT PATH	DIRECT PATH
1974. Molonglo survey identifies CC493 (4C 04.66?). Clark and Caswell note proximity to supernova remnant W50. ↓	**1960s.** Case survey. ↓

INDIRECT PATH

1975. Circinus X-1 identified with pointlike radio source (later found by Caswell to be variable) near a supernova remnant. Optical counterpart later found by Whelan to be a peculiar emission-line star.

↓

1976. Seward and his Leicester colleagues find variable X-ray source A1909+04 in W50. Suggest it may be stellar remnant.

↓

1977. Caswell and Cambridge radio astronomers show that the pointlike radio source CC493 in W50 is highly variable. Data published in late 1978.

↓

1978. May. Erice conference discusses stellar-remnant problem; challenge is set to find other systems like Circinus X-1.

↓

DIRECT PATH

↓

1977. Stephenson and Sanduleak publish list of emission-line stars; number 433 is one of twenty sources noted to have strong H-alpha emission.

↓

INDIRECT PATH	DIRECT PATH
June. Clark and Murdin at AAT find peculiar emission-line star they associate with CC493, A1909+04, and supernova remnant W50; note similarity to Circinus X-1.	**1978. September.** Seaquist (unaware of earlier radio work) announces radio variability of source 433 in Stephenson and Sanduleak catalogue, via IAU circular 3256.
October. Margon, alerted to new discovery by Clark, observes spectral peculiarities in SS433.	**October.** Asiago astronomers, alerted to new discovery by circular 3256, observe spectral peculiarities in SS433.

Late 1978. Margon and colleagues (and, independently, Asiago astronomers) discover motion of peculiar spectral features.

↓

Early 1979. Cambridge and Israeli "jet sets" produce ingenious theories.

↓

Mid-1979. SS433 raised to superstar status.

Many of the steps along each path were accidental, but so it has been with many discoveries in astronomy. On the *direct* path, the Case survey was not a planned search for a stellar object displaying jets—although it was, of course, clearly envisaged that stars displaying strong emission lines were potentially of great interest. Along the *indirect* path, a series of chance and apparently unrelated discoveries merged into a hypothesis for stellar remnants of supernovae; the links between CC493 (4C 04.66?), A1909+04, W50, and a peculiar emission-line star were fused in an attempt to find a system similar to the better-studied Circinus X-1. Many of the steps may have been pure chance, but the separate paths eventually merged when Margon unveiled the moving features.

Most of those who played important roles in the period prior to the direct and indirect paths merging continued to probe the mysteries of SS433 in the years that followed. Sadly, John Whelan did not; he died in 1981, at the age of thirty-six, after a long, courageous battle with cancer. An obituary in the *Quarterly Journal of the Royal Astronomical Society* noted his manifold contributions to astronomy, including the discovery of the optical counterpart of Circinus X-1, though it failed to emphasize that this discovery was a beacon lighting the way for those of us who followed along the indirect path to SS433.

By mid-1979, astronomers had discovered a wealth of strange properties of SS433, and developed a rotating-jet model that seemed to describe satisfactorily most of these. SS433 still had many surprises in store, however.

6
BOMBAY DUCK

If it waddles like a duck, and quacks like a duck—then maybe it is *a duck!*
—SIDNEY VAN DEN BERGH,
on supernova remnant W50
(1980)

Thangasamy Velusamy got his training at the renowned Tata Institute of Fundamental Research, in Bombay, India, and in 1969 went to the University of Maryland to work for a Ph.D. degree in the field of radio observations of supernova remnants in the northern skies. While Jim Caswell and I were making our Molonglo-Parkes observations of Southern Hemisphere radio supernova remnants, Velusamy and his thesis supervisor, Mukul Kundu, were making similar observations of northern supernova remnants, using the 300-foot-diameter and 140-foot-diameter radio telescopes at the U.S. National Radio Astronomy Observatory. In 1974, the same year that Caswell and I published our partial W50 map showing just the northern "banana-shaped" rim, Velusamy published a map of W50 showing its total extent, as explained earlier. The new map was of only modest resolution, and the position of the central pointlike source (incorrectly annotated as 4C 04.66) was not accurately determined, but Velusamy was the first to show the actual structure of radio supernova remnant W50, indicating the central position of the pointlike source.

In the following five years, W50 lay dormant, arousing little or no interest among the supernova-remnant pundits. While astronomers were securing the optical identifications of many supernova remnants, W50 escaped their attention. The X-ray astronomers, too, paid it little heed, although Fred Seward did draw attention to the fact that the point X-ray source A1909+04 lay close to W50 and might be its stellar remnant. But radio astronomers failed to attempt to improve on the observational data of Velusamy, despite the advent of major new radio telescopes capable of doing so. The supernova conference at Erice changed all that, as it had so many other areas of supernova research, including the unveiling of SS433.

A young American radio astronomer, Barry Geldzahler, of the University of Pennsylvania, visited the Max-Planck Institute for Radio Astronomy in Bonn, West Germany, during 1978–79. Since he had been studying some of the pointlike radio sources in supernova remnants in an attempt to link the point sources and extended remnants unambiguously, at Erice he was particularly interested in taking part in discussions on the missing-link mystery. One object had dominated his interest—a pointlike radio source, known as "CL4," near the center of a large old supernova remnant called the "Cygnus Loop." He described his observations of this object at the Erice meeting, arguing that it was but a chance positional coincidence on the sky of the extended supernova remnant and a distant background source. (This interpretation was later confirmed by others.) He was careful not to preclude the possible association of other pointlike radio sources and supernova remnants on the basis of just this one negative result. After his talk, I told him about W50 and its central source and urged him to take new observations of it. This he and his colleagues did on August 3–4, 1978 (two months after the Erice meeting), using the giant 100-meter-diameter radio telescope at Bonn. Others were to comment later on the remarkable coincidence of new W50 observations being made almost simultaneously with the early optical observations of SS433. However, unlike so many of the occurrences in the SS433 saga, this had been *no* coincidence—the AAT observations of SS433 and the Bonn observations of W50 both had their birth in the discussions at Erice.

The Bonn map of W50 (Figure 6.1) was of greatly improved quality compared with the Molonglo and Velusamy maps. As with the latter, the radio frequency used was high enough for the whole remnant to "emerge" from the diffuse galactic background radio emission, and the

FIGURE 6.1. W50

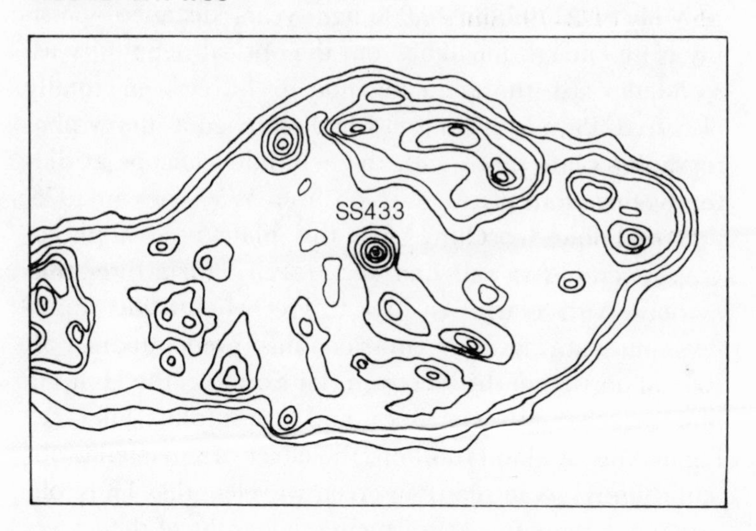

detail displayed on the new map was impressive indeed. Rather than showing the near symmetry of almost all supernova remnants, W50 showed unusual protrusions on its eastern and western edges—"ears" to the remnant, which gave it an overall elliptical structure. Although the bright northern rim originally mapped at Molonglo remained the most conspicuous extended emission feature, other bright "ridges" and "knots" were seen. But dominating all else was the bright pointlike radio source plumb at the remnant's center. SS433 stood out like a bull's-eye on an archery target, tempting observers to shoot at it.

The new Bonn radio map of W50 was released in preprint form in April 1979, about the time the excitement generated by the Doppler interpretation for the moving features in SS433 was spreading through the astronomical community. Five years of observational neglect of W50 were about to be reversed in a few months of feverish activity. The radio data implied that the remnant probably lay within about 10,000 light-years' distance—possibly close enough for light from the optical nebulosity associated with the remnant not to have been totally obscured. Paul Murdin and I had searched a survey photographic plate taken with the Schmidt telescope at Siding Springs for optical emission from W50 back in 1976, and had found nothing. But this plate used a photographic emulsion and had been taken with a filter that made it particularly sensitive to green light. Old supernova remnants display emission lines predominantly in the red portion of the spectrum (for example, the H-alpha line, adjacent nitrogen lines, and red sulphur lines; see Figure 6.2), and, in addition, the effect of interstellar obscuration is less in red than green wavelengths. Thus, old supernova remnants experiencing reddening of their spec-

FIGURE 6.2. TYPICAL SUPERNOVA REMNANT RED SPECTRUM

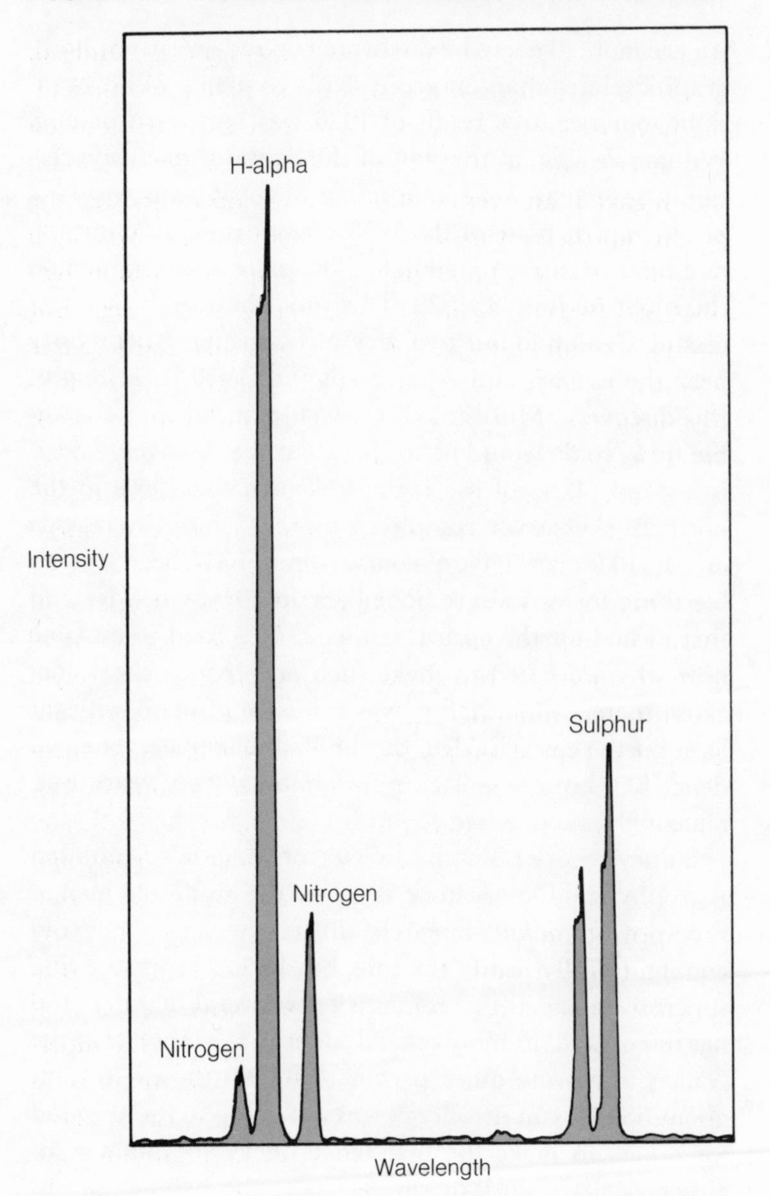

tra are more likely to be discovered on red-sensitive photographic plates than on green-sensitive plates. With hindsight, our negative result of 1976 was hardly surprising. William Zealey, of the staff of the Schmidt telescope certainly appreciated the importance of getting a new survey photographic plate of the W50 region using an emulsion and filter sensitive to red light. The plate was obtained on the night of June 3, 1979. This time the search was successful. Zealey found two arcs of filamentary nebulosity near the eastern and western edges of W50. Learning of this discovery, Murdin and Caswell realized that a sensible thing to do would be to check out the discovery on existing red plates of the region taken in the 1960s in the northern-sky survey completed by the Schmidt telescope on Mt. Palomar. This, of course, would have been a sensible thing for us to have done back in 1976, when we had first looked for the optical remnant. It is hard to imagine now why we failed to make such an obvious check, because there, unbelievably, was evidence of nebulosity (at least on the eastern edge) on the Palomar plate. The evidence had been in existence for almost twenty years, but, amazingly, no one had found it.

Sidney van den Bergh, director of Canada's Dominion Astrophysical Observatory, is one of the grand old men of supernova-remnant research. In truth, he is not old enough to fully justify the title, but he has been studying supernovae and their remnants over several decades, and has discovered far more optical supernova remnants in the Galaxy than any other person. After all the excitement about SS433, van den Bergh was not going to wait around for others to make the first move on W50. Unaware of either Zealey's work or the fact that the nebulosity was present on an existing Palomar plate, he arranged for new

Palomar Schmidt observations to be made. To isolate the optical nebulosity clearly, these were taken through filters that would transmit light only in the vicinity of the H-alpha line and red sulphur lines. The success of the new Palomar search was announced in an IAU circular dated August 17, 1979:

> S. van den Bergh, Dominion Astrophysical Observatory, telexes that H-alpha and [red sulphur line] filter plates of the non-thermal radio source W50 taken with the Palomar Schmidt telescope show faint filamentary nebulosity located approximately 28 arc minutes east and 25 arc minutes west of SS433 along the outer edge of the extended radio source.

Thus he was the first to *announce* the discovery of W50 optical nebulosity, although there can be no doubt that Zealey had found it first. Perhaps the question of precedence in the case of W50 is unimportant; after all, the evidence had existed on the Palomar survey plate for twenty years but had been ignored by us all.

Now that the optical nebulosity associated with W50 had been isolated, it was important to take a spectrum of it as soon as possible. Again, the wait for telescope time would have been many months. But Murdin had a stroke of good fortune. He had been given the job of supervising the construction of a new Image Photon Counting System—an almost exact copy of the sophisticated electronic detector used on the AAT. To give the instrument a thorough testing at a good astronomical site, arrangements had been made for it to be shipped to the South African Astronomical Observatory at Sutherland and mounted on the 1.9-meter telescope there. Murdin traveled to South

Africa in August 1979 to commission the instrument, and at the first opportunity (August 23) used it to get a spectrum of W50. The result was surprising. The vast majority of old supernova remnants display spectra dominated by bright hydrogen lines, with the emission lines from other elements somewhat weaker. The red sulphur lines tend to be rather strong in supernova remnants, and the relative strength of these has often been used in the past to identify them. The two lines of nitrogen that lie on either side of the intense H-alpha line are almost always weaker than the H-alpha line. Murdin's IPCS spectrum of W50 (Figure 6.3) showed only very weak H-alpha emission; the red sulphur lines were comparatively strong, confirming a supernova-remnant identification, but it was dominated

FIGURE 6.3.

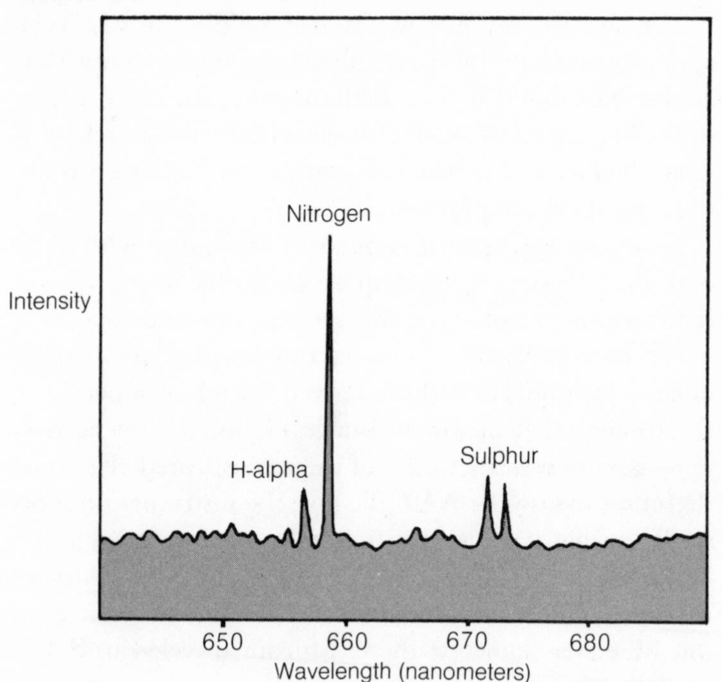

by intense emission from nitrogen. We knew of only one other optical supernova remnant that displayed such an unusual spectrum with intense nitrogen emission—a Southern Hemisphere object called "Puppis-A." The W50 spectrum was heavily reddened, like SS433, strengthening the case for the two being at similar distances from the Earth and physically associated.

Murdin and I were still conscious of the fact that we had been overhesitant in not releasing details of our first AAT spectra of SS433, so on this occasion we rushed through an announcement. The IAU circular of September 10, 1979, read:

> P. Murdin and D. H. Clark, Royal Greenwich Observatory, report that IPCS spectra taken with the South African Astronomical Observatory's 1.9 metre telescope of the eastern filament of W50, independently discovered by van den Bergh and visible on the Palomar Sky Survey [red] plate, show that nitrogen emission is mostly responsible for the apparent H-alpha photographed by him. The ratio [nitrogen/hydrogen] is approximately 5, Puppis-A being the only other known optical remnant showing such nitrogen enhancement. Identification of the nebulosity as the supernova remnant W50 is confirmed by a large [sulphur/hydrogen] ratio. The red lines are the only lines detected in a low-dispersion spectrum suggesting a large reddening, like that of SS433. This is further evidence that W50 and SS433 are associated.

We were unaware that Zealey and his collaborators had taken IPCS spectra of W50 at the AAT one week before Murdin's South African observations. These they announced in an IAU circular dated October 25, 1979. Others were to obtain spectral data of W50 also. Perhaps the best spectra of the W50 nebulosity were obtained by Bob Kirshner and Roger Chevalier in April 1980 (Figure 6.4). All the data confirmed the anomalous intensity of the nitrogen emission lines. Did this indicate that nitrogen was more abundant in the vicinity of W50 (and, for that matter, Puppis-A) than for the vast majority of supernova remnants? And, if so, was this high level of nitrogen something that existed in the interstellar medium prior to the

FIGURE 6.4.

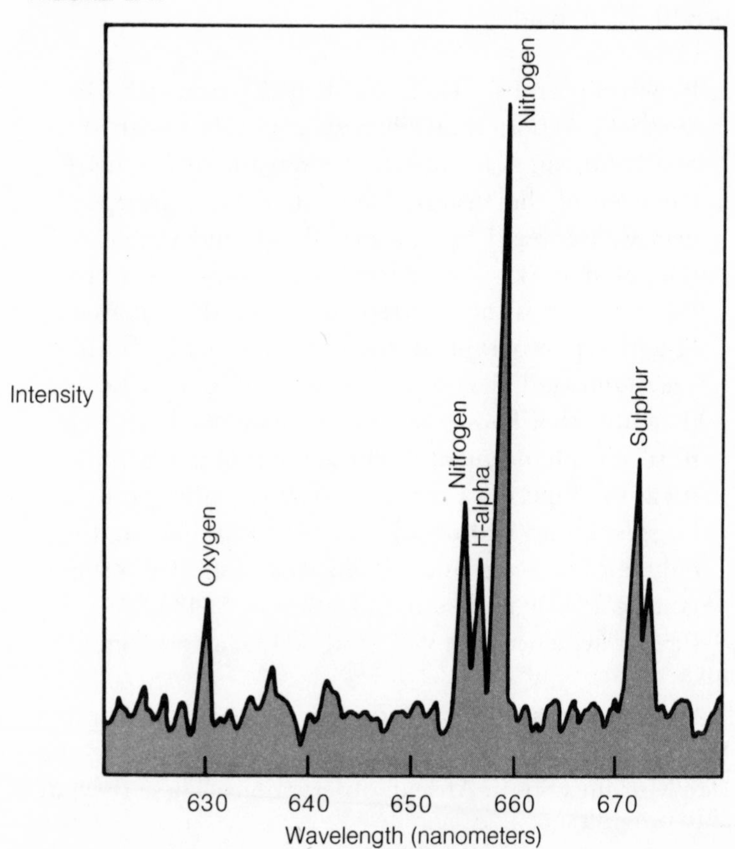

supernova explosion, or an enhancement resulting from the supernova explosion that produced W50? Kirshner and Chevalier suspected the former:

> [The high nitrogen-line intensity] is usually interpreted as an abundance effect, but it is more likely to have its origin in the interstellar medium than in the supernova event that produced W50.

Murdin and I were less certain of this, offering a range of alternatives in a paper published later:

> The abnormal spectrum of Puppis-A has been interpreted as originating in nuclear-processed material which has been ejected from a star. From its diameter W50 is, like Puppis-A, an old supernova remnant (older than ten thousand years). In such an old remnant, the bulk of the ejecta is usually expected to have merged with the interstellar material. Perhaps the abnormal spectrum of W50 is a peculiar, unexplained excitation effect, as presumably would be the spectrum of Puppis-A. But for both W50 and Puppis-A it remains a possibility that dense knots of processed ejecta have retained their identities on an extended time scale.

Van den Bergh calculated that to explain the anomalously strong nitrogen lines in the spectrum of W50, the interstellar material swept up by the expanding supernova remnant would have to have been enriched by a mass of nitrogen comparable to the mass of the sun. If, as Murdin and I had suggested, this nitrogen had been ejected from a precursor star, what sort of star could possibly provide such a large mass of nitrogen? There was one likely source: a Wolf-Rayet star (the type of object we erroneously first thought SS433 might be on that eventful night at the AAT). Wolf-Rayet stars come in two main varieties: so-called WC stars (displaying spectral features indicating an enhanced abundance of carbon) and WN stars (displaying spectral features indicating an enhanced abundance of nitrogen).

Wolf-Rayet stars are exceptionally massive (probably at least twenty times the mass of the sun) and undergo rapid evolution. As in all stars, successive stages of nuclear burning occur in their central cores, with earlier stages of burning occurring in outer layers (see Figure 6.5). However, because of its extreme mass and rapid evolution, a Wolf-Rayet star tends to be extremely unstable, shedding its outer hydrogen layers in the form of a stellar wind, revealing lower layers of partially processed material rich in carbon and nitrogen. The explosion of a Wolf-Rayet star could significantly enrich its environment with carbon or nitrogen. Van den Bergh proposed that the nitrogen overabundance in W50 indicated that it had been produced by the explosion of a WN star.

While so much attention was being focused on the radio data of W50 and the properties of the newly discovered optical filaments, Fred Seward and others were using the instruments on the Einstein Observatory to study both SS433 and its environment. These observations were to prove a milestone in understanding the jets in SS433, but they failed to reveal any X-ray emission from the surrounding supernova remnant. This absence of X-ray emission from W50 could be explained in one of two possible ways: either X-rays were being produced but were being obscured from view by intervening matter, or the material being swept up by the supernova shock wave was so tenuous as to generate insufficient X-ray emission to be

FIGURE 6.5. SHELL STRUCTURE IN MASSIVE STAR

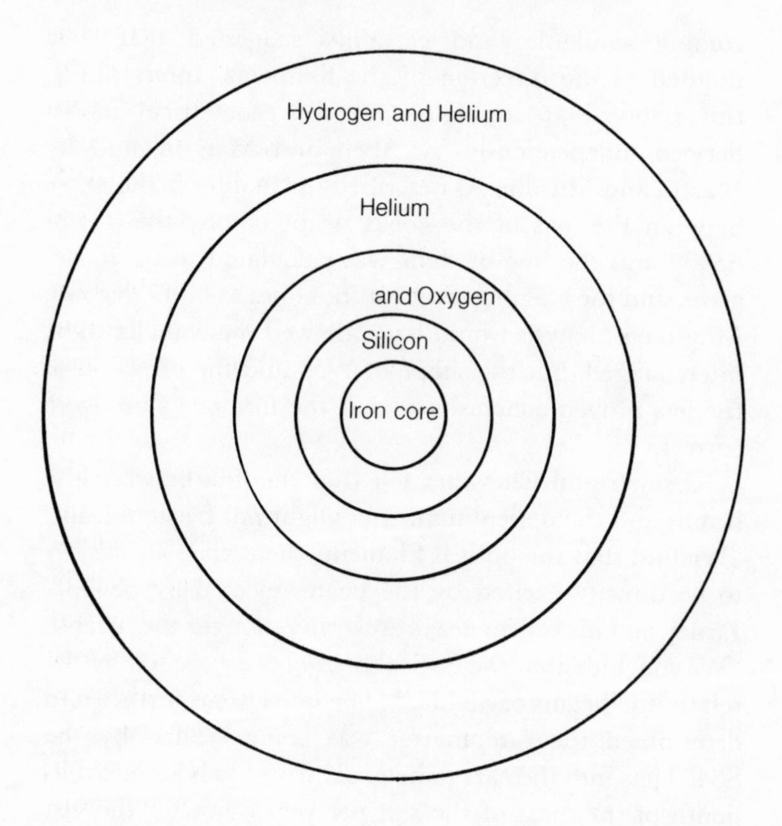

detectable. This latter explanation was the one favored by the theorists.

The peculiar radio shape of W50 compared with other supernova remnants had not escaped attention. Most old supernova remnants maintain something approximating a spherical structure. Yet W50 was highly elongated, displaying peculiar earlike protrusions. What is more, the optical filaments were aligned with the inner edges of the ears. Could the ears and optical filaments be formed by the jets from SS433? Radio data on the jets were now becoming available, and certainly suggested that they pointed in the direction of the filaments. Interestingly, this resolved an ambiguity in the geometrical model derived independently by Abell and Margon, and by Martin and Murdin. As described in Chapter 5, the angle between the axis of the cones swept out by the jets of SS433 and the line of sight was calculated to be 78 degrees, and the opening angle of the cones to be 17 degrees. Milgrom's analysis would have allowed these angles to be interchanged, but the shape of W50 and the direction of the jets proved conclusively that the former values were correct.

Kirshner and Chevalier felt that the link between the beams and the optical filaments might not be significant: "We find that the optical filaments themselves *are unlikely* to be directly excited by the beams ejected by SS433." Zealey and his colleagues in Australia thought the reverse: "We conclude that the optical filaments *are* excited by the relativistic beams of SS433." (The latter went further and determined the rate matter was being ejected by the SS433 jets into the ears to be equivalent to about one-millionth of the mass of the sun per year.) Not for the last time, groups of researchers were reaching totally opposite conclusions about SS433 and W50 from similar data.

The majority of supernova remnants display peripheral brightening—when viewed in the sky, their shape is reminiscent of a doughnut with a hole in the center. This morphology is indicative of an expanding shell of radiating material. However, there is another class of supernova remnant, the Crab Nebula being the best-known example, which is brightest at the center. These centrally bright supernova remnants are known as "plerions." ("Plerion" is derived from the Greek word for "filled center." Its use to describe filled-center supernova remnants was proposed for the first time at the Erice conference.) The central brightening of a plerion is thought to result from injection of energy from an active pulsar at its center.

An intriguing suggestion made about the nature of W50 was that it displayed features in common with both that class of supernova remnants showing peripheral brightening and the plerions. An example of a remnant displaying both properties, called MSH 15-56 (see Figure 6.6)), was in fact known. Although the bright banana-shaped ridge

FIGURE 6.6. SUPERNOVA REMNANT MSH 15-56

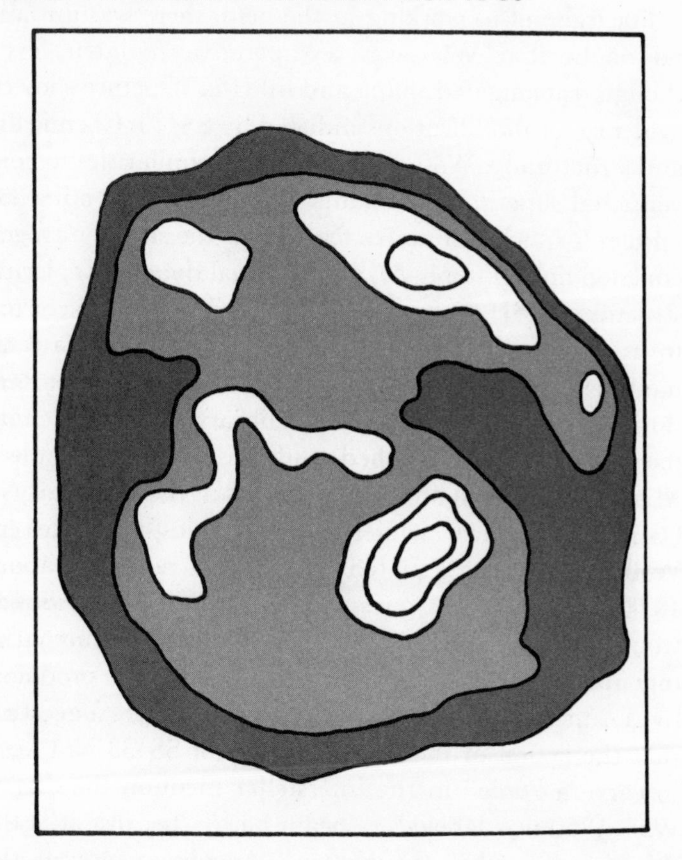

of W50, and even the ears, seemed to be defining a conventional doughnut shape, Kurt Weiler, of the U.S. National Science Foundation (and instigator of the term "plerion"), noted that the central region of W50 was brighter than expected for a conventional remnant, even after allowing for the presence of SS433. While the similarities between W50 and the prototype plerion, the Crab Nebula, are rather tenuous, clearly sources contributing to central brightening are known in each—the central pulsar for the Crab, and SS433 for W50.

For those of us working in the field, there was initially no doubt that W50 was a supernova remnant, even though its elongated shape and filled-in structure showed evidence for modifications induced by SS433. Chemically and structurally, W50 displayed many similarities to conventional supernova remnants; there were even other examples for such distinctive features as the strong nitrogen emission lines (Puppis-A), and the dual doughnut/plerion structure (MSH 15-56). It had, therefore, never occurred to us that perhaps W50 might not be a supernova remnant. The possibility was suggested to me by Martin Rees during a chance encounter in the library at RGO. He told me of a yet-to-be-published study by his former student Mitchell Begelman and his colleagues at the University of California, Berkeley, which proposed a most novel idea for W50. They had calculated that, over a period of about 10,000 years (a best guess for the age of W50), SS433 would have injected as much energy into the surrounding interstellar medium as would have been produced by a supernova explosion. Hence they were suggesting that the action of the jets ("beams") of SS433 had been to carve a "hole" in the interstellar medium the size of W50. W50 was labeled a "beam bag," "because it is the thing that catches the beams." A consequence of the beam-bag model is that the system must be at least a thousand years old (and presumably very much older), because it would take this long for beam material to travel from SS433 to the ears.

Today there is no consensus on whether W50 is the product of a supernova explosion, subsequently modified by the influence of SS433's producing the ears, or whether it is entirely the result of the action of SS433. Perhaps the last word on the subject should be left to Sidney van den Bergh, who supports the former possibility on the basis that W50 resembles a conventional remnant in so many of its properties. At a conference on SS433 held in Rome during October 1980, the nature of W50 was actively debated. Was it a supernova remnant or was it solely a beam bag? Van den Bergh passed his judgment: "If it waddles like a duck, and quacks like a duck—then maybe it *is* a duck."

Velusamy's "duck" may be a "strange bird," and may have taken a long time to show its true plumage, but no one can doubt that, thanks to SS433, it now had much to quack about.

7
TRIAL . . .

In the very middle of the court was a table, with a large dish of tarts upon it; they looked so good that it made Alice quite hungry to look at them—"I wish they'd get the trial done," she thought, "and hand round the refreshments!"
—LEWIS CARROLL,
Alice's Adventures in Wonderland

In early June 1979, I was yet again en route to the Anglo-Australian Telescope. On this occasion Paul Murdin and I had been awarded a generous allocation of observing time specifically (but not exclusively) for extensive observations of SS433.

It is always tempting to break this journey in the United States; on this occasion I decided to stop off in Boston to call on Fred Seward. I was eager to learn how the Einstein Observatory program, which he was helping to organize, was progressing. Already a flood of spectacular results from Einstein was becoming available. A fraction of the observing time on the spacecraft had generously been opened by NASA to astronomers from around the world (guest programs being selected on the usual basis of scientific excellence), and with various collaborators I had been fortunate to have had several applications for Einstein observations awarded time, although no data were yet available. Knowing of Seward's interest in W50 and A1909+04 (SS433?), I had not submitted an application to observe these, but, unaware of Seward's long-standing involvement, Ernie Seaquist had. (Seward and Seaquist collaborated in later X-ray observations of SS433.) Seaquist's Einstein observations of SS433 had been completed in April 1979, with the high-resolution imaging detector on the spacecraft.

A data-reduction facility for the Einstein Observatory had been established at the Center for Astrophysics (CFA) in Cambridge, Massachusetts, and guest observers were encouraged to visit CFA to reduce and analyze their data from the spacecraft. Although none of my data were yet available, Seward showed me how to operate the various data-reduction computer programs, and then left me at one of the computer terminals to gain experience in their use by processing some of his data, so that I would know what was involved. I was surprised to find among the list of objects stored in the computer memory "SS433—E. Seaquist." Usually in a situation like this, one expects the data of others to be protected in some way—a code or key word being required to gain access. Never expecting the computer to respond to my typed command, I called up the SS433 data. To my amazement, the data flashed on the computer display unit. In the center was an X-ray star exactly coincident with the position of SS433. Any lingering doubts I might have had that the X-ray star A1909+04 discovered by Seward and the Leicester X-ray astronomers (but with rather uncertain position) was in fact SS433 were immediately dispelled. I clearly had no right to look at Seaquist's data (I didn't tell Seward of my sneak preview, to avoid making him an "accessory after the fact"), but it was useful to know that Einstein had positively verified the association of the X-ray source A1909+04 and SS433 months before the result was published.

My final two days in Boston coincided with a meeting of the American Astronomical Society in Wellesley. The meeting was dominated by two topics: the initial spectacular results from the Einstein Observatory and SS433. Bruce Margon could not get to the meeting, so he sent a colleague to give a talk on his new results on SS433. I arrived at the lecture theater to find that it was already packed to capacity, with astronomers sitting in the aisles and standing around the periphery of the room—in contrast to the usual modest audiences attracted to specialist talks. Perhaps rather petulantly, leaving SS433 to bathe in its glory, I gathered my bags and headed for the airport.

Murdin was already at the observatory when I arrived some thirty-six hours later. Our strategy for mounting a full-scale attack on SS433 had been carefully planned before leaving England. We obviously had to take account of the extensive work being undertaken elsewhere (particularly in California and Asiago), with Margon now standing colossuslike astride the SS433 scene. But there were many aspects of it that appeared to us to be still worthy of investigation.

1. Although most of the attention so far had been concentrated on the moving features originating in the jets, we wanted to find evidence of the main star system (presumably a binary star) underlying SS433.
2. We wished to study in detail the "stationary" emission features; although these had excited less interest than the "moving" features, they must nevertheless contain important clues to the true nature of SS433.
3. Since our observations would be made at a phase in the

164-day period when the blue-shifted and red-shifted moving features would be approaching each other and lie comparatively close together, we wanted to look at similarities (or perhaps differences) in these features.

4. We hoped to take spectra separated by just minutes or hours to study the variability of SS433 on this range of time scale.
5. If, as was generally assumed, the moving features were emitted from cooling blobs of material in the jets, we wanted to ascertain if the behavior of the moving spectral features could describe the motion of the blobs in the jets.

(It turned out later that all these topics were being studied by others about this time, but with results still to be announced.)

While conclusions based on aspects 1, 2, and 4 would have to await a detailed reduction of the observational data, an improved understanding of aspects 3 and 5 was obtained even as our observations were being made. There were occasions when the blue-shifted and red-shifted features, which were known to vary dramatically in intensity as well as in wavelength, appeared to be almost perfect mirror images of each other (see Figure 7.1), as if the central powerhouse for the jets had simultaneously brightened or faded. They tended in general to be fainter on their "trailing" edge, but this was certainly not always the case. On occasion, the matching blue-shifted and red-shifted features could look spectacularly different. SS433 appeared to have no intention of making its detailed interpretation simpler by being consistent in its behavior.

The new AAT spectra did reveal some startling facts on the nature of the moving blobs making up the jets. It

FIGURE 7.1.

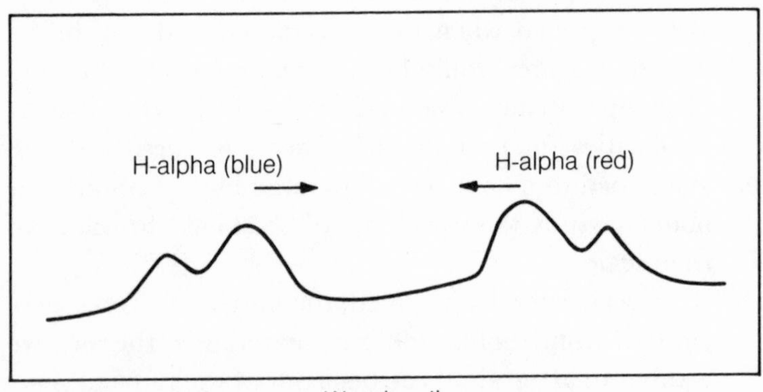

seemed that a moving feature would appear at a particular wavelength in the spectrum, grow in intensity, and fade over a period of several days, but not actually move in wavelength at all. The illusion of wavelength drift resulted from another quite distinct feature, appearing at an adjacent wavelength, brightening somewhat later than the earlier blob, and so on (Figure 7.2). The "shift" was therefore a drift of the wavelength at which a blob was ejected; it seemed that it then traveled "ballistically." The blobs behaved like bullets. Sometimes SS433 "fired from both hips" (producing the mirror image blue- and red-shifted features); sometimes it fired from just one. (This strange behavior could explain the enigmatic result, noted by some observers, that the moving features could occasionally execute an enormous "jump" in wavelength from one night to the next. At a first observation they could be seeing the dying phase of a bullet that had been produced several days previously; since no bullets were produced in the intervening period, when the next one appeared it was at a significantly different wavelength, because the preferred direction of ejection had continued to precess.)

FIGURE 7.2.

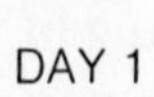

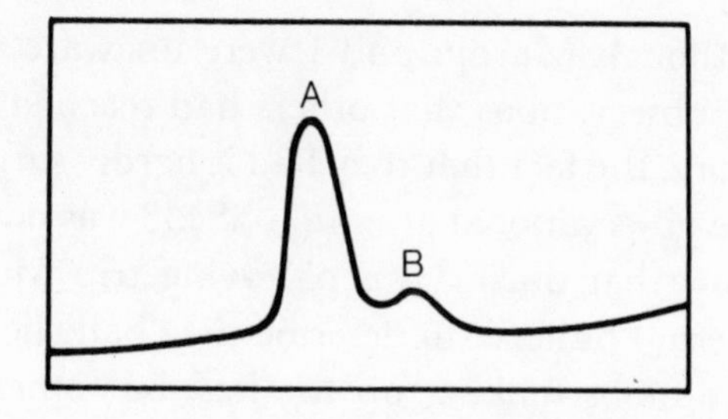

DAY 2

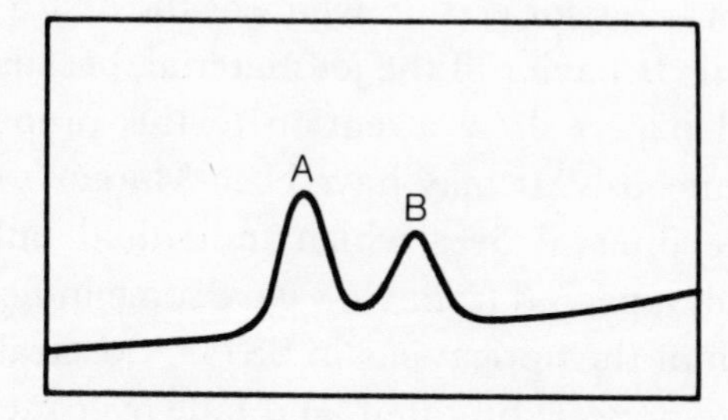

DAY 3

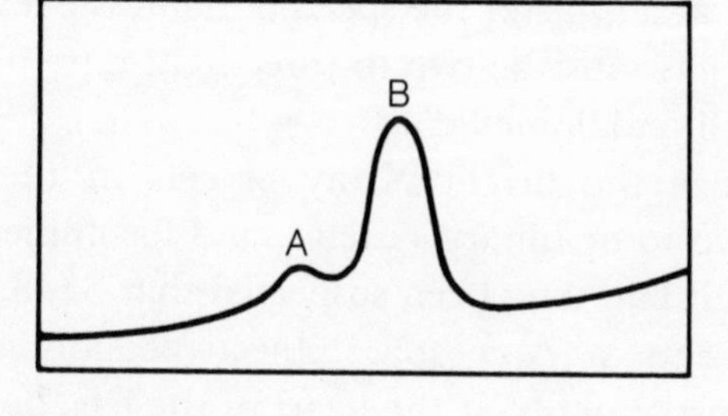

DAY 4

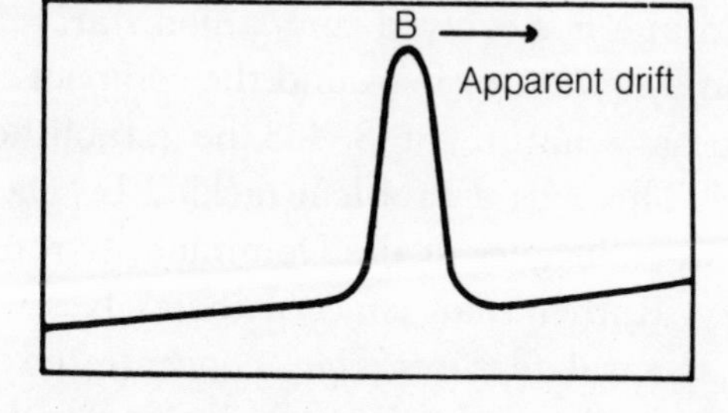

Although Murdin and I were unaware at the time of these observations that others had reached identical conclusions, the fact that they had is hardly surprising in view of the observational attention SS433 was now demanding. I know that during this observing trip Murdin adopted the term "bullets" to describe the "ballistic" propagation of the blobs making up the jets, but other investigators were independently to adopt an identical terminology. I do not know for certain who was the first to recognize the ballistic behavior of the jet material, because several published papers drew attention to this property almost simultaneously. It may have been Margon's co-workers.

The interval over which individual bullets appeared and disappeared from view gave some indication as to the length of the optical jets in SS433. Spectral features were seen to appear, brighten, and fade over intervals of up to about ten days. Since we knew that the bullets were traveling at a quarter the speed of light, the length of the optical jets must be two to three light-days (on the order of 50 billion kilometers).

Since the bright X-ray objects in the Galaxy were known to be binary systems, and for numerous other reasons, it had long been suspected that SS433 must be a binary system. A compact object (possibly a neutron star) was presumably at the heart of the jets, but the jet material (hydrogen and helium) must, it was argued, have originated in a less evolved companion star, reaching the jets via an accretion disk around the compact star. But could the binary nature of SS433 be established unambiguously? This was a problem tackled by David Crampton and his colleagues at the Dominion Astrophysical Observatory. Rather than concern themselves with the "moving" spectral features, they concentrated on the bright "stationary" emission lines. By looking at these night after night (forty-eight spectra in all were obtained between April and July 1979), they discovered that the stationary lines shifted backward and forward in a 13.1-day period. The amount of this shift (certainly due to the Doppler effect) was less than one-thousandth of the enormous Doppler shifts found in the jets. So it was a fairly subtle effect, which required great care for it to be revealed. The origin of this 13.1-day cyclic Doppler shift in the stationary features (more accurately, the *almost* stationary features) could only be the orbital motion of one star about another (see Figure 7.3). There could now be absolutely *no* shadow of doubt that SS433 was a binary system. The

FIGURE 7.3.

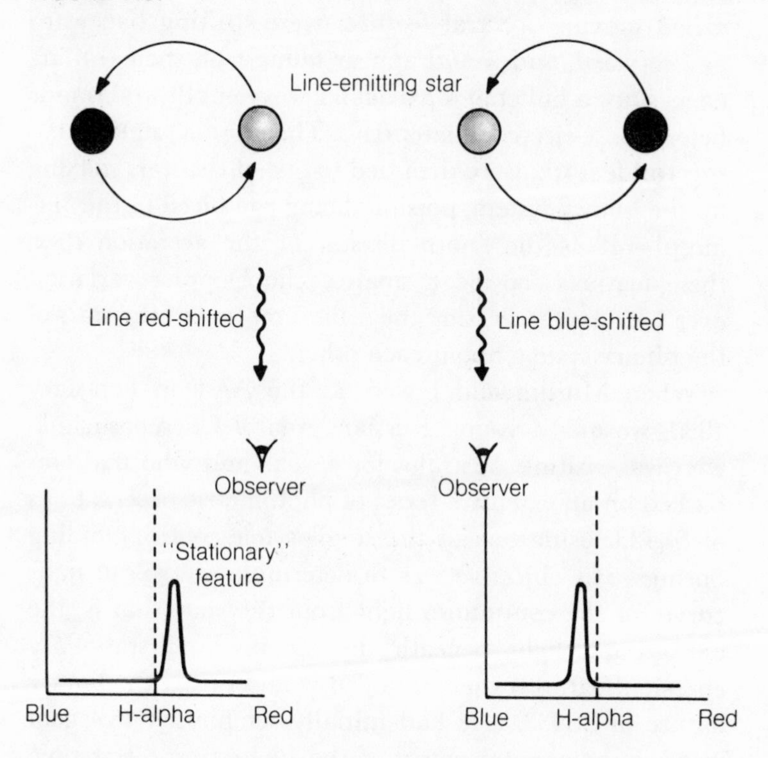

limits of the orbital system determined by Crampton and his collaborators suggested that the binary system comprised a neutron star plus a rather ordinary star of modest mass. The orbital period determined by the Canadians was announced in an IAU circular dated August 6, 1979. More exotic possibilities were soon revealed.

The picture of SS433 had now evolved one stage further. Clearly it *was* a binary system, including "jets," which were a totally new (and unpredicted) stellar phenomenon. The jets contained "bullets" of material responsible for the red-shifted and blue-shifted emission features, the direction of ejection of the bullets precessing with a 164-day period, presenting the illusion that the so-called moving spectral features were drifting backward and forward, and would appear faintest on their trailing edge, since a bullet at a particular wavelength would fade before those ejected in later days. The intense "stationary" spectral features were then tied to one of the stars making up the binary system, possibly being produced in the "atmosphere" of the "normal" star or the accretion disk; these features showed a small cyclic Doppler variation over 13.1 days, reflecting the orbital motion of the stars of the binary system about each other.

When Murdin and I were at the AAT in February 1980, we met a young Russian, Anatol Cherepashchuk, who was visiting Australia for a year and who had embarked on an extensive series of photometric observations of SS433, using one of the smaller telescopes at Siding Springs. His objective was to determine an overall light curve for the continuum light from the star (that is, the background light beneath the moving and stationary emission features) that he hoped would reveal the binary nature of SS433. (He had initially set himself this goal prior to the announcement of the 13.1-day spectroscopic period by Crampton and his colleagues.) We were intrigued to learn about his progress to date. With his observations from 1979 and extending into 1980, he eventually showed convincingly that the continuum brightness of SS433 did indeed vary with the 13.1-day period (see Figure 7.4), displaying both primary and secondary minima. Minima of this form in the light curve of a binary system are assumed to reveal eclipses of one object in the binary system by the other (see Figure 7.5)—perhaps in the case of SS433 the eclipse by the normal star of the accretion disk presumably formed about the compact object, or vice versa. The 13.1-day period was also found, by Margon, in the intensities of the stationary emission lines.

Studies of the variation of the intensity of the light from SS433 were greatly affected by its chaotic behavior. Reports came in of sudden significant brightening over an interval of a few hours, and even factors of two variations in brightness over intervals of just a day. Clearly some observations of varying brightness were contaminated by the moving spectral features drifting into and out of the wave-

FIGURE 7.4.

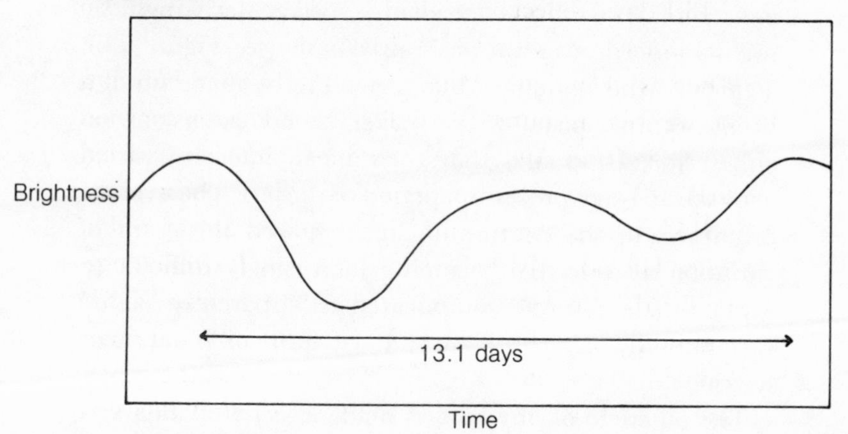

FIGURE 7.5.

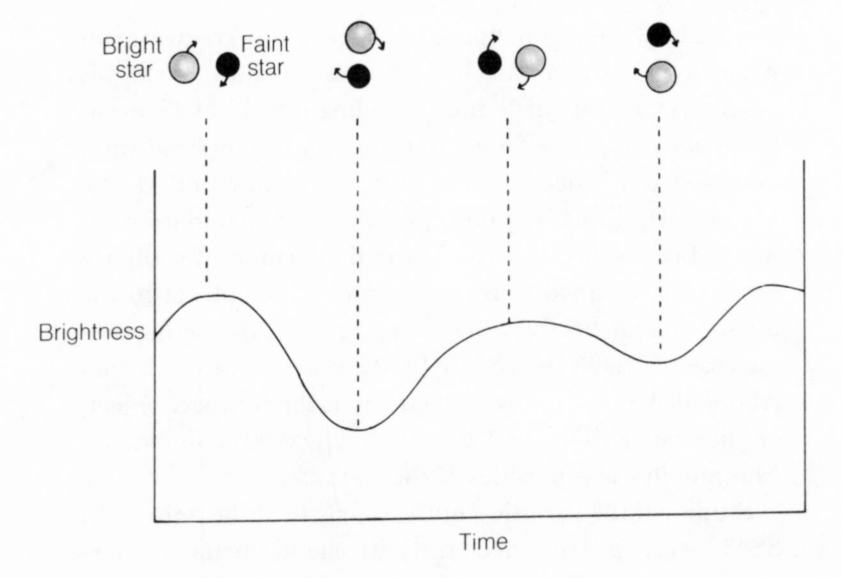

length band being studied photometrically. Within this chaos, an average behavior related to the 13.1-day orbital variation was maintained and confirmed by many independent observers. The shape ("profile") of the stationary emission lines was found to change spectacularly night by night—indeed, even on an hourly basis (see Figure 7.6). Typically, the stationary line seemed to be made up of a bright central peak, with weaker broad extensions on either side. It seemed that their mean intensity varied with the 164-day precession period of the jets. The average brightness of the continuum light showed this form of variation also. It was becoming increasingly difficult to explain these absurdly complicated yet apparently related variations by means of any known form of binary-star system.

The outcome of any trial is made easier if evidence is not seen to be in open conflict. For SS433, as each new

FIGURE 7.6. VARIATIONS OF PROFILE OF "STATIONARY" EMISSION FEATURE

SPECTRUM 1

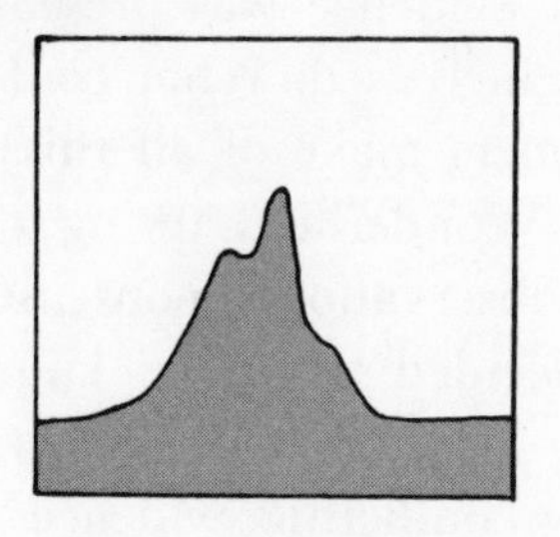

SPECTRUM 2

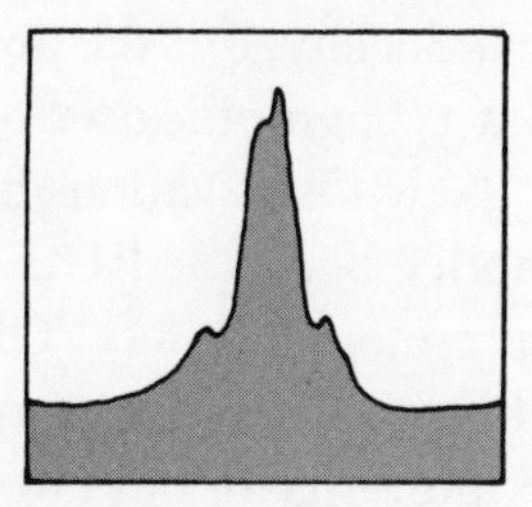

SPECTRUM 3

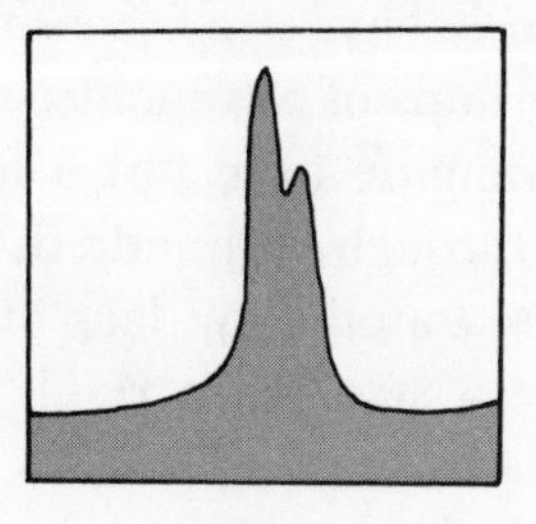

SPECTRUM 4

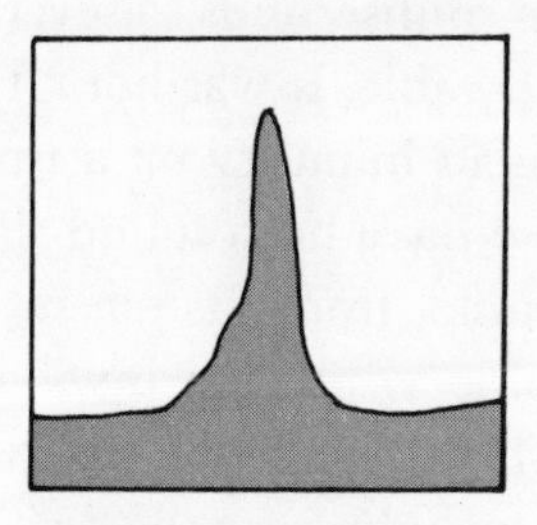

piece of evidence was presented, the degree of conflict steadily increased. What could the jury of international astronomers make of all this? They must have felt like Alice in Wonderland, trying to make some sense of an apparent observational nonsense. One anonymous astronomer decided to make known his frustration at the growing list of bizarre properties for SS433 and the apparently conflicting evidence. I had been invited in late 1979 to talk about our new observations at the Royal Astronomical Society, but the announcement of the meeting included a typographical error. The title of my talk was given as "New Observations of SS443," instead of SS433. On the notice board at RGO, someone had scrawled beneath the announcement: "Oh, God, not another one!!"

If the brightness and spectroscopic variations of SS433 in the period range of days to months was difficult to reconcile, there was one range of times over which SS433 appeared to behave itself. Sensitive searches were made by several groups of astronomers looking for variations with periods ranging from just a few tens of milliseconds extending through to hundreds of seconds. *No* such variations were found. This lack of short time-scale variations was a very significant result. If the compact object in SS433 was a neutron star, its rotational period (presumably in the range of the known rotational period of pulsars, from milliseconds to several seconds) might just have been observable. It was not. "Flickering" (that is, random variations in intensity on a time scale of tens of seconds) might also have been found if the bulk of the light from SS433 came from its accretion disk. Certainly other known binary systems involving a compact object surrounded by an accretion disk were known to display flickering of the light from the disk. SS433 did not. For once, it seemed, SS433 was content not to try to outdo the pulsars and conventional binary systems.

Back in July 1978, soon after we had realized what an interesting object the strange emission-line star we had found associated with A1909+04/CC493 was, Murdin had contacted colleagues he knew could make observations in other important wavelength regions. There was no point in alerting radio astronomers, other than to pass on the news to those we met by chance. We knew that Caswell and the Cambridge radio astronomers were pursuing that route. For the X-ray region, I had undertaken to pass on the new result to Fred Seward during my trip to the United States in early September 1978. Murdin contacted his friend Ian Glass at the South African Astronomical Observatory (with whom he had worked on studies of Circinus X-1), asking him to take infrared observations of the new star. Glass's observations of August 1978 provided the first infrared data on SS433. He showed that not only was the infrared emission highly variable on time scales of days to months (no surprise in that), but also that it was brighter at longer infrared wavelengths than might have been expected by extrapolating the optical continuum and shorter-wavelength infrared continuum (even after allowing for the effect of reddening). The infrared excess and variability were confirmed by other observers during 1979, including Dave Allen, who had completed some of the early spectroscopic observations at the AAT. (Allen also found moving spectral features of hydrogen in the infrared, although the 13.1-day period was not confirmed in this wavelength region.) Murdin then contacted an RGO colleague working at that time at the ground station of an ultraviolet space observatory, the International Ultraviolet Explorer. Not surprisingly, in view of the star being heavily reddened, it could not be seen in the ultraviolet.

So the trial of SS433 progressed through 1979 and 1980, into 1981. The evidence being produced by the prosecution increased steadily: there were five IAU telegram contributions referring to SS433 in 1978, thirty-two in 1979, and eight in 1980; there were two papers published in 1978 (as listed in the compilation of recognized astronomical papers, *Astronomy and Astrophysics Abstracts*), twenty-eight in 1979, seventy-three in 1980, one hundred twenty-two in 1981, and fifty-nine in 1982. If the optical evidence appeared often to be contradictory, new evidence was being produced by the radio astronomers that offered some hope that the international astronomical jury might, even yet, be able to reach a majority verdict.

There is a powerful technique used by radio astronomers to determine the distance to objects in the Galaxy. Neutral hydrogen, permeating the regions between the stars, emits radio waves of a characteristic wavelength of twenty-one centimeters. If a cloud of neutral hydrogen is moving away from us, the twenty-one-centimeter emission will be red-shifted (Doppler-shifted to a longer wavelength); if it is moving toward us, it will be blue-shifted (shifted to a shorter wavelength). Relative motion of neutral hydrogen clouds and the solar system does occur, because of the rotation of the Galaxy. The Milky Way rotates sedately in space, like a gigantic pinwheel. The time for a single rotation depends on the distance from the center of the Galaxy; at the distance of the solar system this period is about 200 million years. If the Doppler shift of a neutral hydrogen cloud is measured, it can be fitted to a model of galactic rotation to determine the distance to the cloud. Suppose there is a source of continuum radio emission (for example, a radio star such as Circinus X-1 or

SS433, or perhaps a supernova remnant) lying behind a neutral hydrogen cloud. The twenty-one-centimeter line will be seen in absorption, and its Doppler shift will provide the distance to the intervening cloud (see Figure 7.7). Of course, this is merely a *minimum* distance to the background source, but even such a minimum distance can be extremely valuable.

American Miller Goss had long had an interest in the mystery of the pointlike radio sources within supernova remnants. Working with Canadian Peter Sheather, he had used the Parkes and Molonglo radio telescopes, in the years prior to my working with Mills in Sydney, to com-

FIGURE 7.7.

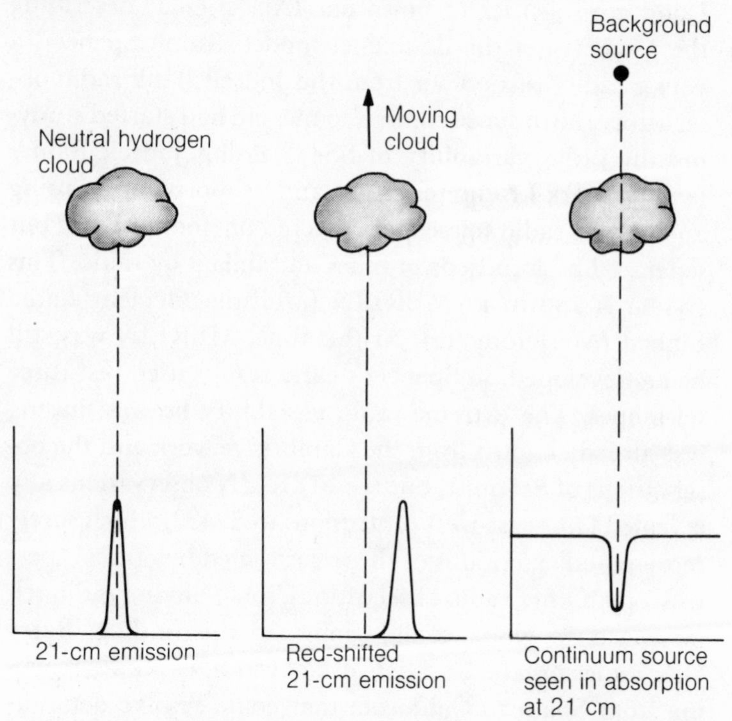

plete some classic work on galactic radio sources, including many supernova remnants. He was now working in the Netherlands and, again in collaboration with Sheather, he used the radio telescope array at Westerbork to estimate the distance to SS433 by the neutral-hydrogen-absorption technique. A minimum distance of about 10,000 light-years was obtained. This was an important result, since estimates of the distance to the supernova remnant W50 were also of this order. This similarity gave further credence to the belief that SS433 and W50 were associated.

At the meeting of the Royal Astronomical Society of May 11, 1979—at which Peter Martin, Paul Murdin, and I had got together to finish our IAU circular describing the geometry of the double-jet model, Ralph Spencer, a young radio astronomer from the Jodrell Bank radio observatory, introduced himself to me. He had started studying the radio variability of SS433, using Jodrell Bank's famous Mark I radio telescope, and its morphology, using an array of radio telescopes centered on Jodrell Bank but separated by hundreds of miles and linked by radio. This system is known as MERLIN (*M*ultiple *E*lement *R*adio *L*inked *IN*terferometer). At this time, MERLIN was still being developed, so Spencer's early results used just three telescopes. The extreme radio variability he was finding was already known from the Cambridge work and the observations of Seaquist, but the MERLIN observations also revealed faint east-west protrusions to SS433, which surely represented extensions of the jets revealed by optical spectroscopy. Other radio observations, some linking radio telescopes on a global scale, confirmed this finding. Barry Geldzahler organized a network of radio telescopes reaching from Spain to California that could resolve detail as fine as a few thousandths of a second of arc, and Australian Richard Schilizzi (whom I had known from my time in Sydney, when he was a Ph.D. candidate working under Mills, but who was now working at Westerbork) used a network of European telescopes. The radio evidence from these observations of the jets was conclusive; they were aligned east-west and pointing in the direction of the ears in W50. The geometrical uncertainty in the alignment of the jets, mentioned earlier, was now resolved.

During 1980, Seaquist and other investigators started using a newly completed giant array of radio telescopes in New Mexico, called the Very Large Array (VLA), to study the radio jets of SS433. Although the fraction-of-arc-second resolution was insufficient to follow the changing orientation of the jets in fine detail, the new data indicated with no doubt that the radio features changed with the 164-day precession period of the jets identified optically. Indeed, the varying radio structure was compatible with having been produced by twin precessing gas streams moving away from the star. Since the "length" of the radio extensions in light-years was many times the 164-day precession period, the extended jets would sweep out helical patterns, since the direction of ejection changes even as ejected material travels outward. SS433 produced two cosmic corkscrews (see Figure 7.8).

The varying structure was not merely the result of precession. Sudden "flares" occurred occasionally, seen as an outward expansion of bright features as the flare evolved

FIGURE 7.8.

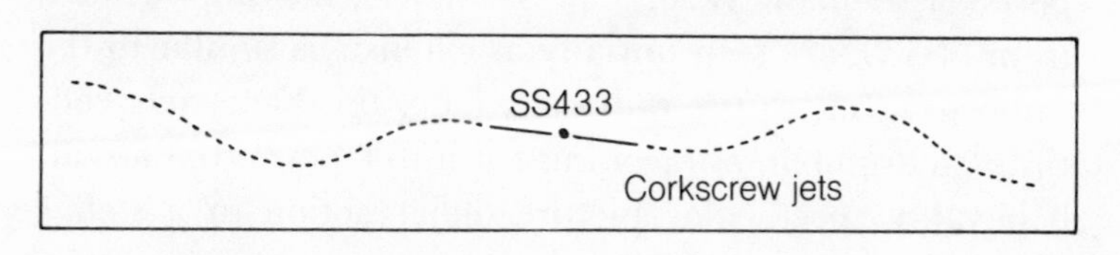

outward in the oppositely directed jets. By measuring the rate of expansion of these flare features, and assuming that the flare gas streaming out into the jets was traveling at the same speed as the material producing the optical "moving" features (that is, at a quarter the speed of light), the radio astronomers determined that SS433 must be at a distance of about 15,000 light-years. This is half again as far as the distance inferred from the neutral-hydrogen-absorption observations, but in view of the considerable uncertainties and assumptions made in each technique, the discrepancy does not raise too many worries (although the larger distance would imply gross obesity for W50).

If the new radio data on the jets were producing startling results, the most spectacular picture of them was to be produced by the X-ray astronomers. The April 1979 Einstein observations had been made with the High-Resolution-Imaging detector (HRI), but there was another detector system, the Imaging Proportional Counter (IPC), that could detect features too faint to be seen with the HRI, although with somewhat poorer resolution. IPC observations of SS433 were made for Seaquist, Seward, and the Leicester X-ray astronomers in October 1979. The pictures they presented for the jets of SS433 were truly spectacular (see Figure 7.9), and reminiscent of the jets and lobes in radio galaxies. The X-ray jets of SS433 stretched across the supernova remnant W50, and were exactly aligned with the ears, directly confirming the beam-bag association of the jets and protrusions of the supernova remnant W50. The X-ray jets, moving outward from SS433, are seen initially as extensions similar to the radio jets, but as the radio jets fade, the X-ray jets continue to brighten, burgeoning out into lobes. What an unbelievably spectacular picture of jet action in a stellar

FIGURE 7.9.

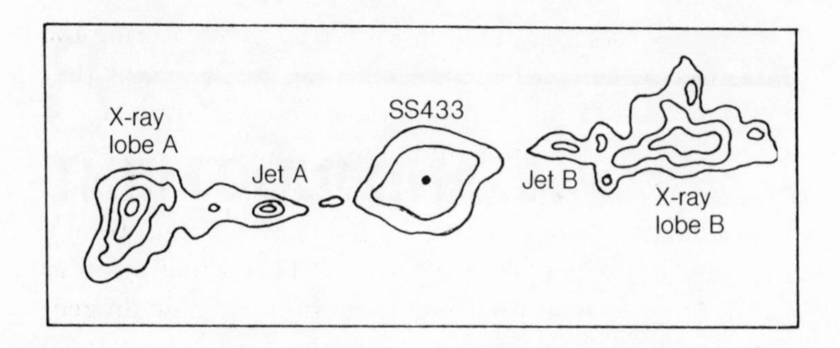

system, a totally unknown and unexpected celestial phenomenon before the discovery of SS433!

The "trial" of SS433 produced these exhibits:

A. X-ray jets and lobes
B. Radio "corkscrew" jets and flares
C. 13.1-day orbital period; 164-day jet precession period; relations between the two
D. "Bullets" in the jets
E. Optical, radio, and X-ray variability over intervals of hours and longer, but not over very short time scales
F. "Beam-bag" link between the "jets" of SS433 and the "ears" of the supernova remnant W50

SS433 stands accused of adopting the guise of a radio galaxy, and failing to reveal its true identity. Ladies and gentlemen of the jury, I ask you to retire to consider your verdict.

8
... AND JUDGMENT

"No! No! Sentence first—verdict afterwards."
—LEWIS CARROLL, *Alice's Adventures in Wonderland*

Against the barrage of new evidence being produced by astronomers around the world, the double-jet model for SS433 stood unflinching. By 1981, the big guns firing in support of massive-black-hole models had fallen silent. Indeed, the detailed model of Abell and Margon (and, in barely discernible form, of Martin and Murdin) describing the geometry of the jets was now accepted almost without question. Precessing jets—yes. A binary system—undoubtedly. An orbital period of 13.1 days—definitely. A "beam-bag" link between the jets and the "ears" of W50—irrefutably. But what types of stars make up the binary system? Why do the jets precess? What is the source of the material in the jets? How is it accelerated to a quarter the speed of light? Why is the material emitted in discrete bullets? Why are the jets observed as most extended in X-rays? What is the relation of SS433 to the radio galaxies? Questions, questions, and more questions—questions about answers, and questions about questions. The double-jet model might be able to describe *what* was going on, but not the whys and wherefores.

If the next piece of the puzzle could be found in the myriad pieces of evidence now accumulated, there was hope that the remaining pieces could be identified and slotted together. But what *was* the critical next piece? Where to begin? Paul Murdin decided that identification of the types of stars making up the binary system was important above all else, and we worked together on this task during the final months of 1979 and early 1980. Our data were principally those we had accumulated from our own AAT observations, but also included results passed on to us by astronomers at RGO and farther afield who had generously agreed to allow us to use their data ahead of publication.

If the stars at the heart of SS433 were to be identified, the first thing we could safely ignore were the moving features; they certainly originated in the jets. What was left? First, there was the strong red continuum—reddened presumably because of interstellar dust, rather than intrinsically red; second, there were the highly variable stationary emission lines, characterized by a narrow bright central peak and fainter extensions.

What could the source of the continuum radiation be? It could be light from one or the other of the two stars making up the binary system (or a contribution from both). Alternatively, it might be emitted by the accretion disk that could be assumed, by analogy with other galactic X-ray sources, to form part of the SS433 system (Figure 8.1). Perhaps the continuum light came from both a star (or stars) *and* the accretion disk. To try to determine this, we carefully calculated how the underlying brightness of SS433 varied with color through the visible and infrared (Figure 8.2). Making some assumptions about how the

FIGURE 8.1.

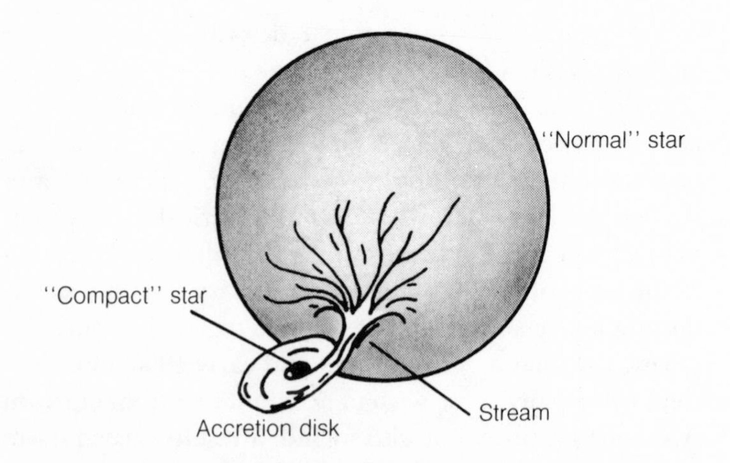

star could be reddened by intervening dust, we could then attempt to decide whether the variation of brightness with color was more characteristic of what one might expect from a star or from an accretion disk. In the visible portion of the spectrum there was nothing to choose between these options (see Figure 8.2); but the available infrared observations coupled with the visible data definitely favored a star, a *very* hot star.

Stars come in a wide range of sizes. Most are of comparable mass to our sun, or up to a few times greater. A small number are much more massive, up to tens or even hundreds of times the mass of the sun. Although there are some spectacular variations from the norm, the tendency is for more massive stars to be hotter, brighter, and shorter-lived. Interpreting the source of the continuum light as an extremely hot star, we were able to infer a likely mass—about 100 times that of the sun. Such a massive star would be expected to display other features, which would confirm that it was indeed as large as this.

FIGURE 8.2.

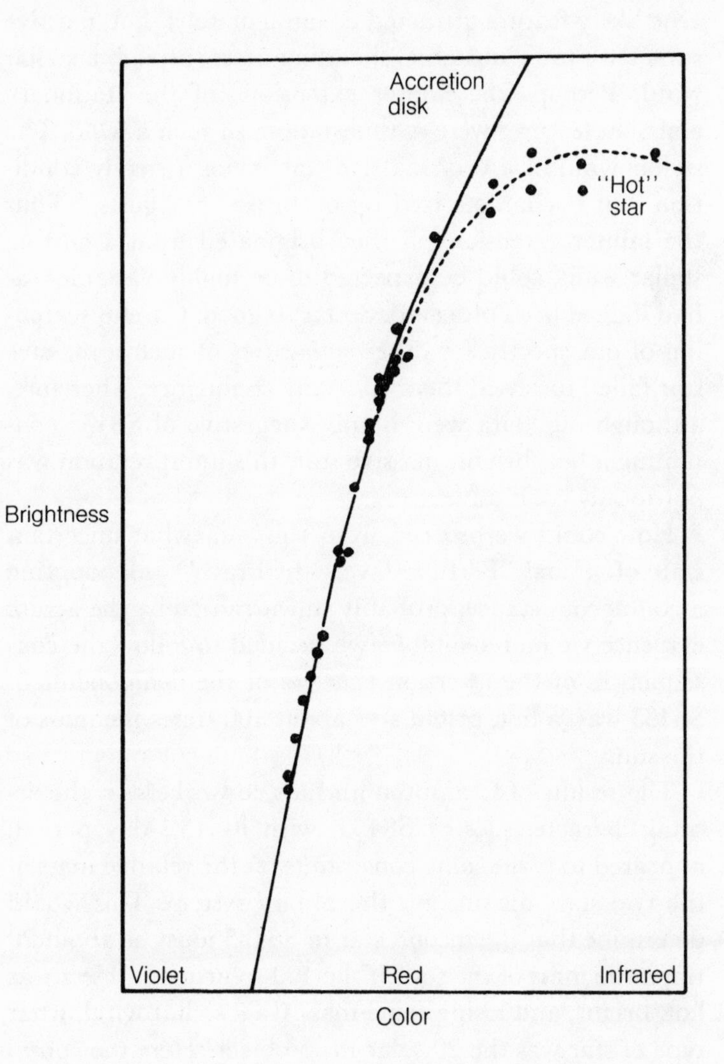
Accretion disk
"Hot" star
Brightness
Violet
Red
Infrared
Color

One likely feature attracted us immediately: hot, massive stars tend to be unstable, shedding mass through a stellar wind. Perhaps the fainter extensions of the stationary emission features were manifestations of such a wind. The stellar wind of a very massive star is not a steady condition, but is characterized by outbursts, or "gusts." Thus the fainter extensions, if they originated from a gusting stellar wind, could be expected to be highly variable—as had indeed been observed. So far so good. Careful searching of our spectra for other signatures of such a massive star failed to reveal them with any confidence. Therefore, although our data were highly suggestive of SS433 containing a hot, bright, massive star, this interpretation was not totally conclusive.

How could we proceed from this somewhat uncertain state of affairs? "Fortune favors the brave"—so, adopting a courageous stance, probably unwarranted by the actual evidence we had available, we decided to follow the consequences of the assertion that *one* of the components of SS433 was a hot, bright star about 100 times the mass of the sun.

The results of Crampton and his co-workers on the orbital characteristics of SS433, with its 13.1-day period, appeared to place some constraints on the relative mass of the two stars making up the binary system. This would determine that the second star in SS433 must be about 20 times the mass of the sun. If the 100-solar-mass object was hot, bright, and losing some mass via a stellar wind, what type of star was the 20-solar-mass object? Here the consequences of our initial interpretation started to get serious. The normal X-ray binary stars contain a normal star and a compact object—a neutron star. But a neutron star cannot be more massive than three to four times the mass of the sun. More massive compact objects undergo total gravitational collapse to become black holes, the ultimate state of compaction of matter.

If we were correct in our assertion that SS433 contained a hot, massive star responsible for most of its light (the "primary" star), a consequence was that the compact companion in the binary system (the "secondary" star) must be a black hole with a mass about 20 times that of the sun. The ingredients of our SS433 mixture (see Figure 8.3) were:

A. A hot, massive star (100 times the mass of the sun) that produces the bulk of the continuum light from SS433
B. A black hole (20 times the mass of the sun) that orbits A
C. A stellar wind emitted by A, seen as the broad extensions to the stationary emission features
D. An accretion disk, through which A loses mass to B, and which possibly produces the narrow central component of the stationary emission features (which might also be produced in the atmosphere of A)
E. Two finely collimated jets of ejected material that produce the bizarre moving features.

In collaboration with Martin, Murdin and I published details of this model in early 1980. We were well aware at the time of various inadequacies and remaining uncertainties in our "massive-binary" model for SS433, but, with a variety of other models being announced, we felt it important at least to put forward our suggestions for consideration.

We were not the only proponents of the massive-binary idea. Ed van den Heuvel of the University of Utrecht and his colleagues independently arrived at a system including a massive star, although it differed in some detail from our system. Their primary star was, like ours, massive (per-

FIGURE 8.3.

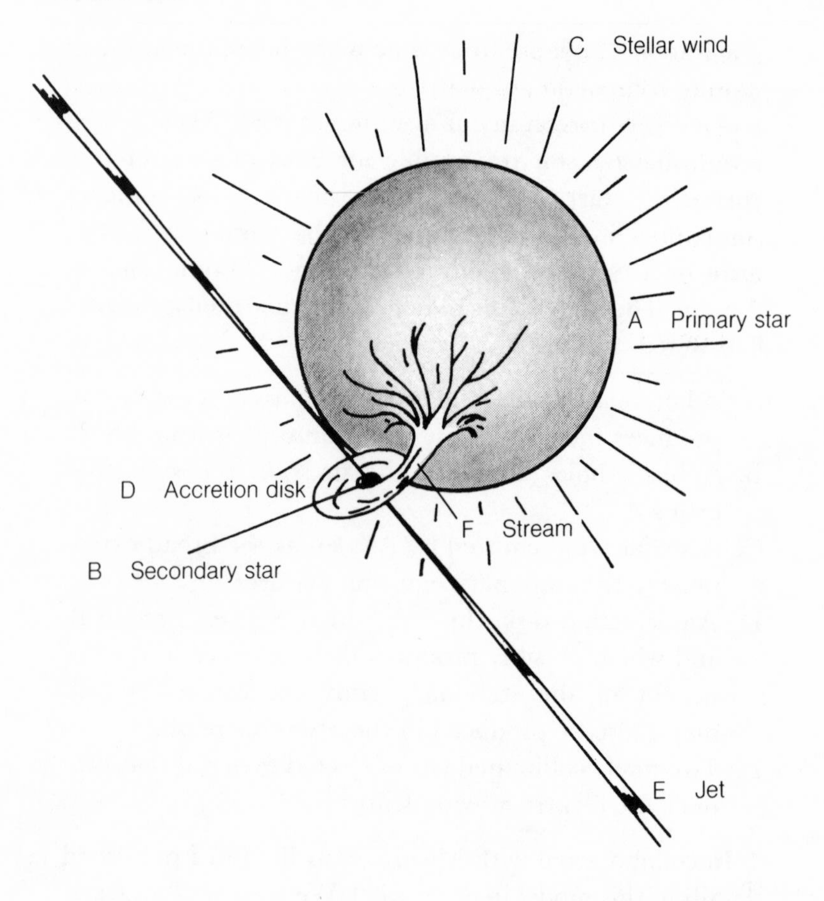

haps 20 solar masses) and shedding material in a wind (producing the broad component of the stationary lines). They suggested, too, that the primary might even be a Wolf-Rayet star (an unexpected theme at this stage, since Murdin and I initially rejected a Wolf-Rayet description for the bastard star at first sighting because the mystery bands did not fit). But they argued that only about half the continuum light came from the primary star, the remainder coming from a bright accretion disk surrounding the secondary. The results of Cherepashchuk, and others, suggesting a "double eclipse" (that is, two objects of about equal brightness eclipsing each other) led them to this conclusion (see Figure 8.4). In addition, they noted that the maximum Doppler deviation of the narrow component of the stationary emission features coincided with the eclipses. This required that these spectral features *must* be

FIGURE 8.4. DOUBLE ECLIPSE

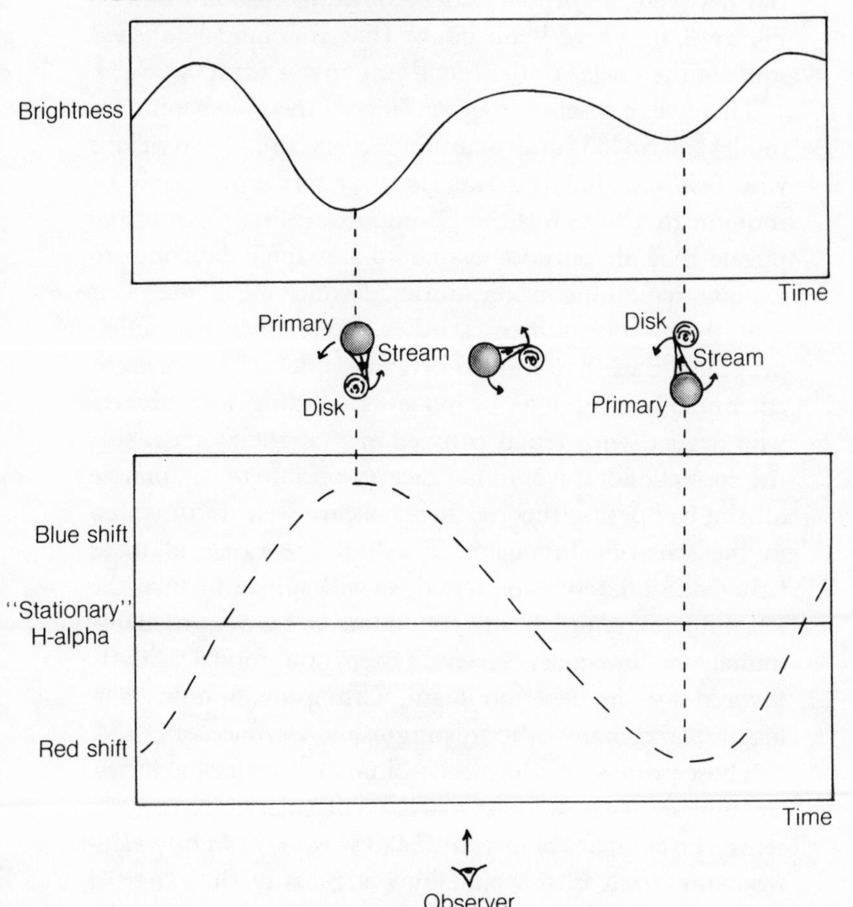

produced in material transferring from the primary star to the disk, and not in the atmosphere of the primary star, as we had suggested. The van den Heuvel system was essentially identical to ours for components A (although less massive), C, and E, but their component B might be just a neutron star, component D might be partly responsible for the total light, and the narrow component of the stationary feature had to be produced in the stream of material between the primary star and the accretion disk (see Figure 8.3). There is no doubt that this model satisfied some of the uncertainties remaining in our ideas of SS433.

There were several other variants of the massive-binary model for SS433, and many observers and theoreticians who believed that this was the way forward. Lest it be thought that here was the all-important first piece of the puzzle that all astronomers could slot their data into to explain remaining uncertainties, it must be made clear that there were numerous other, quite distinct, models proposed. Each had its own brigade of dedicated theoretical and observational proponents, leading astronomers who argued with equal conviction that their model was the correct one. It would not be appropriate to summarize all the competing theories here; all are well documented in the scientific literature. To show the range of ideas being passionately expounded, it will suffice to take the absolute extreme from the massive-binary model—namely, a "low-mass-binary" system, the model initially favored by the Margon team, Crampton and his colleagues, and many other distinguished astronomers.

Those proposing a low-mass-binary system argued that, by analogy with the vast majority of galactic X-ray systems, the compact object in SS433 was likely to be a neutron star—that is, it would have a mass in the range of about 1.5 to 3 solar masses. A direct interpretation of the initial 13.1-day variability data of Crampton and others, as reflecting a true orbital motion, then required that the other star in the binary system must also have a mass about double that of the sun. Such a star would not be particularly bright, and could be expected to contribute little to the intense continuum radiation observed. Nor would it display an intense wind, able to describe the broad stationary emission features.

In the low-mass-binary model for SS433, the accretion disk believed to be surrounding the neutron star played a paramount role, explaining almost all the spectral features other than the moving emission lines, which, not surprisingly, were still ascribed to the jets. The disk provided almost the entire light from SS433, with the complex and highly variable stationary emission features also originating in the disk and indicating considerable structure and turbulence within it. The narrow central component of the stationary features might, again, originate in material from the normal star streaming into the accretion disk, or possibly from a "hot spot" within the disk (see Figure 8.5).

If all the continuum light was coming from the accre-

FIGURE 8.5. LOW-MASS BINARY MODEL

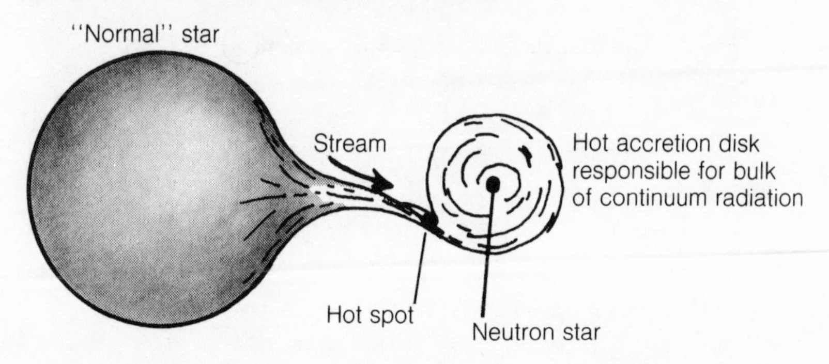

tion disk, how could the variability of the continuum light (the 13.1-day double-eclipse light curve and the 164-day variability) be explained? Partial eclipsing of the accretion disk by the normal star could still play a role, but the main cause of light variation was argued to be the changing "aspect" of an inclined disk (see Figure 8.6). As the disk orbited about the normal star, it would be seen from different directions, and because it is a highly asymmetric

FIGURE 8.6. EFFECT OF INCLINED DISK

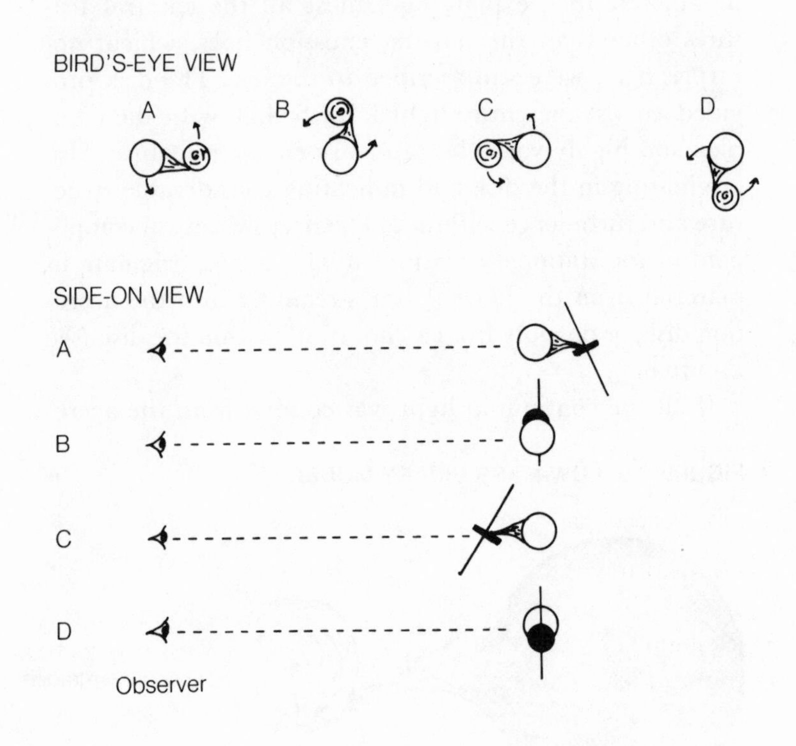

structure, it might be expected that light from it would *not* be emitted uniformly in all directions. Thus, in viewing the disk in changing aspect, it would be expected that it would vary in intensity with the underlying orbital period of the system—that is, 13.1 days. The "disk jockeys" had another strong card to play. Almost everyone agreed that the jets, the source of the moving features, were likely to be pointing directly perpendicular to the plane of the accretion disk. There were both observational and theoretical arguments being presented to support this idea. (Imagine a knitting needle stuck through a hole drilled in the center of a quarter, and you have the picture.) If this was the case, the 164-day precession of the jets advocated to explain the backward and forward drifting of the moving emission features would also be expected to be reflected in a 164-day precessing of the plane of the disk. Thus a 164-day aspect variation would be superimposed on the orbital aspect variation of the disk. Hence the disk might be seen at maximum projection at one time (when it might be expected to be at its brightest), but edge on 41 days later (when it would be expected to be less bright), and so on (see Figure 8.7). This type of 164-day variation had indeed been seen by Margon and his colleagues, as well as by others, in both the intensity of the continuum radiation and the mean intensity of the stationary emission features.

SS433 consistently revealed a knack for arousing professional vehemence within the international astronomical community. The supporters of low-mass-binary models felt that disk radiation plus jets could explain almost all the properties of the spectral variability of SS433. Their opponents argued that the infrared data in particular did not fit a disk (see Figure 8.2). Also there was no evidence that the "color" of SS433 (that is, the "shape" of the vary-

FIGURE 8.7.

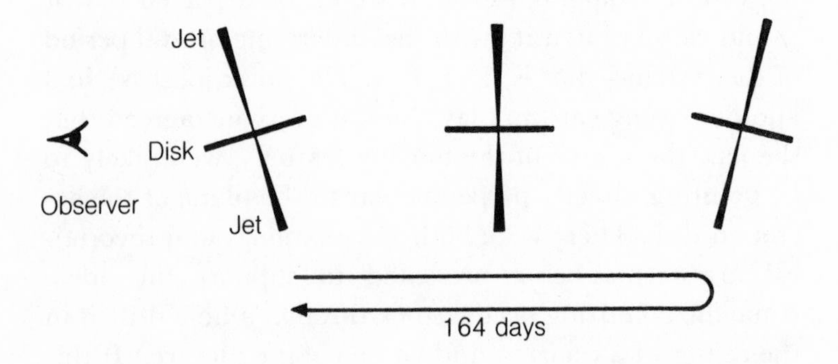

ing continuum radiation with wavelength) changed as its intensity changed (over 13.1 days and 164 days), which it must surely do if the varying aspect of the disk was the origin of intensity variability. There was no evidence of "flickering" expected for a disk. Finally, if the optical continuum of SS433 originated entirely, or even mainly, in the disk, this would outshine the X-ray power (certainly almost entirely from the disk) by more than 1,000 times. Yet all other known galactic X-ray binary sources displayed exactly the opposite characteristic. How *could* the light from SS433 possibly be almost entirely from a disk? There was no way I could ever be convinced of that. Just as persuasively, the low-mass advocates argued against a massive-binary system. The continuum spectra in fine detail just did not match those of any known type of massive star (although they did in broad detail). And where was the natural explanation of the 13.1-day and the 164-day intensity variability (and relationship to other variabilities) that the low-mass model provided?

Between these two extreme stances there were the varying shades of opinion of the converts to alternative models. Eventually there would be some merging of the extremes. Crampton produced refined orbital data that did *not* constrain the two stars in the binary system to about equal mass. This was confirmed by Margon and his colleagues, who consequently conceded that a more massive normal star (of about 15 solar masses) might be present (allowing a wind to produce the broad component of the stationary features), while retaining a neutron star as the accreting object. They also found that their data confirmed that the 13.1-day continuum variation was due, at least in part, to the eclipse phenomenon. For our part, Murdin and I conceded that an accretion disk probably did contribute significantly to the total light (but to nowhere like the extent demanded by some others).

It had not been possible to find a single piece of the SS433 puzzle to which all others could be uniquely mated. But even identifying several not-too-dissimilar pieces that might lead to a final solved puzzle represented quite amazing progress. Although today there is by no means universal agreement on the make-up of SS433, few astronomers would now object to something like the following (referring again to the components of Figure 8.3):

A. A hot, 10-to-20-solar-mass star, contributing to the continuum radiation
B. A neutron star, 1.5 to 3 solar masses
C. A stellar wind from the hot star, producing the broad component of the stationary emission features
D. An accretion disk, contributing to the continuum radiation in about equal measure to the hot star—its varying aspect, linked to the 164-day precession period of the jets, explaining the 164-day variation in total

light, and its partial eclipse describing the variation of light intensity in the 13.1-day orbital period

E. Precessing jets (precession period, 164 days) producing the moving features

F. Matter streaming into the disk seen as the narrow component of the stationary hydrogen lines (although some narrow components behaving rather differently may come from a hot spot on the accretion disk).

As so often appears to have happened in the history of scientific discovery, competing ideas seem to have merged on common ground. A treaty of final settlement has still to be signed, but at least an unofficial ceasefire is being observed.

The suggestion that SS433 might after all contain a massive star had the following attraction: such a massive star would be relatively short-lived (a lifetime of a few million years, compared with the lifetime of billions of years of a solar type of star). The enormous expenditure of energy and mass in SS433 also argued for a short life, but a sweet one. This could explain why no other object quite like SS433 has been discovered.

What about the origin of the jets? There is little doubt in anyone's mind about where the jet material comes from originally. This has to be material from the primary star feeding the accretion disk. But how is the material ejected from the disk into the jets? The energy required to accelerate the material in the jets to a quarter the speed of light was estimated to be fantastic—at least a million times that radiated at all wavelengths from the sun each second. Accretion could provide this energy. But how is it transferred to the bullets in the jets?

An early hypothesis, put forward by Jonathan Katz, one of Margon's colleagues, for the mechanism by which matter in the jets was accelerated to the enormous velocities observed was referred to as "super critical accretion." As matter spirals down into the accretion disk under the action of gravity, locally generated radiation (principally X-rays) becomes so intense that "radiation pressure" overcomes gravity and "blows" matter away. In simple terms, the accretion disk, being force-fed by matter streaming from the primary star, cannot digest it quickly enough, and consequently regurgitates some of it. A "burping accretion disk" as the origin for the jets remains a viable explanation for many astronomers, but there are some difficulties with the argument. By itself, it does not explain the remarkable collimation of the jets; perhaps more important, it does not explain why the material in the jets is observed to have nearly constant velocity (about a quarter that of light). A subtle variation of radiation pressure is one idea, put forward by Mordehai Milgrom. This is known as the "line-locked radiation pressure mechanism." It is an impossible concept to explain simply, depending as it does on many of the detailed properties of the emission and absorption of radiation by atoms. In broad outline, it depends on continuum radiation being produced within the accretion disk close to the compact object. Beyond a certain wavelength, this radiation is absorbed by local atoms, which then relay radiation pressure in a restricted wavelength range that will accelerate matter only up to a certain well-defined velocity. Milgrom pointed out not only that the line-locked radiation pressure mechanism was the only way of achieving a constant uniform velocity, but also that the predicted velocity was calculated to be 0.28 times that of light (in remarkable agreement with the observed value of 0.26). Radiation pressure, in some guise, seems almost certainly to be the source of acceleration in the beams. Final details remain to be resolved between the theoreticians and the observers.

How is the material regurgitated by SS433 confined to highly collimated jets? Perhaps the explanation is very simple. If the accretion disk is very thin, the radiation pressure will be directed out of the plane of the disk (see Figure 8.8), so that the material blown away by radiation pressure will be sent in opposite directions away from the disk. The hiccups of the disk (resulting from supercritical accretion) would then be reflected as simultaneous increases in radiation pressure on both sides—that is, similar bullets of matter would be ejected from each side simultaneously (SS433 firing from both hips). This idea, although simple, was difficult to maintain in the face of evidence suggesting that the disk may have substantial thickness. An alternative suggestion was that matter ejected in the

FIGURE 8.8.

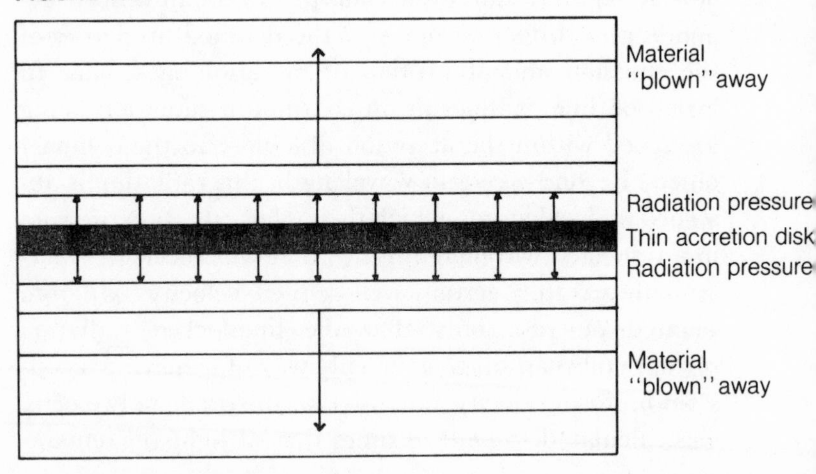

FIGURE 8.9.

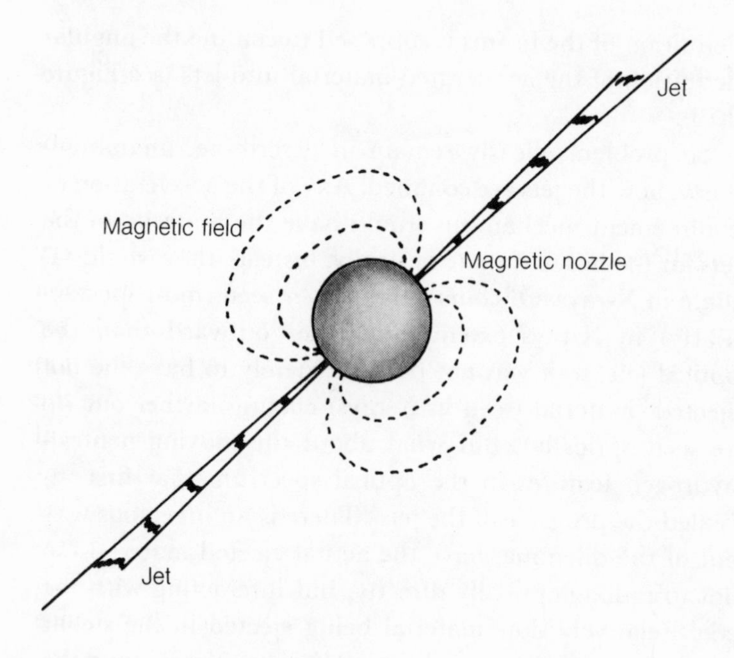

jets is confined by the natural nozzle formed by the magnetic field of the neutron star at the center of the disk (Figure 8.9)—co-alignment of the rotational and magnetic-field axes of the neutron star was proposed. This certainly seemed a possibility, but why the jets should remain so tightly collimated even beyond the region where the neutron star's magnetic field began to diverge was far from obvious. A final explanation, favored by some, but fraught with difficulties, uses collimated radiation to generate collimated jets. We know that pulsars produce tightly collimated beams of radiation that sweep around the sky. Suppose that, as the pulsar rotates, its beam intersects the disk along a line in which matter is then accelerated by the radiation pressure of the beam. The angular definition of the beams is supposed to confine the angular definition of the accelerated material into jets (see Figure 8.10).

So problems clearly remain in describing, unambiguously, how the jets are confined. Any of the acceleration or confinement mechanisms would have the material in the jets far too hot to radiate optically; instead, they would radiate in X-rays. Of course, the jets *are* seen (most spectacularly) in X-rays extending farther outward than the optical jets, so it was not possible merely to have the hot ejected material (seen in X-rays) cooling farther out (to be seen optically). But what about the moving neutral-hydrogen features in the optical spectrum that first revealed the presence of the jets? There is an ingenious way out of the dilemma; have the actual ejected material too hot to radiate optically directly, but interacting with the cool, relatively slow material being ejected in the stellar wind of the primary star. Friction between the jets and the wind produces the optical radiation characteristic of the jets. An attraction of this idea is that a sudden gust of

FIGURE 8.10.

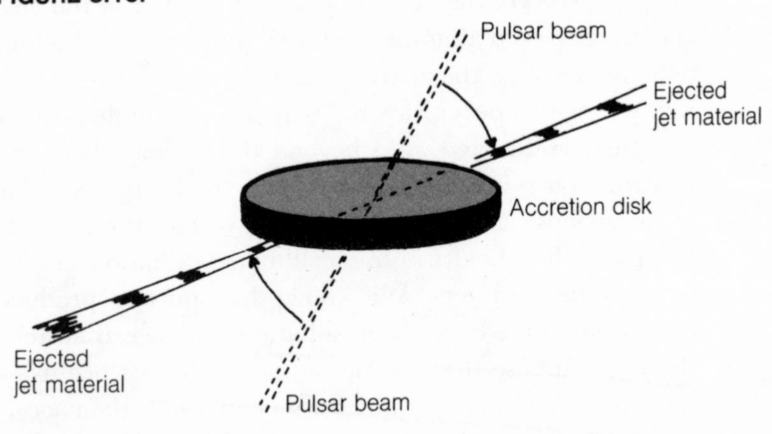

wind would be expected to be seen in both jets—explaining the usual mirror-image symmetry of the moving features. Since the stellar wind is highly variable, the moving features would similarly be highly variable in intensity. Also, with the strength of the stellar wind falling off rapidly with distance from the hot star, the optical jets could be limited in extent while allowing the hot ejected material (seen as the X-ray jets) to extend to vast distances.

Do we yet understand the origin of the 164-day "clock" in SS433? Although early models were based on an inherent stability to this 164-day period, Bruce Margon and his colleagues found that it was not in fact constant, but showed complex variations (with increases and decreases) over extended intervals. (The first detection of this affect, by astronomers at Ohio State University, was incorrectly reported as a rapid "running-down" of the 164-day clock, with the claim that SS433 would "die" within a very few decades.) There was early agreement that the origin of the 164-day clock was almost certainly precession of the jets—"wobbling" of the spin axis of the compact star, like the effect of a spinning top running down (see Figure 8.11). A variety of causes was proposed for the origin of this precession. Van den Heuvel and Katz independently argued that a "tidal interaction" between the primary and secondary stars caused it; Mitchell Begelman thought it might be due to a general relativistic effect ("warping" of space in the vicinity of the compact object by a perilously close companion); others suggested the presence of a third star in SS433 that influences the direction of the jets (by no means an outrageous suggestion—many triple-star systems are known).

Margon and his colleagues also noted that in a binary system where the spin axis of the secondary star was not

FIGURE 8.11.

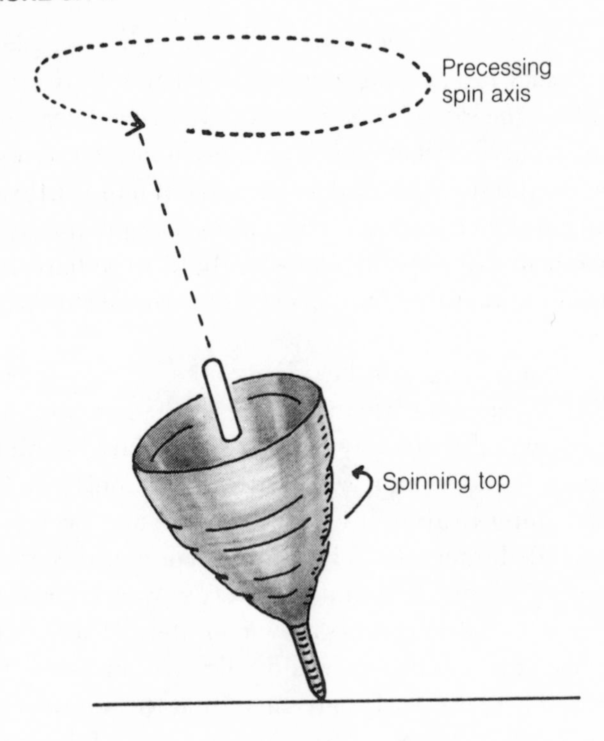

pointing exactly normal to the orbital plane of the stars, and where the orbital period was a significant fraction of the precession period (as it was in SS433), a short-period "nodding" of the accretion disk would occur. For SS433 this was calculated to be a small, but nevertheless significant, effect on a time scale of about 6.3 days, and was indeed found by Margon in his data.

At the present time, no model for the origin of the jets in SS433, their acceleration, collimation, or precession, stands out as compelling above all others. Nevertheless, theoretical investigation and detailed observation continue apace in an attempt to find the definitive description. In the meantime, although the "jury" of international astronomers may have failed to reveal the true identity of SS433 with certainty, it has produced a carefully compiled composite description (Figure 8.12). But what a bizarre image it is, like nothing else previously seen in the heavens! Or is it unique? Could it perhaps be an image in miniature of the giant active galaxies at vast distances?

FIGURE 8.12. COMPOSITE PICTURE OF SS433

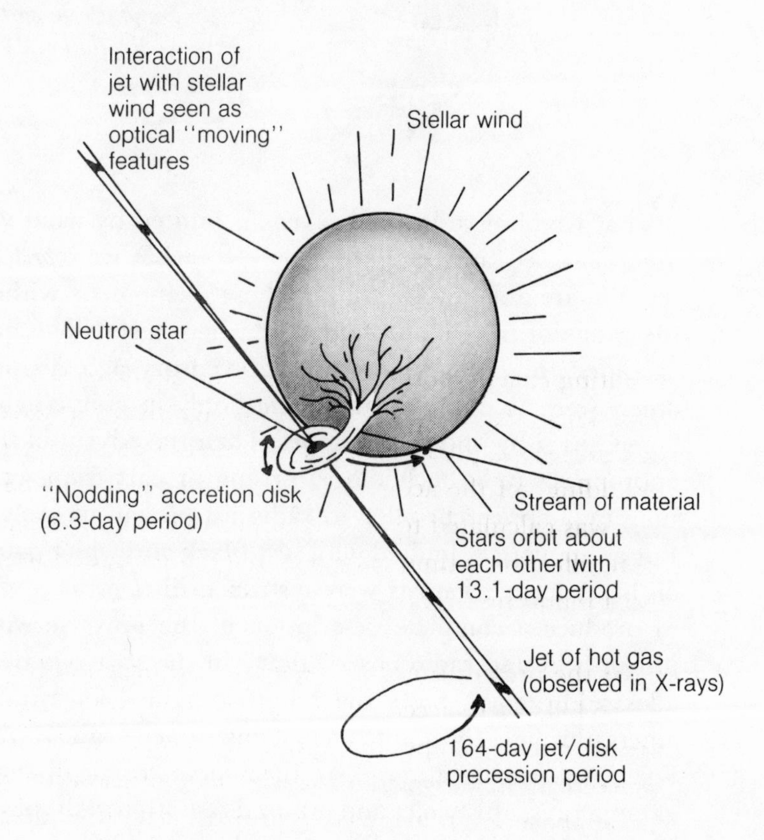

9

THE NEW UNIVERSE

And I saw a new heaven
and a new earth.
—*Revelation* 21:1

What we observe in the heavens is limited by what we are *able* to see, and, to some extent, by what we *expect* to see. We are able to observe just those phenomena within the range of the human senses, or where technology has extended those senses. A mere half-century ago, astronomers were able to view the cosmos only in visible light, albeit aided by optical telescopes. Then the advent of the appropriate radio technology (arising in part from wartime radar research) allowed radio astronomy to evolve. But as an artist is limited with just black and white paint on his palette, scientists were restricted in their attempts to produce a complete description of the universe with just optical and radio observations. In the past two decades, additional "colors" have been provided for astronomers through the launching of instruments above the Earth's obscuring atmosphere to observe cosmic X-rays, gamma rays, ultraviolet and infrared radiations. Although the cosmic canvas is slowly taking shape, there are many forms of information from the heavens still unavailable to us. Every new method of observation has added new objects and phenomena to the known contents of the universe; it is certain that as new technologies and new methods of observation are developed, as new "pigments" are added to the astronomers' "palette," a rich variety of unexpected phenomena will be unveiled.

Many discoveries in astronomy were achieved by unforeseen means; the first detection of cosmic radio waves by Karl Jansky is a classic example. To some extent our preconception of what we can expect to see has held back the discovery process. Often a totally unexpected discovery has had to be made before a new technology is applied to astronomy. For two decades of radio astronomy, receiving equipment was matched to the expectation that any inherent variability in cosmic radio sources would be on comparatively long time scales; no one had foreseen the likelihood of finding pulsing radio sources with periods of a mere fraction of a second (the pulsars), although the technology existed to detect them. Similarly, bright celestial X-ray sources were *not* expected; they were first detected by an experiment designed for a totally different purpose (like Jansky's radio receiver), and gave birth to the powerful new discipline of cosmic X-ray astronomy. Even with the history of radio and X-ray astronomy evolving through totally unexpected discoveries, one complete area of astronomy was overlooked for a decade, because astronomers were convinced there was no chance of being able to see anything. It was thought that very-short-wavelength-ultraviolet radiation (the "extreme-ultraviolet") emitted by stars could never reach the Earth, but would be obscured from view by the interstellar gas between stars. Despite such a pessimistic view, a group of California space astronomers managed to get a small extreme-ultraviolet telescope on the joint U.S.-U.S.S.R. Apollo-Soyuz space mission, and they found extreme ultraviolet emission from certain stars. By sheer good fortune, it seems that the sun lies in a giant void in the Galaxy, where the density of the interstellar medium is uncharacteristically low.

Astronomers often initially see only what they expect to see, rather than what is actually there. This is hardly surprising, since imagination is tempered by experience. The mysterious bands in the SS433 spectra are a classic example of the not so obvious being overlooked. Many extremely able astronomers looked at those bands on the early spectra, and tried to interpret them in a conventional way. No one looked at them and immediately thought "jets." Additional information (on the "drift" of the bands) was needed before that hypothesis evolved. There are numerous similar examples in the history of scientific discovery. Many sightings of a particularly brilliant comet were noted by Far Eastern civilizations since the second century B.C., but it was Edmund Halley who predicted, in the eighteenth century, the periodic return of the interplanetary interloper that now carries his name. The first Astronomer Royal at Greenwich, the Reverend John Flamsteed, observed a particular "star" on numerous occasions, but it was William Herschel who finally detected the subtle movement that identified it as a new planet (Uranus). One could fill a book with similar astronomical near-miss and hard-luck stories. Scientists should always remind themselves of Sherlock Holmes's admonishment "You see, but you do not observe!"

Perhaps surprisingly, the identification of the bizarre properties of SS433, leading to the jet hypothesis, did *not* depend critically on the availability of advanced new technologies. The star is sufficiently bright that it can be seen with a comparatively small telescope, and it lies close to the celestial equator, so it can be seen in both Northern and Southern Hemispheres. Moreover, the most unusual spectral properties are so extreme that they can be identified with a spectrograph of fairly modest performance. Indeed, the type of telescope and spectrograph available early in this century would have been quite sufficient to isolate the unique properties of SS433 and, in particular, the moving bands. So why was it not found half a century earlier? Simply because, before the availability of the new technologies, there was nothing to draw attention to the star as being worthy of detailed study; there was no reason why Edwardian astronomers should have chosen to look at it rather than any other of the tens of millions of stars they could observe. They would never have suspected that such a weird object as SS433 could exist, since identifications of interacting binary systems and accretion disks would have to await X-ray astronomy, and the existence of cosmic jets would have to await radio astronomy. For SS433, it took the new technologies of X-ray and radio astronomy to draw attention to a peculiar star and reveal the startling similarity of some of its properties to those of the radio galaxies.

It is instructive to relate the evolution of scientists' ideas about galaxies before describing in detail the relationship between SS433 and the giant radio galaxies. The first detailed study of the structure of our galaxy, the Milky Way, was attempted in the late eighteenth century by William Herschel, working in England. Herschel argued that those regions of the heavens containing the greatest number of faint stars corresponded to the maximum extensions of the Milky Way, thus concluding that the Milky Way was a flattened disk, with the sun near its center. His observations revealed hundreds of "clouds" of emission, or "nebulae" (of which some examples had been recognized previously), many of which were found to have a characteristic spiral structure. Because most of these seemed to lie away from the central plane of the Milky Way, and some could be resolved into what appeared to be individual stars, Herschel suggested that all the nebulae might be separate, distinct galaxies lying far beyond the Milky Way. (The concept of a universe made up of many star conglomerates like the Milky Way had been alluded to in the mid-eighteenth century by the German philosopher Immanuel Kant, who termed the nebulae "island universes.") Herschel's nebula hypothesis aroused little support among the astronomers of the day, although his theory of the shape of the Milky Way and of the sun's position at its center was accepted without controversy. Interestingly, his rejected nebulae hypothesis eventually proved to be correct, while his accepted Milky Way hypothesis was shown to be wrong.

By the turn of the century, it was still a matter for speculation as to whether the universe extended beyond the Milky Way, but there was general agreement that the sun lay somewhere near its center. Only later was the sun dislodged from this pre-eminent central position, by Harlow Shapley. He studied dense clusters of stars (each containing tens of thousands) lying within the Milky Way and, in particular, the nature of certain stars within these clusters that varied in brightness. From these studies of the cluster variables he found that the star clusters were scattered throughout a "flattened" spherical volume with a diameter of about 100,000 light-years. He calculated that the sun lay about 30,000 light-years from the center of the distribution of star clusters, which was presumably the center of the Galaxy. His work revealed the true enormity of the Milky Way and forced the sun closer to its periphery than its heart. (We now know that Herschel's earlier incorrect determination that the sun was near the center of the Milky Way resulted from the effect of dust along the central plane of the Galaxy, which obscured the light from the distant stars toward and beyond the galactic center.)

But the dispute as to whether the spiral nebulae were island universes or were part of the Milky Way remained unresolved, and was at the center of one of the great debates of twentieth-century science. By looking at certain stars called "novae" in the spiral nebulae, that increased dramatically in brightness before gradually fading over days to weeks, American astronomer Heber Curtis concluded that the nebulae had to be distant galaxies. Shapley argued otherwise. The dispute was finally resolved by one of the greatest observational astronomers of modern times, Edwin Hubble. In 1923, Hubble was able to use the new giant 100-inch telescope at the Mt. Wilson Observatory, in Pasadena, to study the spiral nebulae. On the basis of their populations of stars and on the properties of certain types of stars of variable brightness, he was able to show beyond a shadow of doubt that they were distinct galaxies at vast distances. The majority of nebulae had suddenly become galaxies in their own right, some 170 years after Kant had first suggested such, and an amazing step had been made in appreciating the extreme size of the universe.

The spectra of normal stars show absorption lines, which indicate the composition of the stellar atmosphere, against a continuum background originating from the star's visible surface. For an unresolved conglomerate of stars in a distant galaxy, the composite spectrum is a strong continuum, although the main absorption lines should still be identifiable in addition to emission lines originating in tenuous gas permeating the void between the stars. When, in 1912, Vesto Slipher, in Arizona, obtained spectra of about forty spiral nebulae (subsequently shown to be galaxies), he found to his amazement that although the principal spectral features could be identified, they were displaced toward the red end of the spectra—in other words, the light from these galaxies was red-shifted.

Slipher's red shifts were interpreted as motions of galaxies away from the Milky Way (Figure 9.1). This was already deemed strange, but Hubble was to make an even more startling revelation: that the more distant a galaxy, the greater its red shift, or, the more distant a galaxy from the Milky Way, the greater the speed of recession (Figure 9.2). The recessional speeds of the galaxies are enormous. For example, a galaxy at a distance of fifty million light-

FIGURE 9.1. EXPANDING UNIVERSE

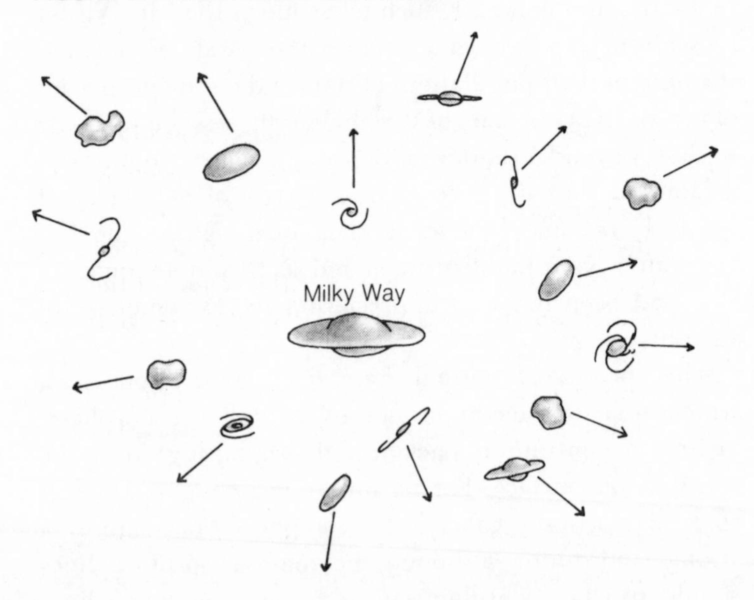

FIGURE 9.2. HUBBLE'S RELATIONSHIP

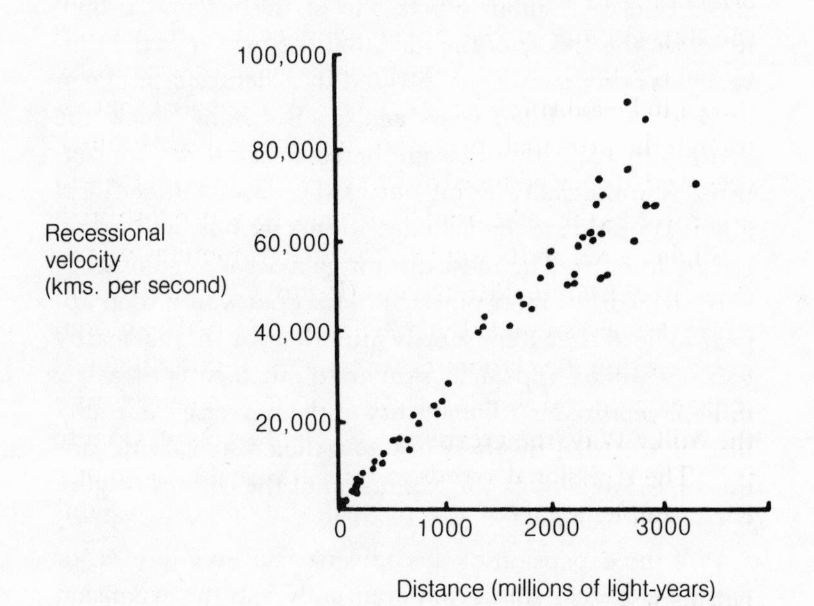

years is moving away from us at about 1,000 kilometers per second; at ten times this distance, the speed will be 10,000 kilometers per second. Although all other galaxies are flying away from the Milky Way at great speed, this does not mean that our galaxy is at the center of the universe. The simplest way to interpret Hubble's revelation is as a general uniform expansion of the universe. Lying within this general expansion, all the galaxies appear to be receding from us; but if we were placed in any other galaxy, we would observe exactly the same effect.

It is tempting to extrapolate the expansion of the galaxies backward, rather like running a movie in reverse, to a time more than 10 billion years ago, when the galaxies would have been tightly packed together. The Belgian cleric Georges Lemaître was one of the original proponents (in the 1930s) of the idea that the matter of the universe was originally concentrated in a dense form. Then more than 10 billion years ago, a "Big Bang" blew the dense primeval system to smithereens. Localized concentrations in the debris flying outward collapsed under local gravity to produce the galaxies of stars we now witness receding from us. The most distant galaxies we can observe with the world's most powerful telescopes would then appear to be as they were shortly after their birth; the nearby galaxies would appear as similar to our own (just a few million years older). The history of the universe can therefore be revealed by the study of galaxies at varying distances, as we witness the expansion of the cosmos (Figure 9.3).

Will the expansion of the universe continue forever, or will gravitational attraction eventually halt the expansion and, indeed, reverse it? The future behavior of the universe depends on the density of the material within it. Although we can observe the stars and galaxies, not all the material lying between the stars (the interstellar medium) and the galaxies (the extremely tenuous "intergalactic medium") is visible to us. It is the exact amount of this invisible "missing mass" that will determine whether the expansion of the universe will eventually halt. If 99 percent of the mass of the universe is invisible, then eventually space will turn in on itself, and the galaxies will be dragged toward each other in a universal contraction. Scientists speculate that such "infall" could eventually precipitate another Big Bang as the galaxies are crushed together, giving birth to a new expanding universe out of the debris of the old. This is the basis of the oscillating-universe theory, in which a Big Bang and an expansion

FIGURE 9.3. THE EXPANDING UNIVERSE

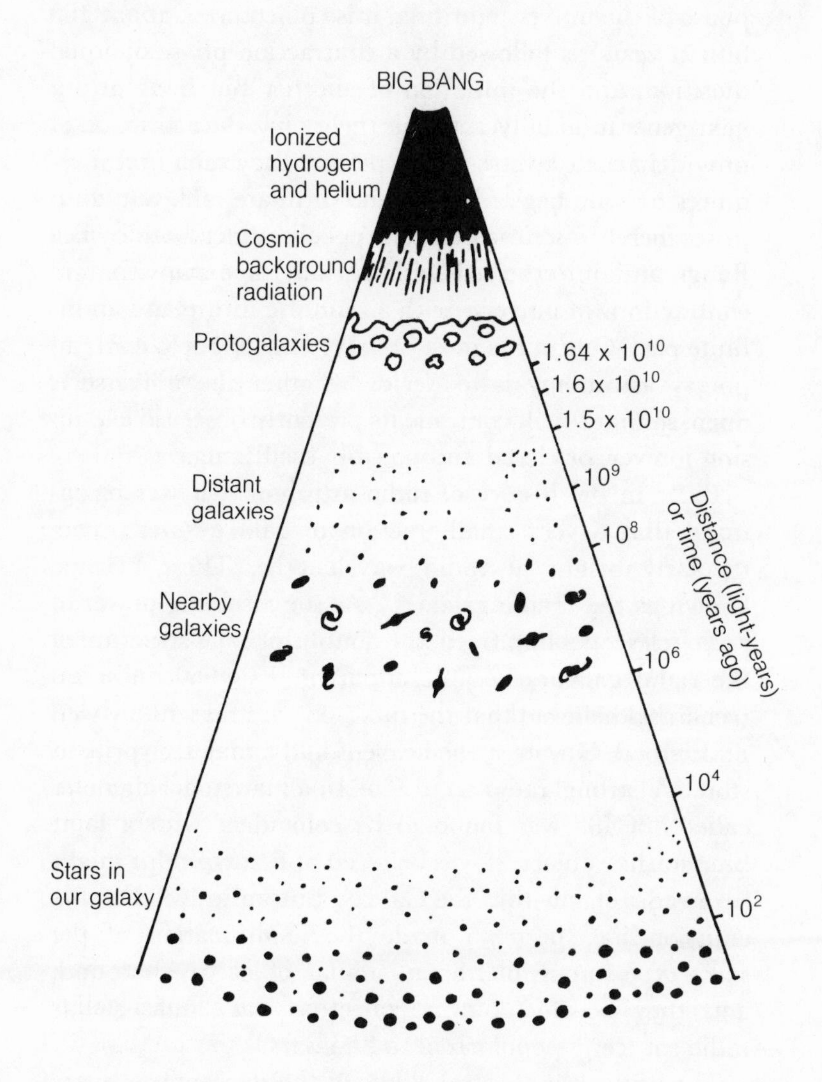

phase of the universe (lasting, it is conjectured, about 100 billion years) is followed by a contraction phase of equal duration, and the initiation of another Big Bang and a next-generation universe. This theory has the attraction of providing the universe with a permanency such that it requires no true beginning and no ultimate end, but comprises merely a series of creative epochs punctuated by Big Bangs and interspersed with periods of expansion and contraction—a universe with an infinite future and an infinite past. One of the most pressing challenges to contemporary astronomy is to decide whether the universe is open, so that it will continue its presently observed expansion forever, or closed and possibly oscillating.

Early in the history of radio astronomy, it was recognized that a very small fraction of galaxies were spectacularly bright at radio wavelengths. These became known as the "radio galaxies." As the resolving power of radio telescopes improved, the double lobe/jet structure of the radio galaxies became apparent. By 1960, most astronomers believed that the radio sky was reasonably well understood. However, the heavens had a major surprise in store. A strong radio source of small angular diameter called "3C48" was found to be coincident with a faint blue starlike object. It was believed at first that this might be a radio star within the Galaxy, but an indecipherable emission-line spectrum made the identification of the star's type impossible. Soon, similar objects were found, and they became known collectively as "quasi-stellar radio sources," popularized to "quasars."

The key to the spectral riddle of the quasars was eventually found by Maarten Schmidt, at the Mt. Palomar Observatory, who recognized in the complex spectrum of a quasar called "3C273" the characteristic pattern of the emission lines of hydrogen. Spectral lines of other elements then revealed themselves. But the entire spectrum was red-shifted. In itself, a large red shift was not particularly surprising, and would be expected merely to reveal extreme distance, but coupled with the observed brightness of the object, the derived distance made quasar 3C273 at least one hundred times brighter intrinsically than any other galaxy ever observed. Schmidt could scarcely believe the reality of the data. Reanalysis of the spectra of other quasars also revealed extreme red shift. If these results seemed difficult to accept, even greater surprises were in store. A search of old photographs dating back to 1890 showed that 3C273 varied significantly in intensity over a period of about ten years. But no object can co-ordinate its activity on its remote side with that on its near side in less time than it takes for light to travel across it. Thus, a change in intensity over a ten-year period implied that 3C273 was no more than ten light-years across, compared with, for example, the 100,000-light-year diameter of our own galaxy. Other quasars were found to have similar dimensions. Here was the dilemma facing astronomers: not only were the quasars superenergetic, apparently emitting at least one hundred times the light of a large galaxy, but this energy had to be concentrated in a mere fraction of the size of a typical galaxy.

The decade following these discoveries resulted in the recognition of many hundreds of quasars, some with enormous red shifts, implying recessional speeds of up to about 90 percent the velocity of light. If the relationship of the red shift to the distance derived by Hubble applied to quasars, some must lie near the edge of the observable universe. Many quasars were found to display jet systems, similar to the radio galaxies. Majority opinion now seems to accept that quasars are the highly active nuclei of nascent galaxies at extreme distances, although the debate as to their true nature and the source of their exceptional power continues. The discovery of SS433 almost twenty years later mimicked in many ways the discovery of the quasars.

Once jets were revealed in SS433, it was entirely natural to search for analogies with the radio galaxies and quasars, which also showed evidence of jet action. But the difference in scale should be emphasized. The mass of the compact object at the heart of SS433 is probably just a few times that of the sun, whereas the central nucleus of a typical radio galaxy has been inferred to have a mass billions of times that of the sun. In SS433, the optical jets extend to a distance of just a few light-days, with the X-ray jets burgeoning out into lobes at a distance of a few tens of light-years. In the radio galaxies, the jets may extend millions of times farther into space, making them the largest entities in the universe. A similar scaling of temporal effects would also be expected. For example, a precession of the jets of a radio galaxy comparable to the 164-day variability in SS433 would be over intervals of millions of years, far too long actually to observe.

If SS433 really is a miniature version of the radio galaxies displaying jets, then clearly understanding the behavior of SS433 would help in understanding the radio galaxies. However, there *must* be significant differences resulting from the enormous disparity in scale, and these must be borne in mind. Although some ideas about the habits of living things can be learned by studying ants under a microscope, if one's principal interest is elephants, one can never get the whole picture merely by studying ants. And although it is much easier to put SS433 "under the microscope" than the radio galaxies (because of the convenient temporal periods, the comparative brightness, ease of observation, and so on), there is no escaping the need to study both in as great detail as possible.

The main components of the radio galaxies are recognized to be the bright central nucleus and the outwardly directed jets, emerging in giant lobes. The central source of energy is uncertain, but the jets are undoubtedly streams of gas squirting out from the nucleus of the galaxy like a jet of water from the nozzle of a hose. The jets push their way out through the galaxy, but as the jet material streams into the tenuous intergalactic medium, it becomes more and more difficult for it to plow its way farther, because the material at the extremities decelerates so that it is traveling more slowly than the gas being fed into the jets. Just as squirting a jet of water into sand carves out a cavity and causes a splash back of the water, so gas in the jets is eventually splashed back to inflate the giant lobes at the ends of the jets.

Jets in radio galaxies come in a variety of forms. Some radio galaxies display a single jet; many are highly curved; some show the corkscrew phenomenon seen in SS433 (see Figure 9.4), again presumably attributable to the ponderous precession of the jets. (Note that the individual clumps of material in the jets actually travel in straight

FIGURE 9.4. CORKSCREW PHENOMENON

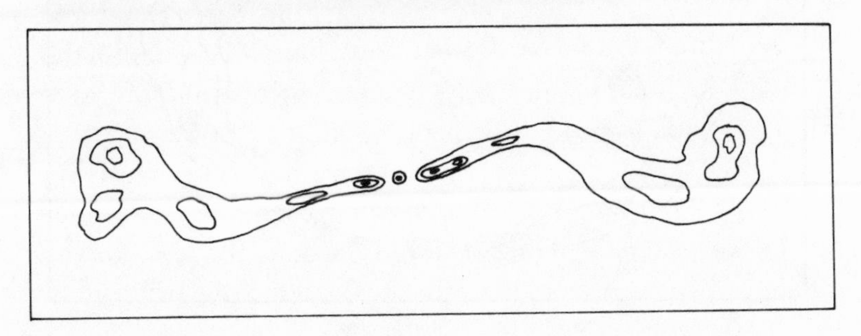

lines, not in helical paths; it is only the direction of ejection of jet material that precesses, presenting the illusion that the jets are following a corkscrew path. As a garden hose is moved backward and forward, the water jet appears to follow a complex path; but, of course, the individual drops of water are traveling in straight paths.)

There are radio galaxies that appear to have giant "tails" (see Figure 9.5), and it is probable that these are formed by low-power jets that are then blown backward because of relative motion between the galaxy and a denser-than-usual intergalactic medium. As the two jets

FIGURE 9.5. RADIO GALAXY WITH "TAIL"

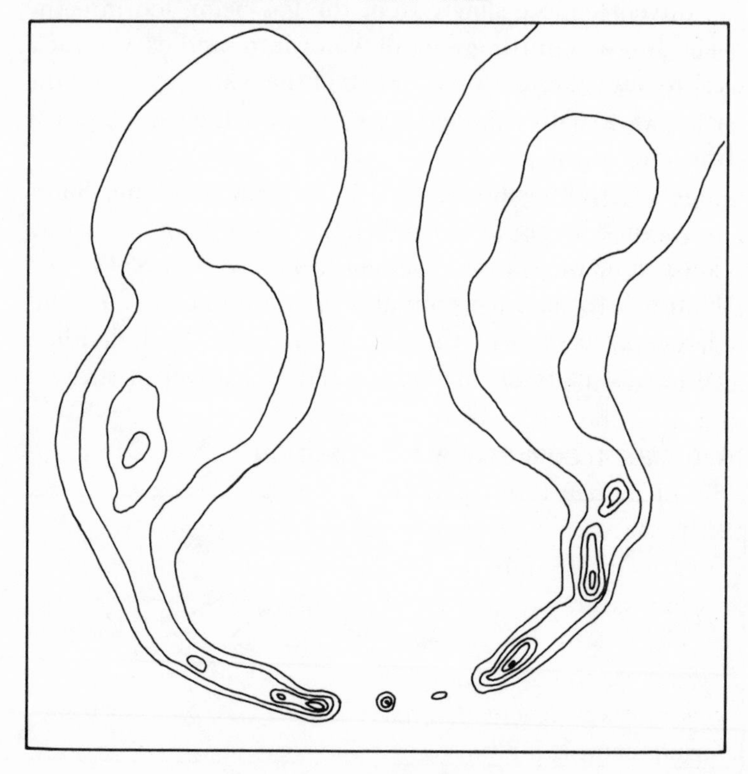

are blown in the same direction, their radio lobes merge to form the tail effect.

Only a small number of galaxies display the enormous energies of the radio galaxies and their superenergetic close relatives the quasars. For 99 percent of the galaxies, their emission can be ascribed entirely to the total radiation from all their stars and the interstellar material. For the remaining 1 percent, the location of the source of their extreme energy is a highly luminous compact central nucleus. Typically, this nucleus of a radio galaxy or quasar radiates more than 1,000 times the combined energy of all the stars in the galaxy. (Some of this energy might be directed to the lobes via the jets.) The emission from the central nucleus is usually highly variable in its intensity on a time scale that might be as short as hours. As previously argued, the central nucleus of a quasar must be only light-hours to light-years in diameter—a minuscule size on the scale of galaxies. What could the compact, highly efficient central powerhouse of the radio galaxies and quasars possibly be? Current thinking favors a massive black hole, formed perhaps by millions of stars coalescing and collapsing under gravity. Such a massive black hole would have an insatiable appetite; surrounding stars and gas would swirl down into it via a giant accretion disk, with the release of vast quantities of energy. It is unlikely that the massive black hole could digest the vast bulk of material swirling into it without "burping" violently. As with SS433, intense radiation pressure is believed to direct some of the accreting material into jets and to accelerate it to velocities approaching that of light (see Figure 9.6).

There is, however, a problem in satisfying the massive black hole's enormous appetite; a normal density of stars is insufficient. But a novel idea has been advanced involv-

FIGURE 9.6.

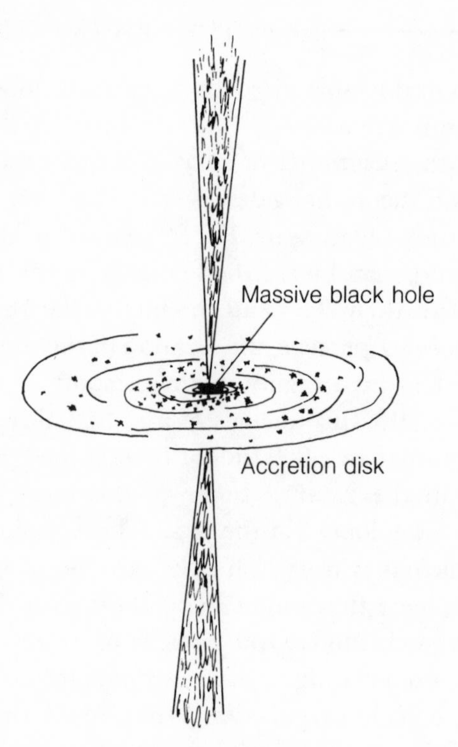

ing the interaction of galaxies. Since the radio galaxies and quasars are known to lie at extreme distances, we are seeing them at an epoch in the evolution of the universe when galaxies were most tightly packed and more likely to interact. A giant galaxy could consume any smaller passing galaxy. The giant galaxy containing the massive black hole is referred to as the "cannibal galaxy," and the innocent unsuspecting passer-by as the "missionary galaxy." Galactic cannibalism is the favored origin of the material consumed by the central powerhouse of the active galaxies, and ejected in part by their jets.

The extreme velocity of material in extragalactic jets has some interesting consequences. Quasar 3C273 (about 1.5 billion light-years away) is famous for its jets. Bright features in the jet have been found to travel rapidly outward, at a rate that seems to imply that they must be moving outward at five times the speed of light. But nothing *can* travel faster than the speed of light, and the apparent "superluminal expansion" of the 3C273 jet (and others) is now believed to be a geometrical illusion. The light from the quasar and the high-velocity bright feature in the jet travel along different paths and hence take different times to reach us. If the jet defines a small angle to the line of sight, it will appear to travel superluminally (see Figure 9.7). These observations indicate not that the jet material is actually traveling faster than the speed of light, but that it must be traveling at a speed approaching that of light.

The vast majority of jets in galaxies are observed only at radio wavelengths, because radio telescopes are comparatively more sensitive than optical or X-ray telescopes. The fact that the SS433 jets manifest themselves in optical, radio, and X-ray phenomena should help to define the relationship between the different emissions and their likely origin, not only for SS433 but also for the jets from active galaxies.

Everything so far learned about SS433 strengthens the conviction that it is a miniature version of the radio galaxies and quasars. The same physical processes, albeit on vastly different scales, must underlie both the active galaxies and SS433. For this reason, SS433 is assured a permanent role in observational astronomy. Not only is it of intrinsic interest, as an intriguing example of the bizarre configuration stellar systems can adopt during their evolution, but its detailed study should reveal some of the secrets of the radio galaxy and quasar phenomena that we could never hope to unravel through direct observation. The mighty ant stands triumphant among the astronomical elephants.

FIGURE 9.7. SUPERLUMINAL EXPANSION

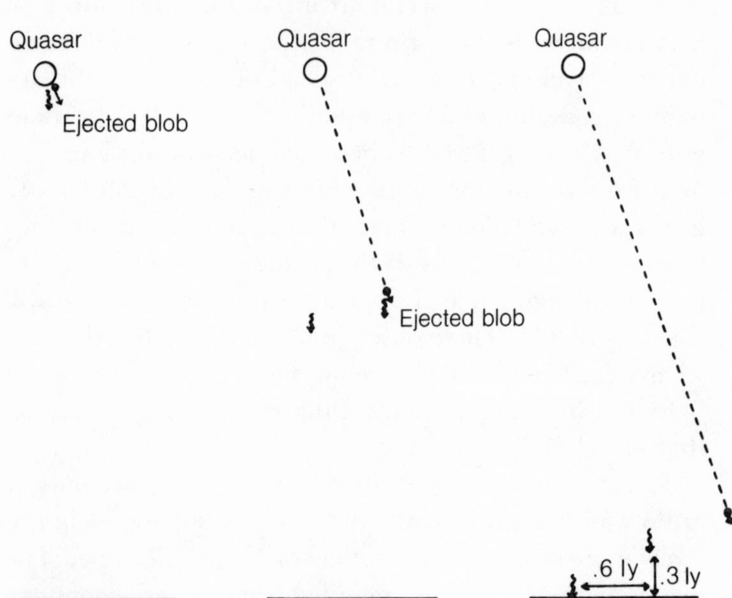

a. Observer is four light-years distant from a quasar, which ejects a blob of material at .9 times the speed of light, almost in the direction of the observer.

b. After two years, observer still sees just a single source; the light from the ejected blob has two years to reach him, while the blob itself has already traveled a distance of 1.8 light-years.

c. Two years later, observer finally sees the blob emerge from the quasar at position a, followed just .3 years later by the light emitted from the blob at position b. The blob will therefore appear to have traveled a horizontal distance of .6 light-years in an interval of .3 years; that is, at twice the speed of light.

EPILOGUE

"Everything's got a moral, if you can only find it."
—LEWIS CARROLL,
Alice's Adventures in Wonderland

SS433 has changed astronomy in a way rarely matched by any other cosmic object; certainly its discovery stands beside those of the pulsars and quasars as being of a fundamentally new and totally unexpected celestial phenomenon. As with the pulsars and quasars, its revelation was essentially accidental, even though in all three cases much planned and persistent study had paved the way to eventual detection. In contrast to the discovery of pulsars (which was made by a single small group), the unveiling of SS433 involved the interaction of several groups of astronomers across the globe.

In the Prologue, I suggested that history must be the ultimate judge of who played the dominant roles in the SS433 saga. Nevertheless, perhaps history may forgive me for expressing a personal point of view. The "direct" route to SS433 was based on the objective prism survey for emission-line objects by Stephenson and Sanduleak. This type of astronomy is demanding and time consuming, and success is far from guaranteed. There have been several attempts to see whether the other objects catalogued by Stephenson and Sanduleak are of special interest, but none have been shown to be so far. Without SS433, it is extremely unlikely that the Stephenson and Sanduleak catalogue would have made any lasting impression on astrophysics; because of SS433, their diligent efforts have justly been assured permanent recognition. E. R. Seaquist and his colleagues had the foresight to realize that among the catalogued optical emission-line stars, they might profitably search for radio emission (their particular interest being the detection of protostars at radio wavelengths). The announcement of their detection of radio emission from SS433 alerted many astronomers to its potential significance, but it was the Asiago workers who took up the challenge of providing first-rate optical spectral data. Their persistence in taking observations over an extended period provided an independent assessment of the spectacular results coming from California.

Along the "indirect" route to SS433, James Caswell and the research teams both in Australia and at Cambridge provided all-important radio observations, first of Circinus X-1, then of its proposed cousin in W50. Without his sixth sense for recognizing what were likely to be the important observations to be made, I doubt whether there could have been an indirect route to SS433. Seward and the Leicester astronomers pioneered the X-ray observations; they extracted from the Ariel V satellite data an elusive X-ray star that had been overlooked initially in the UHURU X-ray survey and then had the remarkable perception (and courage) to propose that it might be an exotic stellar remnant of a supernova. In the optical regime, John Whelan and his colleagues made the discovery of the star associated with Circinus X-1—a peculiar emission-line star that immediately attracted the question "Are there others like it?" The attempt to answer that question plus others raised at the Erice conference, and also link existing X-ray and radio observations, led Paul Murdin and me to SS433. In this endeavor I was privileged to work alongside an optical astronomer of great dedication and exceptional talent.

Bruce Margon's introduction to SS433 may have been mere chance, but, presented with such an opportunity, he was certainly not prepared to let it pass him by. While others failed to appreciate the potential significance of certain peculiarities in the SS433 optical spectrum, he had the perception to realize that here was a mystery that had to be solved. It was a problem perfectly matched to his personal drive and determination. Having seized the initiative, he and his colleagues were never to lose their lead (or even be seriously threatened with losing it) in the race to discover the unique properties of SS433.

To explain the star's bizarre spectral properties, the monumental theoretical contributions of Mordehai Milgrom, and of Andrew Fabian and Martin Rees were produced. There were other ingenious suggestions put forward, but none of these stood the test of time. The "jet set" will be remembered, because their hypotheses turned out to be the only ones that could be adapted to fit the data as more and more refined observations were reported.

History may decide to cast its players differently, since it will ultimately view the path to discovery from a variety of perspectives; but from my viewpoint, the astronomers identified here and their collaborators were the heros of the opening act of the SS433 saga. In later acts, once SS433 was public property, precedence for the various contributions to the discovery process will be less open to personal interpretation. The steady flow of observational and theoretical papers to the scientific literature allow the evolution of new observations and new ideas to be followed with some certainty.

SS433 generated an enormous sense of adventure in the world's astronomical community in the few years following 1979. For those closely involved, in addition to the excitement there were also many disappointments and frustrations. Since scientific discovery involves real people, personal emotions are inevitably part of the process. Interactions between personalities often do play a significant role in science, and this was certainly the case for SS433. Whatever our idealistic conception might be of the scientist who puts the pursuit of scientific discovery before all else, the reality is often very different. Whatever the professional rivalries of the past, or the disappointment, jealousy, and anger experienced, however, time is able to smooth out the differences between emotional extremes. Certainly I am not aware of any lingering animosity between any of those who adopted competing stances during the pursuit of SS433.

The scientific discovery process will never stagnate; it is part of the nature of humankind to pursue the unknown. There will be other "pulsars," "quasars," or "SS433s"—other "VISs." No doubt the path to their discovery will again involve elements of luck, tenacious search, dedicated research, and sheer hard work. For my part, I have gained immense satisfaction from having witnessed one VIS saga from the inside and from having had the chance to share this story with you. After SS433, the universe could never look quite the same again.

INDEX